ROSE WOOD

Sharon Mikeworth

ROSE WOOD

Copyright © 2012, 2013 by Sharon Mikeworth

All rights reserved. No part of this book may be reproduced in any form by any electronic or mechanical means including photocopying, recording, or information storage and retrieval without permission in writing from the author.

This is a work of fiction. Any references to historical events, real people, or real locales are used fictitiously. Other names, characters, places, and incidents are the product of the author's imagination, and any resemblance to actual events or locales or persons, living or dead, is entirely coincidental.

ISBN-13: 978-0-6157257-6-5
ISBN-10: 0615725767

Cover photograph by Dhoxax/Shutterstock.com
Author's photograph by Jessica Ayers
Design and layout by Lighthouse24

Give feedback on the book at:
sharonmikeworth@gmail.com

For my husband

Rose Wood

Prologue

1958

Leeann followed Anita out onto the front porch and settled down beside her in the swing. It would be dark soon, but for now the air still held the last of the afternoon sun's warmth. She pushed off with her foot to set them to swaying. She was about to suggest they call Cindy, whose mom sometimes let her borrow the car, when she heard the crunch of tires. She looked up and saw Ritchie's old blue Chevy making its way down the driveway, front end dipping and bouncing in the ruts.

He swung around to the left and parked sideways, lurching to a stop. His newest girlfriend, Cheryl, peered at them through the passenger window.

They emerged from the car, and Leeann groaned inwardly. Ritchie had brought two cartons of Pabst Blue Ribbon beer. She glanced over at Anita. Stunningly beautiful with dark wavy hair and green eyes, Anita had a tendency to flirt shamelessly with good-looking men whenever she drank—whether they were attached or not. And Ritchie, with his coal-black hair and big brown eyes, was more than good-looking; he was *gorgeous*.

Ritchie mounted the porch steps, towing Cheryl behind him. He barely had time to introduce her before Anita reached over and pulled out one of the beers. She opened it and took a long pull, already eyeing him. Standing beside Anita, Cheryl's ordinary blond prettiness seemed to pale in comparison. She was no match for a tipsy amorous Anita.

Anita was on her second beer when Leeann saw her attention shift from Ritchie to Cheryl. By the time they went to leave for the new drive-in over in Belton, she was on her third and hanging on to Cheryl's every word as if they had become fast friends. But Leeann knew better.

Sure enough, Anita linked arms with Cheryl on the way to the car, then quickly opened the door and slid into the middle of the front seat. She did it as if her only concern was to be close to her new best friend, but she was actually ensuring her place beside Ritchie. It looked like Cheryl was starting to clue in, but she merely shot Ritchie a look and climbed in after Anita, slamming the door, and Leeann got in the back, all-too-familiar irritation sweeping through her.

It didn't help that Ritchie was encouraging Anita, obviously interested in her too, and letting her know it. Anita gave a little squeal and giggled, allowing herself to bounce into him as he swerved to avoid a pothole in the road. Ritchie threw back his head and laughed, his knee coming in contact with hers again as he purposely made another exaggerated swerve. Completely disregarding Cheryl's now furious stare, he took another swig of his beer and switched on the radio. Patsy Cline's throaty voice filled the car.

Anita settled further down in her seat and dropped her head back as if on the verge of passing out. She let her head loll around and then fall over onto Cheryl's shoulder, and when she eased away from her, she turned over and leaned against Ritchie. For a second Leeann thought he was going to put his arm around Anita, but he seemed to catch himself and dropped it along the back of the seat, not quite touching Cheryl, whom he was still pointedly ignoring. Leeann could see the hurt on Cheryl's face as she looked over at Anita curled up against Ritchie, and she felt her irritation sharpen and border on something close to dislike.

She leaned forward. "How much longer, Ritchie?"

"Not as long as it would have been if I hadn't taken this short cut," he said over his shoulder, careful not to disturb Anita.

It seemed like they had been going down the same road forever when the car gave a hard thump and then began the unmistakable rhythmic bumping of a flat tire. Ritchie bumped slowly along the shoulder, turned, and parked the car in front of a cleared area between the trees.

He pulled out the spare tire and jack while Anita, immediately wide-awake and alert, held a completely unnecessary flashlight. The moon hung fat and full in the night sky, almost bright enough to read by. Leeann tried to catch Anita's eye, but she was disregarding her just as much as she was Cheryl, a self-satisfied smirk on her face.

Cheryl abruptly turned around and stomped off in the direction of the clearing. Leeann followed her. She caught up with her after a second, and they walked in silence up the small incline, moonlight fading in and out from behind a cloud.

They stopped beside a low wall surrounding the remains of a cemetery. Some of the old headstones leaned drunkenly, their engravings so weathered and worn they were unreadable in the dimness. The graveyard was small, and Leeann didn't see any remains to indicate a church had once been there. "There must have been a house around here someplace," she said.

Cheryl stood looking down towards the car where, incredibly, Ritchie was still standing and talking with Anita instead of coming after her.

"I'm sorry about that," Leeann said, going over and standing beside her.

"Why are you friends with her?"

"I think the better question would be, why are you with him?"

Cheryl turned around as if she couldn't bring herself to watch any longer and started walking the perimeter of the cemetery. Leeann followed along behind her, their feet crunching through the thick layer of dead leaves covering the ground.

Around the back they found the remains of a path, mostly grown over, leading up through the trees. Even in the winter there was considerable undergrowth; had it been summer it would have been nearly impenetrable.

"You're right," Cheryl said, "I think this must have led up to a house."

They started up the path, which was practically nonexistent and nearly disappeared in some places. Leeann knew Cheryl was upset, but she was starting to get a headache, and she was pretty sure she had just picked a hole in her sweater. A cloud slid in front of the moon, and Cheryl, ahead of her, was swallowed in the darkness. She stumbled after her, trying to see in the added gloom. After a bit she heard the sound of rushing water and stopped.

"Cheryl!" she called out. She called out again, louder this time, "*Cheryl!*"

She heard nothing but the distant murmur of Ritchie and Anita in the distance.

A twig snapped, and Cheryl appeared out of the darkness onto the path in front of her. "Come look, there's a house up here!"

"Shouldn't we get back?"

"We'll hurry. Come on!" Cheryl started off again, and she had no choice but to follow her.

The moon came back out and she saw they were following alongside a stream that was deepening and widening into more of a river the farther along they went. After a short distance, Cheryl veered off onto a more worn section of the path, and they followed it up to the shadow of an old house.

The house seemed to loom above them, flashing in and out, first tall and imposing, then dark and menacing in the shifting moonlight. Leeann felt a flicker of foreboding. They shouldn't be there.

They made their way around to the front of the house through the untended, overgrown hedges and dead withered vines and bushes.

Leeann climbed the stone steps to the front porch. Stepping hesitantly onto the weathered boards, she walked over and twisted the doorknob and found the knob unyielding. "It's locked."

"Maybe the back's open." Cheryl started down the steps, and Leeann turned back around. There were long windows on each side of the door, and she peered first in one, and then the other, amazed that the antique wavy glass was still intact, but could see nothing, only darkness.

"They smell heavenly, don't they?"

Leeann's eyes widened and she went still. She waited a beat, still trying to absorb what she had heard.

That had not been Cheryl's voice. The voice that had just spoken had not been Cheryl's. Not even close, not exactly higher in octave, but *younger*. An icy fingernail of fear scraped its way down her spine.

The same strange, lilting voice spoke again, *"I've always loved roses."*

The hair on the back of her neck stood up.

She could smell them now, too: an overpowering scent of roses with a smell of decay underneath, like an old moldering flower left too long.

She turned around slowly just as the moon appeared again and lit across Cheryl standing in the yard below her. All the previously dead and barren flower bushes were now heavy with roses—blood-red roses, blooming in the dead of winter where moments before there had only been desiccated sticks.

She blinked and they were gone. Once again the lifeless bushes were empty of flowers.

She stood trembling, barely breathing, not sure what she had really seen or heard until the moonlight flickered, threatening to send them into darkness, and broke her paralysis. She shot down the steps and grabbed Cheryl's arm, pulling her. "Let's go!" The scent of the flowers seem to follow her as she hurried around the hedges and crashed through the trees back the way they had come. She had a sense of barely escaping something, and Cheryl seemed to be feeling the same urgency and hurried just as fast.

Leeann was slightly ahead as they rounded a sharp cutback near the riverbank and she saw them first, her feet sliding to a stop as she grabbed a hold of a small tree and tried to stop Cheryl from seeing. The stupid idiot was all over Anita right there on the path. There was a rock outcrop beside the edge of the bank and Ritchie had Anita up against it, kissing her!

She tried to back up, but it was too late; Cheryl had spotted them. Cheryl made a sound like *"Ohh,"* and Leeann grabbed for her as she doubled over, her face contorting. Leeann had just let go of her and turned to yell at Ritchie when Cheryl gave an incoherent cry, shoved by her, and flew at Anita. Ritchie looked out of it, possibly drunker than she had thought, as he stepped almost casually back, but Anita realized exactly what was happening. She just had time to step away from the rock when Cheryl hit her with both arms straight out in front of her and knocked her stumbling back.

Anita stood swaying on the edge of the ravine. She was no longer smirking. She made as if to step towards Cheryl when the bank she was standing on suddenly shifted, started to crumble, and then gave way. Cheryl gasped, threw herself forward and grabbed for her, just missing Anita's outstretched fingers as she shrieked and plummeted down in a cascade of dirt and rocks. There was a brief sound of her crying out and tumbling, followed by a sickening thud, and then nothing.

The ripe, sweet smell of roses wafted down from the house above and settled around them. Leeann looked down in horror at Anita splayed on the boulders below. A dark, glistening circle of blood spread out from the back of her head in a slow stain across the rocks.

PART ONE

It's All In The Cards

The boundaries which divide life from death are at best shadowy and vague. Who shall say where the one ends and the other begins. ~ Edgar Allen Poe

Chapter 1

2010

All of Aileen Whitney's journalism classmates had found decent positions after graduating. One was a reporter for a television station in West Virginia; one was a radio news anchor; and even Tina, the least ambitious of them all, had finally landed a position as a writer for the lifestyle section of her hometown newspaper. They all had nice, normal, *credible* jobs. Aileen wrote a paranormal section for *Southern Aurora* magazine. The glossy bimonthly publication featured the strange and the unknown such as ancient mysteries, UFOs, physic abilities, and homeopathy, as well as the supernatural. The name of her section was called "Skeptical Traveler", and for the sake of her job, she tried to keep the tone not so much that she didn't believe, but that she didn't believe *yet*. But she was finding it increasingly difficult to keep an open mind and justify how she made her living when not once during all her visits to houses, theatres, ghostly inns, asylums, and graveyards had she ever found any evidence of the supernatural.

She nudged Josh, who had immediately fallen asleep as soon as they had started down the long stretch between Atlanta and Augusta. He was dressed as outlandish as usual in black and red chained Tripp pants, long black leather coat, and studded Demonia boots. With the bleached out tips of his hair spiking out above the silver ring piercing his eyebrow, he looked like a skinnier version of Guy Fieri dressed as a Goth.

She turned her little Volvo hatchback onto the unpaved lane that led up to Redhill Plantation. She slowed the car as they passed the old cemetery.

"From graves forgotten stretch their dusty hands, and hold in mortmain still their old estates," said Josh in a pretty good Vincent Price imitation.

"That was actually Henry Wadsworth Longfellow if you were wondering," he said.

"I wasn't."

She stepped on the gas.

The two-story white house appeared, rising up above the row of magnolia trees lining the small lane.

"It's pretty. Bigger than I thought," she said.

"Well it's built up on brick pillars like a lot of lowcountry houses, and there's a widow's walk there at the top between the chimneys."

She pulled around and parked in the small gravel area behind the house. They climbed out, and she stretched and tried to get the kinks out as he rummaged through the equipment in the back. "You want the analog with external mike or the digital?"

"Just the analog, no mike, and the camera." She glanced at her watch. It was already 4:30, which meant they barely had ninety minutes of daylight left and only thirty minutes until the house was closed up for the night. "Let's just get this over with. Take some quick shots out here and then we'll head inside." She hadn't bothered to get permission to tour the house after hours. For this assignment it wasn't really necessary. Many of the supposed sightings and uneasy feelings had occurred outside during the day.

She grabbed the mini recorder, switched it on, and then milled around while Josh set up the tripod and took pictures. She read the marker out front and various other plaques posted here and there as he photographed the triangle-shaped hedges and trees the home was noted for. She felt nothing strange or supernatural, as usual.

A woman with hair dyed an even shade of brown was coming out with a group of people as they mounted the steep steps. They stood to the side as she finished up a tour. Aileen had planned it this way on purpose. Being led around and fed the same tired spiel as everyone else just wouldn't do. She wanted time alone in the house, and she was hoping for some possible inside information. She had found several nice nuggets this way in the past. While she was averse to actually fabricating a ghost experience of her own, she was not averse to occasionally reporting someone else's alleged experience, as long as they were giving what she considered a reliable, believable account.

The tour guide, Gladys according to her nametag, finally turned to them. "I'm afraid that was the last tour of the day. We generally close up the house at 5:00."

"That's okay. If you don't mind, we'll just look around for few minutes?" Without waiting for her reply, Aileen darted in the door and started up the stairs, Josh right on her heels.

Gladys unobtrusively followed them as they walked from room to room, then left them to their own devices to answer a call on her cell phone.

They continued on up to the third floor. Aileen pulled the recorder out of her bag and turned the volume up. Josh began snapping pictures as she took in the view. It was here at this window on the top floor that a shadowy figure had been reported standing as if still looking out on the Savannah River valley below. According to her research, Governor John Hadley Hale, owner of the house and said ghost, had been able to see the bell tower in downtown Augusta nearly fifteen miles away. The only thing she could see was the outskirts of town in the distance under a layer of smog.

She moved out into the hallway and stood posing for Josh as he captured her where the Governor's ghost was also reported to pace up and down on occasion.

"Maybe there'll be something in the pictures later when I develop them," he said.

"Right."

Gladys thumped up the stairs and emerged onto the landing where they stood. Aileen saw her eying the recorder and camera and knew they only had moments before being ejected from the house.

"So how long have you worked here?" she asked quickly, steering her back down the steps.

As they moved into the library, she questioned her steadily on the background of the house and the rumors of paranormal activity. Josh did his part, his camera emitting quiet flashes of light in the darkening room.

Gladys shot a look at Josh over in the corner clicking pictures of an old typewriter.

"Some people claim they've heard the sound of the typewriter, for instance."

Gladys shook her head. "Well I've never heard anything like that."

She looked down at her watch, and Aileen knew they had pushed it as far as they could. "Thank you for your time," she said, and they shook hands, her signal to Josh that they were finished. She headed for the front door, and then realized she was alone.

She turned around and went back to the library.

Josh stood with his back to her, staring out the window.

"Josh?"

He stood motionless, making no sign that he had heard her. The digital camera had slid out of his hand and fallen to the floor.

"Josh?" she said again, coming around beside him and taking hold of his arm. He seemed to be aware of her this time, the muscles in his arm contracting as she touched him, but his eyes remained focused on whatever he was looking at so intently. She peered out, seeing nothing at first, and then she spotted them: three lone trees standing all by themselves in an otherwise empty field. *Oh*. The triangular-patterned hedges and trees hadn't been what were rumored to be so unnerving; it was these three trees. She vaguely remembered something about them during her preliminary research.

She pulled her gaze away and looked at Josh again. His face was pale with beads of sweat standing out on his forehead and upper lip.

"Josh? We need to go," she said, tugging gently on his arm.

"What? Oh, yeah." He suddenly seemed to come to and abruptly pivoted and walked out, leaving the camera lying on the floor. She grabbed it and followed him. He had almost made it to the car by the time she was coming out the front door. *What had gotten into him?* And he hadn't taken any shots of the right trees.

The light was going, and she hurried to remember how to work the camera. She managed to get it set on what approximated a twilight setting, zoomed in, and snapped the pictures.

Gladys stood in the shadows of the front porch watching them as she backed up and drove slowly down the dirt drive. Josh still hadn't said anything. He sat slumped down in his seat with his eyes closed.

"So what happened back there?"

"Stop the car," he mumbled, pulling on the door handle. She jerked to a stop. He flung the door open, leaned out, and vomited.

"You okay?" she asked when he had finished, handing him a tissue and a bottle of water.

"I think I'm okay now. I don't know. I was looking out the window at those trees, and the next thing I knew, you were there and I was sick to my stomach." He swished some water around in his mouth then spat it out on the ground. "Oh my God, the camera!" he suddenly exclaimed, sitting bolt upright in his seat.

"Don't worry, I got it," she said, and he slumped back down in relief.

She waited on him to elaborate like he had in the past when he had claimed to have supernatural feelings, but this time he said nothing. Not even hours later when they stopped for something to eat and he was obviously feeling better.

Chapter 2

Aileen spent most of Saturday at her apartment writing and editing her piece on Redhill, alternating work with small breaks outside on the balcony. It was a beautiful clear day and she enjoyed the sun on her face despite the cool air.

She still hadn't talked with Josh about what had happened to him that day. He had not seemed interested in the audiotape. She had been the one to transfer the sound files and analyze them, as usual hearing nothing but the sound of their voices and the empty electronic hiss of the recorder. She took what had happened, and his uncharacteristic reticence, and chalked it up to a mild case of food poisoning or a virus and left the incident out.

By lunchtime the next day she was finished, and she decided to go home and visit her mother.

Now that her father, Thaddeus, had died, her mother, Betty Jean, lived alone in the house that Aileen had grew up in. She worried about her mother living there all by herself and tried to visit as often as she could.

The dark suburban highways gave way to bleached out interstates and old cement squares of coastal roads as she left Atlanta and headed into the boggy low country of South Carolina.

Black swamp water snaked along both sides of the road, winding around and occasionally passing under the low bridges she crossed.

The land thickened and huge oak trees draped with Spanish moss began appearing, and soon she was driving up the long drive. The house came into view and she noted, not for the first time, that it needed painting and the porch was sagging a bit. At first glance the house appeared grand despite its slide into disrepair, but there were actually only two stories of somewhat cramped and cluttered rooms leading off a large staircase. Above that there was a two-room attic space, and this plus the wraparound porch added to the effect of being more than it was.

Her great-grandparents had farmed tobacco and had built the house in 1938. By the time Aileen was a teenager, all the money and most of the family and the land had been long gone. Now the only thing left was the house and black-and-white snapshots and sepia-toned memories.

Betty Jean was in the kitchen mixing potatoes, her dog, Chigger, sprawled out at her feet. He was a Pit Bull that one of her friends had given her after Aileen's father died. He had been the runt of the litter, and even now, fully grown, he was a little on the small side for a Pit—hence the name Chigger. But what he was missing in size he made up for in ferociousness.

He was fiercely protective of her mother, and Aileen was thankful for that and rested easier for it in her apartment all the way back in Atlanta.

"I thought we'd just have a little supper, since it's too late for dinner. You haven't eaten, have you?" Betty Jean asked, adding another half a stick of butter.

"No, ma'am. I haven't had much of anything all day."

Her mother missed cooking for her family. With Dad gone, her brother living in Washington, and now her living in Atlanta, Betty Jean had no one to cook for anymore. So for the sake of her waistline, Aileen always showed up hungry, because her mother always cooked, and always expected her to eat.

Aileen poured herself a glass of iced tea and perched on one of the kitchen counter stools. "You need me to do anything?"

"No. I think I about got it all ready." Betty Jean pointed to a large pot of simmering green beans on the stove. "The beans are on and I just need to finish the steak and make the gravy. And for dessert I made a butternut pound cake."

She seemed to be going to a lot of trouble for just a little supper. Aileen looked closer at her mother. Was that a new dress? And her blond hair looked recently colored, minus the usual gray strands.

"You don't have to go to so much trouble just for me."

"Oh, didn't I tell you Steven was coming?" Betty Jean asked, pulling open the refrigerator and burying her head inside.

"Nooo, you did not tell me anyone was coming." *She could not be doing this to me again*, Aileen thought.

"Remember, Miriam's son, the one I told you about? He's moved back to work at his father's practice until he gets back on his feet. From his stroke, you know."

No, she didn't know, but she was sure she would hear all about it. Mentally she was nodding, yes, yes, this is exactly why she had moved out. She really should be thanking her mother for reminding her once again. She looked down at her wrinkled shirt and athletic pants and sighed.

Without another word, she climbed the stairs and resigned herself to a tedious and quite possibly excruciating evening ahead. There was no sense in entertaining false hope and what-ifs. It just wasn't in the cards for her. She threw herself down on her old bed she still used when she slept over and unsuccessfully tried to block out the past results of her mother's matchmaking.

There had been the time she had fixed her up with the guy named Lenny (the name should have been an indication, really, and the fact that he suggested she could just pick him up, which she had let go because she wasn't sure if she wanted to ride in some strange guy's car anyway) who was not only an alcoholic, but who was technically *still in jail*, only out on some kind of work pass. This he tells her in the middle of dinner. And if that wasn't bad enough, he had four cocktails with his shrimp scampi that he dragged out for over two hours and then ignored her polite requests to leave when the busboys began clearing and straightening the empty tables around them. She had been acutely embarrassed. She had smiled apologetically at their waitress and urged Lenny to go repeatedly. When they started shutting off lights in the back, she'd thrown down a twenty-dollar tip, got up, and walked out. Lenny managed to stagger out behind her, and she drove him back as fast as she could. But when she got him to his brother's house, she couldn't get him out of her car. He just kept sitting there talking nonsense until finally she had to knock loudly on the door and rouse his brother so she could get him to pull Lenny out of her car, which he did, appearing just as furious and disgusted as she was.

She got up and started searching through the few clothes she had left in her closet for something that wasn't too small or outdated.

And then there was the time her mother had encouraged her to pursue a man named Richard that Aileen had met on one of her Skeptic Traveler expeditions. He was working as a historian over at one of the paranormal sites, and she had listened to her mother when she pointed out his professional credentials and had initiated a meeting with him so she could "interview" him. Unfortunately, during the *interview* and subsequent meeting for lunch, which again Aileen had to initiate, he spent the whole time lecturing her on his work and was clearly just humoring her when she tried to take part in the conversation. He wasn't quite able to hide his amusement at her occupation. But it was when she turned to walk back to her car that he had done it. He had swatted her on the behind. He had followed that up by pushing her up against the car and trying to kiss her. It wasn't that she had anything against kissing, it was that she had something against kissing a man who obviously didn't think she was worthy of dating and getting to know on a personal level for a possible real relationship. In short, he was treating her like a floozy. He had confirmed her suspicions by murmuring "Hey, how about we go inside and you show *me* a little professional courtesy, babe," while trying to pull her close again. He had such an inflated sense of his own importance that he thought she *owed* him.

She pulled out a pair of faded blue jeans she hoped she could still wear and a cami she could layer under a low V-neck shirt.

And, there was her all time personal favorite: the night she had ended up in a high-speed chase running from the law when her date had decided it would be fun to run from a possible speeding ticket. She shouldn't have gone out with him, but her mother had set it up with his mother who thought Aileen, being an "older" woman (she had been all of twenty-two, only two years older than him), would be a responsible influence on her son. He had certainly proven his mother's worries were founded when instead of pulling over and waiting on the cop who had just flipped on his lights and spun it around in the road, he had stomped down on the gas and punched his souped-up Mustang. She had held on for dear life as he blew through a red light and slung it sideways down a side road. Zooming from side to side to avoid the parked cars in the street, he had executed the fastest parallel parking she had ever seen, flipped off his headlights, and yelled "DUCK!" She had obeyed on instinct, and that was how her date had ended; down on the floorboard, hiding from the law.

She looked critically in the full-length mirror mounted behind the door. Not too bad, but not great either. She could definitely stand to lose a few pounds. But at least her hair was finally growing out from the spectacularly bad haircut she had gotten at the mall two summers before.

She showered off, put on a minimum amount of make-up, and ran a brush through her hair. She wasn't about to dress up for this guy. She would just go about her business like she always did. She had nothing to do with this. If her mother wanted to invite someone to supper, then let her entertain him.

She clomped down the stairs just as Steven was coming in, not caring if she should be waiting upstairs for a moment in order to not appear too eager. This wasn't a date, anyway. She barely glanced in his direction as she continued on around through the den and into the kitchen. She made a show of checking everything on the stove, lifting lids and stirring until she began to feel guilty. She was being rude. She had just turned around when her mother came in leading Steven behind her.

"Aileen, this is Steven, you remember, Miriam Robert's son?"

"How do you do?" she asked, holding out her hand, and then felt ridiculous. Who the hell did she just sound like, Scarlet O'Hara? Blanch Dubois?

He had a good handshake, she noted, not soft or perfunctory—and mercifully quick. *One plus mark for him.* He pulled out a chair at the worn kitchen table that had been there for as long as she could remember and sat down while Betty Jean got him a glass of tea.

His dark blond hair was cut stylishly short, and she supposed he was good-looking in a slender, urban kind of way. He might have lived there some time as a child but there didn't seem to be much of the country left in him now. He was wearing a suit, with the jacket now hanging delicately from the coat rack in the foyer, that she suspected cost more than she earned in a month. There would be no mistaking him for the country bumpkin GP he probably saw his father as. From what her mother had told her, she gathered that Steven had left home and gone to live with a more affluent member of the family as soon as he was old enough to have a say. He had attended medical school and done his residency away from his father, which had to have been hard on him—having his son to follow in his footsteps but at such a distance that he couldn't share in it.

"How's your father?" she asked quietly.

Steven started nodding his head. "He's doing fine, showing some improvement. Shouldn't be too long and he can start some rounds of physical and speech therapy."

She started to ask him how long he would be in town then stopped herself, not wanting to pry, knowing it would lead to the whole issue of whether or not his father would ever be able to fully recover and take back over his practice, and what Steven would do if he didn't.

"Well, I hope you're hungry," said Betty Jean, coming back in from putting Chigger out. "We've got country-style steak, homemade mashed potatoes, green beans, biscuits, and butternut pound cake."

Aileen winced; her mother was *so* country. She sounded like she was reciting the menu from Cracker Barrel. Steven's eyebrows went up momentarily at the mention of all the bad-for-you, artery-clogging food, but he recovered quickly, and his face was impassive when they began to eat.

His face didn't remain impassive long. He was clearly enjoying the food, complimenting Betty Jean, and asking for another biscuit, even. *Another plus mark for him.* Her mother *was* a fabulous cook.

After eating about half of what was on her plate, Aileen sat back, stuffed, and considered unbuttoning her pants.

"So, where do you work—do you work?" Steven asked, sliding his plate away and taking a drink of his iced tea.

Aileen froze.

Oh how she hated this question. It was never a simple question and answer like it would be for most people when questioned about how they made their living. She always had to explain, and then to *justify*.

And she particularly hated the way he had just worded it: *"did she work"* as if she couldn't possibly have a real career, just some menial job. *Minus number one.*

"I work for *Southern Aurora* magazine."

"Oh? What do you do for them?"

She took a deep breath. "I write a travel section for them. So what kind of medicine do you specialize in?"

"Reaallly," he said, insultingly surprised, ignoring her attempt to change the subject. "What places have you written about?"

Oh for God's sake, why couldn't he be self-involved and talk only about himself. "My section is called 'Skeptical Traveler'. I visit paranormal sites."

"Oh really?" he said, this time with an incredulous lift on the end.

Minus number two. "Here we go," she muttered under her breath, and her mother kicked her under the table.

He stared at her, probably not sure how to respond, waiting on her to elaborate. When she didn't, Betty Jean jumped up, glaring at her from behind his back, and began carrying dishes into the kitchen. Steven made as if to stand, but before he had a chance to even think about leaving, Betty Jean poked her head back through. "Coffee's on, dessert will be a few minutes." He settled back down in his chair, looking as if he wanted to be anywhere but there.

She decided to try again, for her mother's sake. "I'm really not one of those ghost hunters like you see on television. I don't see or communicate with ghosts."

"Well that's good," he said, and gave a laugh, obviously relieved that she might not be a nutcase after all.

"I don't think there is such a thing as a supernatural phenomena, only mysteries we have yet to explain. Many supposed ghost sightings have natural explanations. Glowing lights produced by gases in a swamp, for example."

"Oh, you don't actually believe in all that yourself, you . . . what, uncover hoaxes?"

"I have," she said. He didn't get it. "But I don't seek to discredit or debunk anything. You're confusing skepticism with cynicism. Cynics believe that just because something is unexplainable does not mean that paranormal forces must be involved, only that an explanation has not been found yet. And conversely, just because something doesn't have a natural explanation, it doesn't mean that it didn't happen or that it's due to misconception, hallucinations, or fraud."

"Doesn't it? I mean, ghosts can't be proved by any scientific method or natural law."

"Not yet, but even Einstein proved a *law of nature* can be overturned. He found out with the detonation of the thermonuclear bomb that the conservation of energy law that stated that energy could neither be created nor destroyed but only changed in form was wrong. You could convert matter into energy. And what about the Big Bang theory? Scientists have never really been able to completely explain that. So with our knowledge so limited, how can we deny the possibility of the existence of the paranormal? After all, it can't be objectively proved that there is no afterlife."

"Well, that's one thing, but surely Occam's Razor can be applied here."

She practically gritted her teeth in frustration. Cynical pseudo-skeptics frequently used Occam's Razor, the principle that basically states that when you have competing theories then the simplest explanation is usually the right one, as an absolute rule for denying the existence of God or anything supernatural.

"So you're saying that if someone just happens to stop by a fortune teller and gets a cold reading, and they get a very specific prediction that the psychic reader had no way of knowing, and it proves true, then—"

"Then the fortune teller must have gotten the information some other way."

"You would rather believe some complicated, convoluted, *simpler* explanation that somehow, someone must have tipped the fortune teller off that they were coming even though they didn't know beforehand themselves, or that a spy in the room must have overheard some detail before the reading along with noticing something in their appearance that gave away clues, rather than believe it was simply a psychic experience?"

"I'm just saying that people have been known to remember and perceive things wrongly, and you have to admit, these people that say they believe in the paranormal are often charlatans or obviously irrational."

Minus, minus, minus. "First off, anecdotal evidence like eye witness accounts is used in the court of law all the time, why not for this? I admit some of them, like that Sylvia Browne lady, are a bit over the top and hard to believe, but having a spiritual and cultural view does not make someone less intelligent or rational than nonbelievers! Forty percent of all Americans attend church. Does that make them childish and unintelligent or crazy?" She took a breath and tried to calm down.

"I did not say that." A trace of irritation was coming into his voice now, too.

Betty Jean came back in and set two cups of coffee down in front of them, gave her another look, and walked right back out. This was one argument she had heard many times before.

"Look," Steven said in a conciliatory tone, "maybe Shakespeare's quote would be more appropriate: 'There are more things in Heaven and Earth, Horatio, than—'"

"—are dreamt of in your philosophy," she finished with him, trying to smile. "It's just that there seems to be a lot more evidence for the paranormal, than against it."

"Who are you trying to convince, me, or you?"

Chapter 3

Aileen nosed her car down the front of the tall building on Peachtree Court where the magazine offices were located, hoping for a rare parking space, then gave up and drove three blocks over to the nearest parking garage. By the time she walked into the front entrance, her feet were killing her. She had on new shoes and they were rubbing a blister on her heel. She stepped gingerly over to Colleen's front desk just as Mackenzie walked by on staggeringly high stiletto heels. She didn't seem to be having any trouble with her feet, she noted.

"I see CFM Shoes is in early for a change," Colleen said, making no effort to lower her voice.

Aileen snickered in spite of herself. Mackenzie "Come Fuck Me Shoes" worked in the human resources department and was famous for living up to her footwear and rarely made it in before 9:30 or 10:00. They watched her for a moment as she undulated down the hall, her long legs perfect.

"Hey, want to meet at the Pearl tonight?" Colleen asked. "I'm buying."

Aileen hated it when she did that. Early on in their friendship she had noticed that Colleen had a tendency to buy her things and pick up the check whenever they went out. At first she had thought maybe Colleen felt like she had to buy her friendship, but now that they were good friends she sometimes wondered if Colleen did it to remind her that even though she was just a secretary and Aileen was the writer with a journalism degree, she made more money. Or maybe Colleen was just being considerate of her tight financial situation.

"Sure, but dutch."

After agreeing on a time, she headed back to Ed's office. Ed, six foot two with iron-gray hair, was part owner and editor-in-chief of the magazine, and Aileen reported directly to him. When she had finally cut ties to the university where she graduated and left the part-time job she had been working as a paranormal field investigator for experience, she had approached Ed with the idea for a regular section that featured her visiting and evaluating paranormal sites. She had told him it would surely boost sales since the paranormal was so hot right then. And she didn't think it had hurt that she looked a little like Ed's daughter, who, she found out later, had died five years before in a car accident just after graduating from high school. She had seen him glance between her and a photograph of a brown-haired girl on his desk during the interview. Eventually, she was hired as a writer for a new "Skeptical Traveler" section. She had wanted the job mainly for her bank account, since a lucrative journalistic position had remained stubbornly elusive.

And now something she had merely dabbled in as she worked her way through college had somehow become her life.

She felt the first inkling that something wasn't right when she opened the door and walked in after Ed's barked assent. He threw the printout he had been holding down on the desk, and she saw it was the piece she had e-mailed him the night before.

"Is this it? Is this all we're ever going to get?" he asked, a look of disapproval replacing his usual placid expression.

Aileen was thrown. She had seen Ed displeased before, certainly, but never at *her*.

"Well, I . . . I can't . . . *lie*. If there isn't any evidence . . ." she stammered.

"Maybe you just don't want to see it." He sat back in his chair, observing her through narrowed eyes.

She thought of her heated discussion with Steven and flushed guiltily. She had not really done a decent investigation of Redhill. She had automatically assumed the whole thing was bogus, exactly like the cynical and frequently inept people she often complained about.

"Maybe this isn't the job for you, Aileen. I thought in time . . ." Ed didn't finish his sentence, letting it trail off as he looked at her coldly

Was he about to fire her?

Aileen dug deep. She dug down and reached for the one thing that would stop him in his tracks. "I'll do the piece on Crystal Edwards," she blurted.

He started back at her, apparently unmoved.

"And I'll do a full investigation this time."

Still nothing, his expression remained impenetrable. "And I'll do the damn show."

"That's my girl!" he exclaimed, smiling broadly, his formidable expression instantly vanishing.

Did he just play her? Ed had suggested her doing a piece on Crystal many times before, but she had always refused. Crystal was a "sensitive" with a penchant for flamboyant gypsy skirts who claimed she communicated with the dead. She performed paranormal cleansings, supposedly to remove or calm the paranormal entity, that were the kind of sensationalistic, merely for show investigations that gave professional paranormal investigators a bad name, and Aileen hated to cater to that by association. *And she probably charged a fee too*, she thought nastily. Sometimes she really didn't like her job.

She left Ed busy making phone calls and arrangements and wandered back up front. She was still trying to come to terms with what she had just gotten herself into when Mackenzie came tottering up the hall towards her.

"Oh there you are. Here, I ran across this at a yard sale. Now you can say you finally captured a ghost." She tossed a little green object at her as she walked by and Aileen caught it out of reflex. It was a small glow in the dark Casper the Friendly Ghost bobblehead. OH, the BITCH! She winged it across the reception area towards the wastebasket, missed, and landed it with a clang in the potted plant instead. Mackenzie pealed laughter behind her as Aileen wrenched the door open and stalked out.

Chapter 4

When Aileen walked into the Pearl at five minutes after seven, the place was hopping with the after-work crowd. She didn't see Colleen, so she weaved her way through the throng of people over to the bar and ordered a margarita. As she sipped her drink, she looked around and spotted Josh sitting in a booth by himself. She ordered a plate of nachos to be sent over, picked up her drink, and went to join him.

"You alone?" she asked, sliding into the booth across from him.

"Yeah, you?"

"Colleen's supposed to meet me here." She waited for him to make some remark about getting the hell out of there before she came, but he merely drank the last of his drink and said nothing.

Colleen had been after Josh since he came to work at the magazine three years earlier. She was constantly coming on to him at every opportunity even though he was nearly ten years younger than her. Josh was gorgeous, despite his radical hairdo, with a dark complexion that was currently enhanced by a five o'clock shadow that gave him even more of the kind of dangerous appeal that attracted many women, including Aileen. In the beginning when they had first started working together, they had gotten a little too close one night, had become a little too familiar with each other, and the inevitable had happened and they had ended up making out in the car like two teenagers. Aileen had been tempted, but not wanting to be just another notch on his bedpost, she had reluctantly pulled away, telling him she didn't like to get involved with her coworkers.

She spotted Colleen coming towards them as the waitress set her order of nachos on the table. She started to make room for her when Josh unexpectedly moved over and patted the seat cushion beside him. Aileen's mouth fell open. There was definitely something wrong with him—and with Colleen. She acted like she didn't even notice Josh pouring on the charm, throwing his arm about her shoulders, listening attentively to everything she said. She just ignored him, and barely said, "Thanks Josh" when he complimented her on her dress.

As they talked, Aileen touched only briefly on work, trying not to think too much about the expedition, on camera no less, to be shown on Crystal Edward's upcoming television series *Spirit Hunters*. A group called The Eastern Paranormal Service ran the show, and the episode with her working in tandem with Crystal was supposed to be a joint endeavor to promote both the show and the magazine. *Southern Aurora* would promote the premier of the new television series, guest starring their very own Aileen Whitney, and viewers of the show were invited to visit the *Spirit Hunters* website, where a link directed them to *Southern Aurora*, for more information on the supernatural.

Josh interrupted their conversation and gave her a chance to speak to Colleen when he got up, excused himself, and wandered off, probably tiring of Colleen's inattention.

As soon as Josh was out of earshot, Aileen leaned forward. "Okay, what gives?"

"*What?*" Colleen asked, smiling broadly.

"Josh is on the prowl and you don't care?"

Colleen continued to smile in a knowing way.

"And you're in way too good a mood." It suddenly dawned on her. "Did you meet someone?"

"Yes!" Colleen shrieked. She proceeded to breathlessly tell her all about her chance meeting with "Bobby" that had led to a dinner date that now seemed to finally be a real relationship.

"He calls me all the time. We do everything together. He even helps me with my work. He seems really interested in what I do."

"I'm so glad for you Colleen," she said, and meant it. Colleen had been going through what was as close to a depression as her energetic, friendly personality would allow, not going out as much and occasionally showing up for work disheveled and uncharacteristically moody. She was glad to see her looking so well and in such good spirits. Colleen was certainly pretty, but in no way a great beauty. Her best attributes were her long blond hair and slender figure, but her nose was a little too large and her age was starting to show in the lines around her eyes and mouth. But the quality that detracted the most from her attributes was her lack of self-confidence. That old saying that you can never find love when you are looking for it seemed to be especially true for Colleen, for no matter how hard she tried to attract a potential mate, it was as if she walked around with a sign that said "desperate and needy" printed on her forehead.

Colleen's phone went off, and she began exchanging text messages with Bobby. Aileen got up to go look for Josh.

She found him at the bar, knocking back another drink. "Don't you think you should slow down? The night's still young."

He shot her a look. "Hey, I'm just trying to take a little break here, have a li'l fun," he said, slurring his words ever so slightly.

"What, with Colleen now?"

He didn't even bother to reply to that and just when she was going to give up and walk away and leave him to whatever he was brooding about, he spoke.

"I just want to forget," he said in a low voice she had to lean over to catch.

"Forget what Josh?" She was truly concerned now. Something was really bothering him.

"I can't forget that day at Redhill. You don't know, Aileen. *I* didn't know."

"What are you talking about?"

"I never really believed, you see," he said, looking at her in consternation. "And now I do."

She looked into his disturbed eyes and knew that he was telling the absolute truth.

"What was it, Josh?" she whispered.

He looked at her as if afraid to speak it aloud. He shook his head. "I can't explain it. It was a feeling I had. Just a horrible feeling like I had been sucked down into this *black void*. It was like the worst, most horrible feeling of apprehension, of, of dread, of fear. I can't describe it, but I know I have never felt anything like it before, and I never want to again."

"My God, Josh," she said, not knowing quite what to say.

"I'm quitting."

"What! No!" *Surely not*, she thought, shocked. Josh had worked long and hard to achieve his position as their chief technical specialist, and his giving up what he had always loved so much seemed inconceivable.

"I'll stay for the show. For you. Then I'm gone." He swiveled around to face her. "'Sometimes horror chills our blood. To be near such mystic things.'"

She looked at him uncertainly, not knowing the reference.

"Elizabeth Barrett Browning."

Chapter 5

Aileen and her team showed up at the private home that had been chosen at 5:00 p.m. and began setting up their equipment. They had the property to themselves for the moment. Tracy and Christine Johnson, their teenage daughter, Michelle, and Christine's mother, Alice, were gone doing their on-camera interviews.

Crystal and her crew hadn't arrived yet, and this gave her time to walk around and record a few observations into her mini recorder and get the feel of the place. She and her team would provide the scientific and technical expertise—testing, monitoring, and recording any evidence of paranormal activity—but she fully intended to report the facts and only the facts as she saw them.

The Johnsons hadn't moved all the way in yet, and the house still had the uncared for look of abandonment about it. The lawn had only been mowed in a small patch around the house and stood overgrown and nearly waist-high in other areas. The weatherworn house was nearly devoid of color with only a few curling flakes of white paint left here and there on the old wooden planks, and the roof needed work. A fixer-upper bought for nearly nothing, no doubt. She had found only a few obscure references of the locals reporting strange and inexplicable noises and shadowy apparitions. Apparently all the recent hoopla had been started when a green blob that resembled a smudge of ectoplasm had been caught in a picture taken by Tracy right after purchasing the home.

They spent the next hour calibrating equipment and taking a few readings outside since they didn't have a key. Colleen, ecstatic at being included, was serving as investigative assistant and manned their best video camera, filming everybody and everything as they went about their various jobs. Dena, an amateur investigator who sometimes volunteered with them, walked around pointing and shooting with the pistol-type thermometer, occasionally stopping to take a picture, while Aileen tried out Josh's newest toy, a portable EVP (electronic voice phenomenon) listener that somewhat resembled a small guitar amplifier.

Josh grabbed the motion sensor and headed around back. Curious, Aileen followed him. As she came around the side of the house, she saw him drop it into a bush by the back door. He had already traversed the back yard and slipped around the corner before she had a chance to question him.

It was twilight before the Johnson family, followed by Crystal Edwards and her entourage, showed up. The cameramen piled out first, already filming Crystal. This time she was wearing a multitude of bangles and pendants and a long skirt of what looked like a bunch of pastel scarves sown together.

Crystal wasted no time lining the family up in front of the house and holding forth. "Beware all those who forget the past for you shall pay the price for not heeding the spirits of the deceased," she proclaimed majestically, the cameraman centering on her as she raised her arms. "The other side has touched this place. A spiritual force that is not of this world has contacted you. You will be the ones to see this, to witness, and to remember.

"And I ask you," she called out, raising her voice, "are you ready to help guide this spirit to a more peaceful place?" She waited until one by one, all of the family members answered, "Yes".

"Then let us come together," Crystal commanded. The Johnsons linked hands and began to pray, all of them swaying slightly, their eyes closed.

Crystal led the way as they started into the house. Pausing before stepping over the threshold, she removed a small bottle of what Aileen could only assume was holy water, splashed a liberal amount on her hand, then made a broad sign of the cross in the doorway.

Feeling like she was in a bad *Exorcist* movie, Aileen followed the group into the house. One of Crystal's minions carrying a large stick of incense and another cameraman trailed behind her. Aileen carried a handheld EVP recorder and compact thermal camera that had a full color display for hot or cold spots. She knew that Colleen or Dena would get any pictures or video they might need, and Josh would monitor the EMF (electromagnetic field) levels.

They had barely gotten in the door when Josh began arguing with one of Crystal's investigators who insisted on leaving the power on with just the lights off, while Josh wanted to shut it off to avoid false electrical readings. He showed Josh the new state-of-the-art EMF meter he was using—the only piece of equipment they appeared to have other than a video camera—that blocked out common power lines and household electricity. The rest of them waited while the technician demonstrated by switching the meter from "Sum" to "Filter" until Josh was grudgingly satisfied. Colleen and the film crew, who were eagerly catching everything, caught all of this on camera, of course.

"I don't like it. He's up to something," Josh muttered.

She decided to call them on it, camera or no camera. "If the power doesn't need to be off, then why are we in the dark?" Both Colleen and Crystal's cameraman swiveled in her direction.

There was a tense silence, and then Crystal spoke, recovering fast, "It is necessary to engage the spirits in a manner they will be more receptive to."

Aileen rolled her eyes at Josh and said no more.

After instructing all nonessential persons to stay in the front room, Crystal's cool blond assistant came forward and addressed the family in an affected voice, "I have come to accompany you as you journey with the spirits. We will guide you through the center of this house. This path will lead you as you search for knowledge. This is what the spirits require. This is why you are here. Let us go on our mission."

With that she turned and began handing out two-way radios and flashlights. After each family member had theirs, they were led off separately to different parts of the house.

Aileen and Josh moved around taking their readings while trying not to get in anyone's way. She went up the stairs with her thermal camera and recorder, where Christine and Michelle had been taken, and Josh headed down towards the basement.

She navigated around as best she could in the dark, but found no meaningful cold or hot spots. She noticed that Crystal and her team appeared to have vanished into the woodwork.

She had just reached the end of the hall when a door slammed back in the direction of the room Christine had just gone into. She heard a muffled cry, "*Hey!*"

She heard her again, this time faintly over the crackle of someone's radio downstairs. "I can't get out! Someone shut the door and it won't open. Oh Lord."

Suddenly there was a loud bang in the direction of the cellar and she heard several screams throughout the house.

The ghosts had arrived right on cue.

She shot back down the stairs and met Josh coming back up. "What's going on?'

"I don't know. But I haven't had any abnormal readings. Have you?"

"No," she just had time to say when there came the sound of another loud slam and more screams, from Christine and Michelle, from the sound of it. Suddenly the air was filled with the crackle and hiss of the radios as the family called back and forth to each other.

"Something's behind me!' shrieked Michelle in some unknown room above them. "I'm serious!"

"Oh Lord, I'm feeling cold air. It's getting cold in here!" came Christine.

Now praying from the grandmother, Alice, "Help me to be strong, Lord. God deliver us from evil. God deliver me."

"God deliver me," Michelle repeated like a mantra, apparently not too scared to press the button on her radio.

After that the situation rapidly deteriorated into a mass of confusing bangs, loud screams, and Michelle's hysterical crying. Crystal's team suddenly reappeared and ran to and fro, up and down the stairs, confusing everything as they tried to "calm the apparition".

Aileen gave up, switched off her camera and EVP, and went outside on the porch to wait out the ridiculous farce that was playing out inside. After a few minutes, Josh came out and sat down on the steps beside her.

"You believe it?" she asked.

"*Hell* no. Even if there were a ghost, you'd never know it with all of that going on," he said, jabbing a thumb at the sound of screaming and running feet thundering throughout the house behind them.

"No feelings this time?" She had to ask to be sure.

"No. This was no haunting. Right after we went in, the motion sensor by the back door went off."

"What do you think it means?"

"I think it means that someone snuck in or out the back door. And I cornered that tech guy coming back upstairs and got a look at that new EMF before he could stop me, and you know what? He had set it back to "Sum" so it would look like it was picking something up. He said it was an accident, but I don't believe him."

"This whole thing has been staged for the show," she said.

They heard a sound behind them and turned to find Colleen and one of Crystal's crew pointing their cameras right on them, recording everything they said.

Chapter 6

Ed slammed down the phone. "Do you have any idea how many calls I've been getting? Crystal herself has already called three times. She has taken this whole thing as a direct attack on her reputation, and she is threatening to sue for slander!"

"Can't they just cut it out for the show?"

"They can, and they will, I'm sure. But we agreed to do this show and now they're threatening breach of contract. It was leaked to an online tabloid." He thrust a printout at her. The headline across the top read: *New Spirit Hunters Series Bogus?*

Aileen stared down at a picture of her and Josh in front of the Johnson house. Josh was frowning up at the camera and she looked particularly disgruntled.

Aileen read the caption across the top. *Skeptical Traveler Goes to the Other Side.* She skimmed down. *Southern Aurora's Aileen Whitney may have traveled into the paranormal realm in her recent guest appearance on the new television series Spirit Hunters, but the only side she has gone over to is the cynical side. Has the skeptical traveler joined the ranks of pseudo-*

skeptics everywhere? Aileen Whitney's investigations have gone from the scientific quest for knowledge to downright unfounded accusations of fraud. It was reported that while filming, she accused popular medium Crystal Edwards of being a charlatan then went on to call the entire show a "hoax". Witnesses confirmed . . ." Aileen threw the printout down in disgust.

"I did not say that! Well, not exactly," she protested. "The whole thing was staged, I tell you! You can ask Josh."

"I already have. Which is one of the reasons you still have a job despite your obvious effort to ruin this for us. The best thing to do at this point is to let Crystal give whatever take she wants on this whole thing and let it all die down."

"I'm sorry, Ed, the last thing I want is to cause you any problems. You gave me a job wh—"

"Have I ever shown you a picture of my daughter?" Ed asked, stopping her apology in its tracks. She had heard rumors that something had happened after his daughter died that caused him to devote his life to the paranormal, but this was the first time that he had ever mentioned her.

He picked up a framed picture out of the group of family photos he had arranged on his desk and turned it around for her to see.

His daughter Regina gazed out from the picture, smiling softly. Aileen thought it might be her senior picture taken right before she was killed in the accident. They did look a little alike. Regina's hair had been the same brownish color, only longer and wavier.

She leaned forward to see it better and spotted a smaller photo stuck in the corner. A younger, chubbier version of Regina grinned gleefully, holding out what looked like a dirty piece of rock.

"That was the day she found the arrowhead. She always said she wanted to be an archaeologist, and after that there was no stopping her. She dug holes all over our yard. We had holes everywhere." He grinned faintly at the memory, and then his expression faded and became somber.

"She was beautiful," she said.

"After the wreck she visited me."

"You saw her ghost?" she asked, careful to keep any hint of disbelief out of her voice. The last thing she wanted to do was offend this kind man who had given her a chance.

"No, nothing like that. I saw her in a dream. I was devastated after she passed. It was bad. I . . . I was a mess. I couldn't eat. I couldn't sleep. Until finally one night I did . . . and she came to me. She was sitting right in front of me like you are now. She talked to me and she told me 'Daddy, it's okay, it's okay. I'm all right and everything's fine now. It's okay, I'm *all right*,' his voice cracked and then broke. He took of his glasses and wiped his eyes. "I woke up still hearing the sound of her voice, and now I try to remember—" He stopped again, swallowing. "I try to remember her words and the reassurance I felt," he finished, his voice thick.

Aileen felt her throat tighten, and she blinked back tears.

Ed slipped his glasses back on. "I have never before or since had a dream that was such a vivid, clear conversation. And I have never dreamed about her again. Not once." Ed placed the photo back with the others. "Never, ever make the mistake of not believing in anything, Aileen. Don't make the mistake of dismissing a mystical experience, because we don't know. We can't know. It is impossible."

"Here," he said, handing her a piece of paper. "Now get out of my office."

The slip of paper had two words on it: *Crybaby Bridge*. Her next assignment.

Chapter 7

The location of Crybaby Bridge was listed simply as River Road, Andersonville County, South Carolina. After a little more searching, she found a description that stated it was the rusty steel bridge over the Tugaloo River. Just about every region had its own "Crybaby Bridge" legend, and this one claimed to be haunted by the spirit of a woman who had thrown her baby over the bridge to spite her husband and then instantly regretted it. Supposedly you could occasionally encounter her leaning over the bridge looking for it and sometimes even hear the sound of the baby crying.

The rain it had been misting suddenly turned into a deluge as she crossed the state line and started down River Road, the old back road that led into Andersonville. Her windshield wipers worked overtime to keep up but were no match for the driving rain, and she struggled to see the road.

She had just decided to pull over when she spotted the bleary outline of a bridge up ahead. She slowed to a crawl and bumped up on the bridge, trying to get a better look at it through the partially fogged windows. She flipped the heater to defrost and felt the car falter. She gave it more gas and it lurched forward, hitched a few more times, and then quit, rolling slowly to a stop in the middle of the bridge.

She turned the key a few times, but the engine wouldn't start. Maybe something had gotten too wet? She would just have to wait it out. She picked up her cell phone and looked at the display. She had been down to one bar before she had started down the long road, and now there was nothing except the No Signal icon in the upper left corner.

She turned on her hazards even though there was virtually no traffic on the road and prepared to wait.

The rain thundered on the bridge around her.

As suddenly as it started, the rainstorm was over. She cracked open her door and tentatively stepped out into the weird dripping silence that followed in the wake of a good hard rain.

Brown murky water rushed beneath her, fast and furious from the storm. The bridge looked nothing like the description she had read, but the river and surrounding area looked similar. It was possible the bridge had been rebuilt since then. There was a small white sign posted on the other side, but it was too far away for her to read.

She tried the car again with no luck and then went to check the sign.

When she got close enough to read it, she saw it was indeed the Tugaloo River. So this was it. She turned around and looked back to where her car sat, yellow emergency lights flashing in the stillness. There was still no sign of any traffic, which was starting to seem odd, despite the weather.

She took her time getting back to the car, listening, but heard nothing but the rushing of the river. She tried to keep an open mind and clear her head of all thoughts. But the crying baby remained elusive.

She grabbed her camera and took pictures from both sides, capturing the bridge and the river it crossed from all angles.

After nearly two and a half hours, she was beyond frustrated. The car refused to start, and it was getting close to dark. She was going to have to walk, and sooner rather than later from the looks of the deepening shadows along the road.

She knew she had not passed any houses back the way she had come, so she started off in the other direction.

About a half a mile on the other side of the bridge, the rain came again with no warning. One minute she was berating herself with second thoughts about leaving the car, and the next stinging needles of rain were pelting her, drenching her in seconds. It was coming down so hard she could barely see.

The rain ran freely down her face and body in a steady stream. She was starting to get scared. The road and surrounding area were beginning to flood. Water pooled in the lower lying ground on either side of her and ran in cascades down the sloping road.

It was almost dark now, and she decided she had better get off the road and look for higher ground. She stepped over a half-filled muddy ditch, climbed the small bank, and ducked under the dead brown leaves of a large oak.

Thunder rumbled in the distance.

The cold rain had chilled her, and she shivered as she contemplated her situation. Going back to the car probably wouldn't be a good idea since the rising river was liable to wash the bridge, and it, away. She turned in a slow circle, looking through the almost pitch black trees behind her, and spotted the distant flicker of light. Her spirits instantly lifted.

Trying to keep the small flicker of light in sight, she followed along the tree line looking for a path or driveway in.

The storm wasn't abating as she had hoped, but getting worse and now seemed to center right above her. Jagged lightning arced and lit up the dark sky like a heavenly strobe light. Distant thunder rumbled and drew closer, louder with each passing minute.

Incredibly, amidst the thundering and lightning, it began to hail. First tiny pieces of ice and then larger chunks rained down on her, striking her painfully on the head and shoulders.

She stumbled along the road, desperate to get out of the storm. She almost passed the dirt and gravel driveway when lightning flashed again and she spotted it. She hurried up the drive, trying unsuccessfully to protect herself from the falling chunks of ice, her shoes slipping and sliding in the mud.

The driveway wound through the trees, the distant light appearing then disappearing as it curved around and back again, until finally, she reached the end and found herself at the edge of a clearing around a large old house.

The source of the light she had been following was the headlights of a car parked in a gravel area at the side. She huddled underneath another tree, momentarily escaping the stinging hail. She could just make out the figure of an elderly man standing on the porch, his hunched figure leaning on a cane.

She jumped and cried out as a particularly loud crash of lightning hit the ground maybe ten yards from her, the concussion deafening. It was immediately followed by another bolt slamming down even closer.

She navigated towards the old man on the porch at a dead run, bolts of lightning shooting down from the sky and zapping the ground around her. She made it about halfway when there was another blinding flash, and she just had time to hear the beginning of the loudest sound she had ever heard in her life—and then she knew no more.

Chapter 8

Aileen couldn't hear, see, or feel a thing. She lay in the quietness of utter dark and realized she wasn't breathing. It felt as if the wind had been knocked out of her. After concentrating for several long seconds, she finally managed a breath and her eyesight returned, but she still couldn't move and her whole body felt numb. She noticed a sweet burning smell and oddly, the intense scent of roses.

After a minute or two, she was able to lift up her head, and she saw that tendrils of steam were rising from her body. Another minute, and she was able to struggle up into a sitting position, but she still couldn't feel her legs. A loud ringing punctuated the eerie silence. She reached up and felt something wet coming from her ear. It was blood; her eardrum, possible both of them, had been ruptured.

From what she could see in the darkness, she had been blown back about ten feet from where she had been standing. Thankfully, the storm was dying down, the night sky only occasionally punctuated by distant flashes of light.

Something shifted in her peripheral vision. She turned her head and her heart nearly jumped out of her chest. She felt her mind slip in sheer horror at the unnaturalness of this *thing* that could not possibly *be*. The girl-thing's eyes were solid white with tiny pinpoint pupils staring dead at her, its awareness and regard of Aileen flooding her with mindless dread. She could feel her mouth and vocal cords straining but could hear nothing as she screamed silently, scrambling backwards.

The inhuman form disappeared.

She looked frantically on either side of her, but there was no sign of the thing.

Then she felt an almost imperceptible movement on the back of her neck, a small breath of air, and her skin crawled.

It was behind her!

She twisted around and there it was—its dead mouth moving, saying something, as it scuttled towards her. She began shrieking again and her mind slipped some more. She screamed soundlessly in terror, the rational world turned into a nightmare.

Aileen snapped to, the old man shaking her, looming above her. He was mouthing something at her, but she couldn't make him out. She whipped her head around, but there was nothing there.

Whatever she had seen was now gone, if it had ever been there at all.

The doctor in the emergency room where she'd been taken said she was probably still alive due to the silver locket she had been wearing. The lightning had been diverted down into the necklace and then across her body, instead of into it, which would have stopped her heart. She had been lucky. Her shoes had been split open and blown off. She had burns on both her ankles and around her neck where her necklace had been. A weird parody of bright red lightning bolts traced down her chest and branched down her abdomen in fern-like patterns. And one of her eardrums had burst but would hopefully heal.

By ten o'clock that evening, she had been moved into a room and had spoken on the phone to Colleen and then to Ed, who had agreed to drive up with Josh the next morning to retrieve her car. She called her mother last, and with difficulty finally convinced her to wait until the next morning to come, when they would be releasing her.

Despite the drugs they had given her for the pain, Aileen found herself unable to sleep. She kept coming back to the nightmare image of the girl-thing. Her mind shied away from the horrific image of its milky white eyes trained on her. It had seemed so real—her coming to after she was hit, the wet ground beneath her, the distant flashes of light, the girl-thing, all of it. She clicked off the television mounted on the wall, lowered the bed some, and gingerly turned over. She had one more thought before pushing it away and finally drifting off to sleep. If Ed's dream was a real visit from his daughter, then did that mean her nightmare encounter was also real?

She awoke some time later and turned painfully over onto her back. Her pain meds had worn off, and she smelled that cloying scent of roses again. When she had mentioned it, the doctor had told her that strange smells were a common response to being hit by lightning and would eventually go away. She pressed the button to call the nurse and waited, but the customary "Yes?" through the speaker behind her bed never came. She pressed it again. Still no response.

Carefully, she climbed out of bed and walked over and pulled the door to her room open. The long hallway stretched out in front of her. The lights had been dimmed for the evening and pockets of shadow pooled between the meager reach of the small lights above each of the doors. There were no sounds coming from any of the other rooms. All was quiet, unusually so, from her past experiences with hospitals. How anyone had ever been able to sleep in a hospital with all the noise, and a nurse waking you up for your vital signs every few hours even if you did manage to sleep, was beyond her.

She started slowly forward, still hearing nothing. It was like a cloak of silence had fallen over the hospital. The first room she passed was empty, the room clearly unoccupied. And so was the next one. And the next. All the way down the hall, she found all the rooms vacant, even the ones with closed doors. When she reached the nursing station, there was no one there either.

She stood in the bright florescent light, unwilling to go back and enter the void of the darkened wing behind her. It was deathly quiet with no sign of any hospital personal anywhere. She was completely alone. *Anyone could just walk right in off the streets and—*

The elevator dinged loudly in the silence behind her. Aileen jumped and cried out.

She stepped back fearfully and waited for it to open.

The doors swished apart. The elevator was empty. She let out the breath she had subconsciously been holding. She was letting her imagination get the best of her. The nurse was probably only gone to the restroom.

She turned to go wait in her room and met the hideous eyes of the girl-thing standing behind her.

This time her terror was so great her body's fight or flight instinct failed her, and she froze in place, petrified. She realized vaguely that the odd keening sound she was hearing was coming from her own throat.

She finally managed to move her feet and stumbled back against the wall. It responded by moving inhumanly fast from several feet away to inches from her face with no discernable steps in between. Its ghost face stared into hers, and she felt a scream building. The unnatural orbs of its eyes shifted down. Slowly, the girl-thing reached for her throat . . . Aileen let loose a guttural cry of abject terror.

Her scream scared the nurse who was coming in so badly that she flung the tray of medications she had been carrying up in the air. It landed with a crash back out in the hallway. Excited voices sounded up and down the floor as frightened patients called out. Several nurses and one doctor filled her door, all of them staring in at her in amazement.

"Sorry!" Aileen shook her head and tried to clear it. "It was . . ." She couldn't think of the word nightmare. It wouldn't come to her at all. Finally she gasped out, *"Bad dream. Bad dream."*

She took in the amused relief on everyone's face and had never been more embarrassed in her life. She came back down off the back of the bed where she had climbed in her terror.

Her nurse adjusted her IV, and mopped the sweat off her brow. "I think we might need to cut down on your pain medication, sweetie."

"Well, I don't think she's had anything recently," said one of the other nurses, looking at her chart.

"Well maybe we need to get you some then," her nurse said, and they both laughed.

Aileen was grateful for their good humor. The bad dream was already fading, replaced by the reality of their laughter.

Chapter 9

Aileen was finally discharged late the next day. Betty Jean drove her reluctantly to her apartment after Aileen firmly deflected her plans for taking her back home with her. She had been more freaked out by the nightmare incident at the hospital than she had realized. She had barely slept the whole time she had been there, and as much as she loved her mother, Betty Jean had been glued to her side nearly the entire time, and all she wanted at this point was some peace and quiet and some alone time to think and process everything that had happened. Her burns hurt all the time despite the pain meds, and her left ear where her eardrum had been ruptured throbbed and she could barely hear out of it. She just wanted to lie down and sleep for about three days.

Despite the fact that her eyelids were drooping from exhaustion, she lay down on the couch instead of going straight to bed and surreptitiously texted Colleen while her mother fussed with pillows and pulled out blankets.

She was wrapped in a comforter and sipping chicken soup when Colleen arrived. She threw her bag down and leaned over to give her a quick hug, and Aileen caught a whiff of the Channel Coco she always wore. Her sense of smell seemed to have been somehow enhanced by the lightning strike and didn't seem to be diminishing any. She had continued to be plagued by the cloying scent of flowers—in particular roses—since the strike, and now it was all she could do not to recoil from the strong perfume.

"Thank you," she whispered as Colleen pulled away.

"No problem," Colleen whispered back, then raised her voice as Betty Jean came back into the room. "I talked to Ed and he gave me the rest of the week off, so I brought some things so I could stay and help out for a few days."

"Well that's not necessary. Why, I'm already here—" Betty Jean started to say, and Aileen quickly turned to Colleen. "Could you? Oh, good, that would be great, like a sleepover!" she said, interjecting as much enthusiasm as she could considering the depths of her exhaustion. She turned back to Betty Jean. "And you must need a break by now. I know how tired you must be."

"Well, if you're sure..."

"Really. Go. I've got it. And I will call you if I have any problems," Colleen said, and after another ten minutes of reassurances and promises to make sure Aileen rested and phoned her daily, Betty Jean finally departed.

Aileen slumped back down on the couch. "You don't really have to stay. I'm not an invalid, despite what my mother thinks."

"I know."

The first thing Colleen did was pour out the cold chicken soup her mother had fixed and replace it with a cup of one of her herbal concoctions. Colleen firmly believed in herbal supplements and natural healing and was constantly touting the merits of some kind of smoothie or new supplement. This one was some kind of tea that was supposed to promote healing, and after tentatively taking a sip, she had to admit it was pretty good.

Colleen quietly moved about the apartment, shutting curtains and blinds and turning off lamps. She fetched a glass of ice water and placed it beside Aileen's bed, where she had already pulled back the covers. Aileen slipped gratefully between the cool sheets. She felt like she could sleep for days.

Colleen pulled the covers up around her, murmured, "goodnight," and then clicked the door shut, and Aileen was out.

The next morning she awoke stiff and sore to the outline of sunlight streaming in around her bedroom blinds. She was so thirsty her tongue was stuck to the roof of her mouth. She reached for the glass of water and gasped. Her skin felt like it was cracking and splitting where she had been burned, and the dull headache that had persisted since she was struck had advanced to a full-blown throbbing. Wincing, she sat up in bed, trying not to move her head any more than necessary, and drank half the water. Digging around in her pocketbook where she had dropped it the day before, she found the bottle of pain pills she had gotten filled at the hospital. She twisted the cap off, shook one into her hand and swallowed it with the other half of the water.

After a few minutes, she managed to make it into the living room, and after a few minutes more, she felt well enough to struggle into the kitchen and start some coffee. Colleen had left a note on the table saying she actually did have to leave early for work and would check on her later.

When the coffee finished, she fixed herself a cup and swallowed another half of a pain pill. She flicked on the television and that's where she stayed for the next half hour or so until she finally began to feel the numbing buzz of the pain medication.

Another half hour, plus some juice and a piece of toast, and she was feeling marginally human again. She thought of the inhuman girl in her dream. She felt the outline of the burn around her neck. Two faint red lines trailed down to a small round patch of singed skin where her necklace had been burned into her. The white disjointed limbs and dead white eyes of the ghost-girl rose up in her mind, and she shuddered and pushed the image away. Ed's lost daughter visiting him was one thing, but this was something else entirely. Thankfully, the nightmare had not returned the night before. She'd slept so hard that if she dreamed at all she didn't remember it. She thought about those dream catcher things the Native Americans used and wondered where she could find one. Just in case.

Chapter 10

After sitting around the apartment the next two weeks and pretty much doing nothing but sleeping, eating, and watching TV, she was starting to get a little stir-crazy. The weird trace patterns had mostly disappeared from her chest and abdomen, her burns were healing nicely, and the infernal ringing in her ear had finally subsided.

After showering, she tried to make an effort. She blow-dried her hair, dressed in a flattering pair of pants and a new shirt, and put on some makeup.

Technically she was still supposed to be recovering, but the prospect of spending another weekend cooped up in her apartment alone certainly didn't appeal to her, so at about four o'clock she phoned Colleen at the office with an idea she had been kicking around for a while. Her disbelief had been shaken by Ed's certainty that his daughter had visited him in a dream, and she had begun to take her job more seriously and was anxious to get back to work in some capacity, even if it was really just for fun.

"Um, I'll have to check something and then I'll call you right back, okay?"

Aileen waited impatiently on her to ring back. She had forgotten about Colleen's new boyfriend, and now that she had made the decision to go, and gotten all excited about it, it was probably for nothing.

But whatever it was that Colleen had been worried about, she managed to work it out because she called right back.

"Let the games begin!" she said, laughing. "I'm on my way."

The ghost walk Aileen had chosen was held in Greenville, South Carolina, about two and half hours from Atlanta. She had gotten the idea from some brochures she had plucked out of a stand in her hotel lobby the last time she had been in Charleston. There were several walking haunted history tours advertised in the Charleston area—one even offered a haunted boat ride around the harbor—but they weren't held in the winter, plus she wasn't really up to such a long drive, so she had chosen Greenville instead. Greenville was also a historic town, only smaller, and surprisingly sophisticated.

From what she had gathered on the website, this particular tour around and about the downtown area was a fairly new endeavor from an enterprising fellow by the name of Jacob Priestly. The website included only a few photos of him talking to a group of people standing in front of various buildings, so she was unprepared for the renovation downtown Greenville had undergone since the last time she had visited.

It was dark by the time she and Colleen emerged from her car on the upper end where she had gotten lucky and snagged one of the parking spaces angled along Main Street. They took their time walking along the wide sidewalk, and she marveled at the near magical quality of all the lights and people and cars cruising by. The street was lit with old-fashioned street lamps, and tiny iridescent bulbs were interspersed in the thick boughs of the trees in a glittering canopy above them. High heels and smart boots clattered on the sidewalk as elegantly dressed women hurried by in the cool night air accompanied by men in suits and dress clothes on their way to or from one of the many destinations that lined the quaint old street.

Music spilled from the doorways of pubs and coffee shops where younger, more casually dressed men and women gathered, talking and laughing, beneath the neon glow of signs with names like The Beaded Frog, Lemongrass, and The Underground. The latter pointed down a flight of stone steps that led one level down to a narrow rock-lined passageway where tiny wrought-iron tables and chairs had been set up along the wall. Tea bars, wine cafés, art galleries, clothiers, jewelers, and deli-bakeries crowded the street, with small plazas offering outside dining dotted here and there amongst them.

A long white limousine slid by amidst the unmistakable clatter of a horse-drawn carriage, and the vibration and whump of a helicopter flying overhead seemed to complete the image of a truly metropolitan city.

The elevated pedestrian bridge, held up by thick white cables rising up in the air above the park and river falls below, seemed almost overkill after the fountains, statues, and art they had already passed. Laughter floated down as they walked alongside the river rushing and splashing over the rocks.

By this time, they had made it all the way to the newly revitalized south end, where the traffic and shops were thin enough to allow for larger, more upscale restaurants with the coup de grâce of actual valet parking. Aileen couldn't help but stare at the young men in their immaculate attire of black pants, white shirts, and matching black ties standing in front of the long red carpet that preceded the High Cotton, a restaurant so fine, so discriminating, that she knew she could never afford to dine there.

Two more blocks and they found the old general store where they were supposed to meet. Aileen spotted their contact, Jacob Priestly himself, as they crossed the street. He straightened from the wall he had been leaning against and offered first her, then Colleen his hand as she introduced herself and then Colleen. He was a good-looking man despite the few extra pounds he carried. He was dressed warmly in a mid-length leather coat and stocking hat. The extra weight didn't show in his face or chin, and his even features, full lips, and straight white teeth gave him an appealing attractiveness.

They stood and chatted while they waited on a couple that hadn't shown yet. Aileen found herself liking the guy, who seemed polite, well-read, and smiled often, nothing like the faintly nefarious character she had halfway been expecting.

The other couple, a middle-aged man and woman, came rushing up, apologizing for their lateness. Apparently the woman had been fooled by the mildness of the day and had left her coat back in the car, and they'd had to go back and retrieve it.

The tour began right where they were standing with Jacob briefly discussing the beginnings of the ghost walk idea from a friend of his whose father had built the store and continued to inhabit the place even after his death. After treating them to a short story about drawers that were nailed shut but were continuously found open with items moved to their proper, original place, they were led around the block into a narrow alley behind it.

"Now I'm going to have to ask everyone to stay to the left. Those valet guys are notorious for flying up through here to park the cars—except for the Jaguars and Lamborghinis, which are parked right out in front, of course," he said with a laugh.

He stopped in front of some kind of warehouse-looking structure and waited on a car to whip by, narrowly missing the backs of their legs as they crowded around him to listen. The supposed paranormal activity four years before had been a benevolent manifestation involving the movement of hazardous electrical wires during a sprinkler system malfunction. The owner had been saved from sure electrocution.

They slowly made their way back up the side alleys and streets perpendicular to Main Street, stopping here and there to listen to Jason orate on the history and hauntings of some of the older buildings.

It had been growing steadily colder as the night wore on, and a brisk wind had kicked up by the time they stopped in front of the darkened windows between the lights of Bartoli's pizzeria on one side and a crystal shop on the other.

It was a nondescript three-story storefront devoid of ornament, except for three light fixtures long since burned out mounted across the top floor.

The wind seemed to be blowing even harder now. Aileen shivered a little and buttoned her coat. This story seemed more interesting, and she listened as she gazed up at the dingy windows above.

"The establishment was originally called the Green Room and eventually evolved into Greenville's version of a speakeasy during prohibition times." Jacob pointed up to the top floor. "A man was kept on watch at all times. All he did was walk back and forth in front of these windows all night long, keeping watch in case of trouble, ready to sound the alert."

She gazed up at the dark windows, imagining what it must have been like standing there years ago and looking up in just the same spot she was standing in now and seeing...

Aileen flinched and stepped back. There had been the flicker of something in one of the second-floor windows.

"—and now people frequently report a feeling of being watched down here on the street from the windows above."

She looked back up at the window and saw it again. There was definitely someone standing there. She nudged Colleen. "There's someone up there," she whispered, not wanting to disturb Jacob who was still speaking.

"What?"

"There's someone up there," she repeated, indicated the window where she could still see the unmistakable outline of a figure. Colleen squinted up and Aileen saw the shadowed outline shift and move, disappearing and then reappearing in the window beside it.

"There! On the second floor!"

"Where? I don't see anything."

How could she not see it? Whoever it was, they were clearly discernable even in the gloom of the unlit room behind them. The shadow moved once more and this time appeared almost directly in front of Colleen in the middle window right above them, and still Colleen continued her perusal, obviously not seeing what Aileen was seeing. Nor was anybody else, it seemed. Jacob was no longer talking. He and the other couple were now standing behind her looking up at the darkened building with interest. But they weren't looking in the right place. It was right there, moving closer to the window now, a face becoming clearer—chin, nose, eyes—eyes that were black for a moment then bloodshot, the red striations blending and forming into two gleaming blood-red eyes.

Aileen jerked and accidentally backed into Jacob. "*Oh*. Sorry."

Everyone was looking from the building to her and back again with a curious mix of bewilderment, excitement, and disbelief, except for Colleen who merely looked worried.

"Sorry," she said again. "I thought I saw something but it must have been a shadow or a reflection."

The older couple moved up the sidewalk a little ways and stood whispering to each other, but Jacob remained standing in front of her, as if debating whether or not to speak, before he too moved off and continued the tour, herding everyone down yet another side street.

Colleen waited until they were all marching down a particularly long stretch of road, then sidled up to her and asked in a low voice, "Are you all right?"

"Yeah, I'm fine."

The other lady must have heard them because she glanced back curiously. Colleen didn't speak for the next few steps, then started to whisper, "Did you really see some—" and Aileen cut her off with a barely audible "Later," and she dropped it.

She was beginning to get tired by the time they made it down a long hill and starting climbing back up again. She was still feeling the effects from the lightning strike, and she was seriously starting to regret their little escapade. At least they were finally reaching their destination. They followed Jacob towards a large stone archway leading into ... *no, it couldn't be ...* but it was: the unmistakable entrance to a large cemetery. If what she had just experienced was any indication, this did not bode well.

They passed through the gates while Jacob started giving the history of the old municipal graveyard. "There are over eight thousand people buried here, over two thousand in unmarked graves. It started out as a private cemetery for the Daniel family—you've heard of the Landmark building?" he asked, indicating a tall faintly gothic-looking building one street over. They hadn't, not being from the area, but the other couple had, and Jacob expounded and answered questions as they moved farther in.

She had been in graveyards before, but never one quite like this. The cemetery was big and stretched into the distance. And it wasn't flat; it was hilly. The crowded graves, with barely enough room for a stone at the head and foot, were packed across rolling hills that would have looked at home in San Francisco. She lagged behind and looked down across all the many graves that rose and fell before her and wondered how fast she could make it to the other end without attracting any more attention than she already had.

She followed the others for a while, then murmured, "I'll meet you at the gate," to Colleen, who looked slightly put out at being abandoned. She veered away towards the far exit that Jacob seemed to be heading towards in a roundabout way.

The narrow sloping road she was on meandered in a long curving path throughout the cemetery, and she decided to take a short cut. Not wanting to step on any graves, she chose one of the smaller lanes that dissected the cemetery into segments and began to follow it.

This part of the graveyard was older she noted from the headstones closest to her, with names like Swinger and Townes and Collins dating back to the early 1800s. Large flat granite crosses covered some of the graves, while others were marked with simple fieldstones. The style and type of headstones she saw seemed to vary greatly and ranged from contemporary marble ones to elaborate raised brick tombs.

She stopped at the top of a hill to catch her breath and noticed a tall Victorian-style monument beside a low stone wall. She stepped over to take a look, still trying to catch her breath. She was starting to not feel well at all. Her head was hurting, and her thighs and calves were beginning to cramp. She really wasn't up to this. She desperately craved something cold to drink and about four aspirins.

The statue atop the monument was of a young girl with long flowing hair leaning against a tall cross draped in some kind of cloth. She seemed to be looking sadly down on the grave beneath it. Aileen stepped closer to read the stone. *George Heldermann.* There was nothing else, just the name. Who was the girl supposed to be? She didn't see any wings, so not an angel. Maybe his wife, or his daughter?

Aileen stepped up on the edge of the monument and looked out as far as she could see in the dim light from the surrounding streets for any sign of the others or the elusive back gate. She had just spotted the top of the stone archway behind another large tomb in the distance when a section that had been previously hidden to her caught her eye. The low wall surrounding the cemetery broke off into an opening into what looked like an empty field.

She jumped down and made her way over. The wall continued on around the empty section, effectively blocking the grassy area off by itself. It was obviously part of the graveyard, yet there were no headstones or markers of any kind.

The noise and traffic of the city seemed to fall away as soon as she stepped through the opening and walked around the perimeter towards a small cluster of trees ahead.

It was darker here under the trees away from the lights, and even if she could find some kind of marker or sign, she wouldn't be able to read it.

She decided to head back when she heard a low growl behind her.

Oh God, a dog. And it didn't sound like a very nice one, either.

No one had said anything about dogs guarding the place, so it was probably a stray. She turned around slowly, knowing better than to make any sudden movements.

The dog was big, completely black and probably was a stray from the looks of it. It appeared to be on the verge of starvation. Scars and scratches marred its coat, and one of its ears looked torn. As she began to back away, it advanced towards her, and she halted. The dog's barking now had a hysterical sound to it, and it was punctuating it with growls deep in its throat. She had just decided to run and take her chances up one of the trees when she realized that the dog's eyes didn't seem to be trained on *her*. She looked back over her shoulder.

A man was hanging from the tree behind her.

Aileen gasped and bit back a scream. He dangled about a foot off the ground, held up by the thick rope embedded into the skin around his broken neck. His tongue protruded from his blackened, swollen face. As she stood rooted in place, staring in horror, the dead man's slitted eyes winked open.

This time she did scream, and fell over the dog as she jumped back. The dog, who had apparently had enough, gave a shrill cry of its own—*how 'bout that, dogs really could scream*—and turned tail and ran, streaking across the grass. She decided to do the same. The hanging man's eyes remained trained on her, and he began to sway from side to side, first slowly, then wildly back and forth by the time she made it to her feet.

She was still running full out when she blew through the opening in the wall, barely registering the sign that said *Potter's Field* she had missed before.

She didn't stop running until her lungs were about to burst and she had made it almost to the back exit. She avoided looking at any of the graves or surrounding areas, afraid of what she might see.

She shuddered and heaved a sigh of relief when at last she made it out and onto the street, where she leaned against the brightest lamppost she could find and tried to catch her breath and block out the image of the dead man. And that's where she stayed, studiously ignoring the graveyard, keeping her eyes focused on the thinning traffic and the few lone stragglers making their way back up Main Street. She was losing her mind, or she was having hallucinations, or else she, the queen of skepticism, had just seen a ghost. Or some kind of reverberation—a distant echo left over from the past like the vibration of fading music. On and on she tried to wrap her mind around it until she heard the sound of voices, and Colleen and the others finally joined her.

She didn't say a word about what had happened, making out like she had just been tired and needed a breather, but it was clear from the worried looks Colleen kept darting her way that she suspected something.

They made a loop back around and stopped at the corner of a new building across from the Hyatt, which was, thankfully, the last stop of the tour. She didn't know how much more she could take. It was clear she had not fully recovered, either physically or psychologically, from what had happened to her the night of the storm.

Jacob moved under a streetlight, unfolded a newspaper clipping, and began to read. "Police are investigating the circumstances surrounding the death of a woman found dead near a downtown Greenville building. A security guard found the body at about 1:30 a.m. Thursday morning near 1 Patriot Circle and called the police. By 2:00 a.m. officers were on the roof investigating the death. Witnesses say the woman who jumped from the seven-story building was from the Greenville area but police have yet to confirm this.'" He pointed at the building behind them. "That was this building right here," he said, passing the newspaper article around for everyone to see.

Aileen turned and craned her neck up, her eyes traveling the length of the mirrored side all the way to the top. Seven floors; there was no way she would have survived that.

"The police ruled it a suicide, but this wasn't the first time something like this happened here. This was originally the site of the Weslon hotel back in the early twenties. It was torn down in 1985 to make room for this office building and the one beside it." Jacob indicated a similar structure. "In the past eighty years, there have been several suicides, three well-publicized murders, and over ten accidents, some resulting in death, from pedestrians being run down or stepping out in front of vehicles. There was even one man who was hit and killed by a falling flowerpot over on the south side. If you'll follow me, I'll show you what's left of the original courtyard." He motioned for everyone to follow.

Aileen decided to stay where she was and rest and let the others go on around without her. She gazed up at the roof once more while Jacob, Colleen, and the other couple disappeared around the side.

The triangular building seemed to rise up gently in a circle of soft white light. The building's deceptively small height was diminished even further by the much larger structures that dwarfed it on either side. Inviting patches of clipped grass and peaceful park benches bordered it on all sides.

She looked up once again and found the spot where the woman had jumped, and traced it down to the white path between the two hedges where she had been found.

She could almost see it.

She could see her being compelled to enter the bright oasis amidst the bustle of the crowded city around it.

It would have been so easy to walk across the manicured squares of clipped grass and pull the tall glass door open.

So easy to walk past the empty front desk, enter the elevator, and ride it all the way to the top.

So easy, so inevitable, to look down at the soft green rug of grass beneath her and imagine hooking a leg over the low wall and just giving a little leap out into the clear night air . . .

Colleen's distant shriek echoing up from far below jolted her back to reality like a slap.

Her heart leaped in her chest, and she let out a wheezy cry of terror. What hadn't looked like far from the ground now looked like the Grand Canyon from the top of the building where she found herself. A blast of wind and vertigo hit her at the same time she realized she was standing on the very edge of the roof, and she fought to keep her balance. For a minute it was touch and go and she teetered on the verge of going over. She swayed in sick horror, then, eyes rolling in her head, she reeled backwards and fell onto the rooftop, landing hard on her back.

She lay there, her body still seizing in fear, and tried to drag in air. *My God, how had she gotten on the roof?*

Her body shook at the enormity of what had almost happened. *Jesus.* She had almost fallen to her death.

And the worst part about it was, she had felt a compulsion to just give in and had almost succumbed and let herself drop, but at the last second some instinct had made her jerk back the other way.

She struggled to her feet, feeling dizzy, the edge of the roof looming close, too close, as the wind whipped and blew into her. Afraid to chance waiting on the elevator, she jerked the staircase door open and practically fell down the stairs in her haste to get away.

PART TWO

I See Dead People

Then away out in the woods I heard that kind of sound that a ghost makes when it wants to tell about something that's on its mind and can't make itself understood, and so can't rest easy in its grave, and has to go about that way every night grieving.

~ *The Adventures of Huckleberry Finn,* Mark Twain

Chapter 11

Aileen locked the door behind Colleen and surveyed her apartment uneasily. What had once been her little bit of space in the world, her home away from home, now seemed full of unseen depths and shadows. There was no doubt about it. Something had happened to her the night she had been hit by lightning that somehow allowed her to tap into and perceive what normally couldn't be seen.

There was a click and a hum, startling her, as the refrigerator kicked on, sounding abnormally loud in the still apartment.

She worked her way through the rooms, switching on lamps and turning on lights, afraid to look too hard into corners and behind doors, but more afraid to not look.

She made a cup of chamomile tea that Colleen had given her and drank it sitting at the kitchen table under the bright overhead light. It had all started the night of the storm. She knew virtually nothing about the old man who had called the ambulance for her or the house where she'd been hit. She had avoided even thinking about what had happened right after the strike, preferring to chalk it up to nightmares brought on by shock and trauma. But after what had happened that evening she was forced to rethink things. Horrible as it was, she had to face the possibility that the girl-thing had not been a figment of her unconscious mind, but something else.

She was seeing ghosts. And not only that, she apparently had such a deep connection that she was in danger of being possessed by them. During her trance-like climb onto the roof it had been like she was someone else. She had been so completely in the other woman's mindset that she, Aileen, had faded away. If it hadn't been for Colleen, she would probably be dead now.

Her mind still whirling with everything that had happened, and the deeper implications of it, she forced herself to go to bed, and she finally fell into a fitful sleep sometime around dawn.

They always say everything looks better in the morning, but in her case, the morning light seemed to bring a fresh wave of horror at how close she had come to dying the night before. There was no denying what had happened during the ghost walk.

After clicking on the Internet Explorer icon, she typed *Crybaby Bridge* into the search box and went to work. She found several sites that briefly listed the bridge as a paranormal site, but only one that included directions stating it was near the Rose Wood plantation on the same road. After briefly being sidetracked by a story about a girl who had died in a fall at Rose

Wood in 1958, she called up an image of the house. It looked like an older picture. It was black and white and there didn't seem to be as many trees around it, but it looked like the same place.

She called up the corresponding website and read the caption underneath another picture of the home, this time in full color.

> ***Rose Wood Plantation Historic Site***
> *This Greek Revival-style house was the home of Senator Walter Gage, a prominent political figure of the Civil War. Its original period furnishings, heirloom rose bushes, and historic magnolia trees allow a look back into the decadent antebellum south. Walk the grounds and trails, explore the preserved slave quarters, or tour the restored mansion. Tours are held ever day on the hour from 1:00 – 5:00 pm.*

After making sure she had enough cash on hand to pay for the tour, she stuffed her camera into her bag and grabbed her keys.

Just a little over two hours later, she turned in through the black iron gates at the front and followed the narrow winding drive around to the side and parked in the gravel parking area provided. There was no sign of anyone around when she got out, and she made quick use of the facilities located in a rustic wooden building beside the small parking area.

In the time since the lightning strike, she had built the place up in her mind until it resembled a massive, looming specter of a house. Looking at it now in the daytime, she saw it wasn't as big as she remembered and the forest around it looked more idyllic than menacing. She pulled out her small digital camera and clicked a few pictures. The simple all brick three-story façade was painted a pale yellow set off by white columns supporting the two-level portico in front and the two smaller porches on either side beside the exterior chimneys. Another two-level portico came off the back exactly like the front one, and the wrought-iron railing surrounding the second-floor balcony matched the gleaming white columns.

As she started around the side, a gust of wind sprang up, flapping the flag flying on the tall pole beside it. She saw that it wasn't a rebel flag like she had thought. It was actually a red design with a blue cross containing white stars, a palmetto tree, and small crescent moon in the upper left corner.

"It's called the Sovereignty Flag."

Aileen turned. A man wearing a park ranger's uniform was coming out of a wooden building connected to the big house by a narrow path of small white rocks. From its proximity to the house, it was probably originally the kitchen, which she knew was always located in a separate building because of the heat and the odors. The large gun on his side and a small gold nametag identified him as Constable Carter. His brown hair was longish like he was overdue for a cut. She took him to be in his early to mid-thirties. He was reasonably handsome in a rough sort of way that was somehow at odds with his uniform.

She was searching for an appropriate response when he spoke again.

"It was the unofficial South Carolina flag before the war. The fifteen stars represent the fifteen slave states."

She squinted up at the flag and tried in vain to think of something to say. She sufficed by holding out her hand and introducing herself.

"Carter Connell." His hand felt hot and tight. For a second she wondered if the rest of his body was as hot as his hands and felt a dull flush spread across her face. As he regarded her, she could have sworn she detected a hint of amusement as if he knew exactly what she had been thinking.

"Are you here for the tour?" he asked.

"Um, yeah, I had a few minutes so I was just looking around." She glanced at her watch. "In fact, I'd better head on up if I'm going to catch it."

He fell into step beside her. "You'll like Jane. She's the interpretive guide today. She's really good. She's actually just volunteering part time, but we're trying to convince her to stay on permanently."

The old plantation was beautifully kept. She was finding it hard to reconcile the way it looked now in the daytime with the black nightmare impression she had been left with the night of her stormy experience. The inlaid brick walkway they were following connected all the out buildings to the main brick path that led around the house and branched off to a small courtyard surrounding the flagpole. Short fences of gnarly wood and low stone walls separated the various areas of the property, and the house and immediate trees were bordered by bushes and raised beds of now dormant flowers.

Halfway around the house, Carter stopped at a neat little patch of cultivated dirt. A small wooden sign posted low to the ground identified it as the *Authentic Heirloom Garden.*

"You'll have to come out in the summer some time and see the garden and flowers and rose bushes when they're blooming."

Rose bushes. She remembered the intense smell she had been plagued with off and on since the lightning strike and suppressed a shudder.

"Okay, just head on up and Jane will meet you at the front door." He pointed towards the lower level and main entranceway.

She thanked him and strolled towards the front steps. Even in the winter, the large tangled magnolia trees were magnificent, their glossy green leaves reaching across the walkway and covering the entire front lawn. Seeing no sign of the aforementioned Jane, she walked down to the front gate. She clicked a nice picture of the trees and the house just as a youngish woman with dark blond hair pulled back into a ponytail came out the front door.

There was a group of people coming around the side as Aileen hurried up to meet her, and by the time she stepped up to pay, another car was pulling in. All in all, there were seven of them, counting Jane. After taking their money, Jane opened the door and led them inside.

Just inside the front door, she had everyone—a group of three little old ladies, a woman and her teen-aged daughter, and Aileen—leave their pocketbooks just inside the foyer. She reassured them it was only for security purposes. *In case someone wants to lift something*, Aileen read between the lines. "No one will touch them. We're the only ones in the house and I have the doors locked," Jane said as they reluctantly piled their purses up.

"What about my camera?" Aileen asked as they filed into the first room to the left of the sturdy circular staircase rising up through the middle of the house.

"Pictures are usually frowned upon, but I will allow you to take some. Just don't let Carter, our park manager, catch you using a flash on any of the oil paintings. It can damage them. He had trouble with someone a while back using a flash on them, even after they had been told it would harm the paintings, and he had to ask them to leave."

She reassured her that she wouldn't do that and followed her into the small parlor.

The room was sparsely furnished. There was a small center table, a few chairs arranged here and there, and an antique pianoforte against the right wall. Still, it was a pretty room. Red brocade curtains gave the room some color and complemented the gold trim and gleaming hardwood floors.

Jane talked for a while about the architecture of the home and how it had started out as a plain federal-style building and then had been renovated in the 1850s into the then modern Greek Revival style. As she led them around the rooms on the bottom floor, she touched briefly on the Civil War background of the family. "State Senator Walter Gage was a prominent political figure during the time before the Civil War. He was a strong supporter to the succession of South Carolina and lived in the home during the war and after until his death in 1876. The home was still owned by one of Gage's descendants until 1960 when it was donated to the Parks Department and later extensively restored and furnished with period pieces, including some owned by the Gage family." She indicated a large, definitely oil, painting of the Senator and his wife, Louisa, hanging in the dim hallway running behind the stairs.

Jane led them up the staircase to the second floor, which was divided into two large rooms on the left, and a large ballroom on the right. The long rectangular ballroom, which encompassed the entire right side of the house, was bare except for two settees placed across the room from each other against the far walls, and according to Jane, the original Gage family L. Rickell's piano. All the rooms had fireplaces, and this one had two, one for each half of the room. Elaborate gilded mirrors sat above each of the fireplaces, and the magnificent glass chandelier dripping with crystals and the gold candelabra placed atop the piano still managed to convey the opulent feel the place must have once had.

Aileen glanced into a small inset room containing a marble-topped washstand and sofa that Jane explained was where the ladies freshened up whenever a ball was being held, then crossed the length of the floor, her heels tapping on the polished wood. She tried to imagine what life must have been like living in this house. Beautifully dressed women and men twirling around the dance floor, waltzing and fanning themselves in the heat, the large airy rooms and tall ceilings and windows only marginally dissipating the sultry heat.

She had already made it several steps past one of the large mirrors when she realized that something was wrong with the reflection she had barely registered out of the corner of her eye.

She looked behind her. There was no one else in the room. She thought for a minute that the dim lighting had merely caused her hair to appear darker, but when she backed back up and looked at her own reflection, it appeared just as mousy brown as always.

Part of her must have wanted something to happen, or else she wouldn't be there, but actually confronting whoever or whatever she had seen that fateful night suddenly filled her with trepidation. Many times she had heard from other paranormal investigators, psychics, and such that inexperienced people not familiar with the proper techniques should never try to make contact with the spirit world for fear of bringing something into their lives that they had no control over and couldn't rid themselves of later. Well, if it wasn't for the fact that it was her job and had invaded her life, which suddenly seemed to be heading in an unexpected and unwanted direction, she would immediately cease and desist. Her loss of control had scared her the night she and Colleen had gone on the ghost walk, and if she couldn't learn to control her newfound connection to the previously unseen world around her, then the next time she decided to fling herself off a tall building there might not be anyone around to stop her.

For years she had made it her business to search and connect with the unknown spiritual realm, and now when she had finally achieved that, all she wanted to do was to run screaming back to the shallow and superficial life she had once led.

No longer wanting to be alone, she quickly walked back across the ballroom to join Jane and the others on the back balcony. She went to step out when a black-and-white picture hanging on the wall above the settee snagged her attention. Unlike many of the early photographs she had seen where no one was ever smiling due to such long camera exposure times, this one showed a small boy grinning impishly at the camera. He looked to be around five or six years old. He was wearing a vaguely sailor-type outfit with a wide white collar and a darker tie. It was a close up, only showing from the waist up, but it looked like it was taken outside from what she could see of the background and the light behind him. The wind must have been blowing because a small section of hair in the back was standing up. She thought he was adorable with his slightly jug ears and Alfalfa twig of hair. She wondered who he was and made a mental note to ask Jane.

"If you look out across the back left, you can see what is left of the slave quarters that made up what they called 'slave row'. They were later converted to tenant houses and servant quarters, and the few that are left are now used mainly for storage. Feel free to walk about and take a look on your way out," Jane was saying.

Aileen only half listened as she discussed the heirloom rose bushes and hedges planted in a battle flag design that Mrs. Gage had planted. She tuned back in when Jane led the way through another door that connected the balcony to the other side of the house.

"This was the children's bedroom, undoubtedly a very sad room. Of the eight children born to Mrs. Gage, only two made it past the age of seven, and only one to adulthood, who became the grandfather of the last living descendant—still alive today—to have actually lived in the home."

Aileen squeezed by one of the older ladies and stood beside the authentic Courier and Ives sleigh bed. She was careful not to look too closely at the tiny infant garments on display across the child's cradle in the corner. Dead ghost babies she could not handle. That was something she definitely thought might send her screaming from the house.

Period toys were placed around the room. An old-fashioned wooden top sat on the mantle and a ball and some marbles were scattered around a detailed girl's dollhouse on the hearth below. She wondered again who the little boy in the picture had been and if he had once played with the toys in that room. It was heartbreaking to think of all the children who had once lived, and then died there.

She edged out of the nursery farther into the adjoining room, mentally urging Jane to finish up and *come on.*

Finally she did, and after giving a short-lived sigh of relief, Aileen started to follow the others out of the room when a strange noise caught her attention. It was kind of like a rolling, scraping sound. She looked back over her shoulder, and as she cast her eyes about for the source of the noise, one of the marbles rolled out from behind the dollhouse.

It continued its slow purposeful roll across the floor as if propelled by an unseen force, scraping against the wooden boards as it proceeded relentlessly across the room towards her.

Aileen stared in horrified fascination as it moved in a steady path straight for her. Right before it touched the tip of her shoe, she whipped around and quickly marched away, trying to ignore the sound of it, which she could still hear. It sounded as if it was going to come on into the room after her.

The master bedroom they were in now was darker, more somber. Heavy curtains hung down around closed shutters on all the windows. A massive mahogany canopy bed and a huge matching wardrobe dominated the room.

They milled around as Jane filled them in and answered questions on why all the beds were so short—people weren't as tall then, and who had worn the amazing, hard to believe dress with the 22-inch waist displayed on a dress dummy—Mrs. Gage, even after eight children.

But the most interesting item in the room was the mourning portrait of Louisa Gage painted after her death. Aileen had never seen anything like it. She stepped closer. Louisa wore a high-necked black dress with a cameo pinned to her breast. Noticing her interest, Jane began to explain that although she had been painted as if still alive, certain items in the painting depicted death. "If you'll notice, there is a tombstone behind her inscribed with a mourning poem, and a weeping willow which further signifies death, along with the gardenia, another signifier of mortality."

Aileen shivered as she imagined someone doing that for a living. Whoever had painted the picture had sat surrounded by so much death, so much *grief*, time after time, trying to capture a loved one's likeness before they were gone forever.

And this house had seen more than its share of death: Louisa's poor dead children, the countless slaves that had undoubtedly died there, the generations before and after. She felt it coming off the house in waves.

She was ready to get out of there. What exactly did she think she would accomplish? There was no way she was going to be able to control something like this. She would just be drawn in deeper and deeper until she was one of those barking-mad people who believed in all kinds of batshit-crazy things and ended up being ostracized from polite society.

She hurried to find the others, who had left the room while she had been staring morbidly at the funeral painting. She was just about to step through the doorway out onto the upstairs landing when her foot slipped on something on the floor and she almost fell. She caught herself on a dresser standing by the door, nearly knocking several items off as she grabbed hold of it. She looked down. The blue-and-white glass marble sat halfway between her and the dresser she was now holding onto. Her heart lurched then began to thump loudly in her chest. Trying to keep an eye on the murderous marble, she quickly straightened the oil lamp and book she had jarred. She picked up a lock of hair tied with a faded yellow ribbon that had nearly slid off, and suddenly the floor seemed to buck beneath her feet. She had to shut her eyes as a sickening wave of nausea rolled over her.

When she opened her eyes, the wooden floor, the walls, and the house around her had fallen away. She found herself under a nighttime sky filled with what looked like a thousand stars. The grass and trees dripped, the air washed clean by recent rain.

A woman's wail rent the air. She stood alone on a nearby hilltop, crying and screaming at the distant pinpoints of light. The earth trembled and moved, the distant tremors rumbling across the landscape. And still the woman screamed out her fury and her grief and her sorrow at the cold night sky.

The woman fell to her knees, sobbing, and the earth trembled once more. A bell began to ring in the distance, and the woman's sobs rang out anew. Each tortured clang of the bell seemed to knife into the woman as she shrieked and pummeled the ground. *Clang-clang, Clang-clang, Clang—*

Clang. Aileen jerked away, the sound of the bell still reverberating in her ears, and dropped the lock of hair as if it were a burning ember. She fled the room, almost stumbling on the stairs. She smelled the odor of roses again, and the ringing in her ears had returned, even worse than before. *My God it was a cacophony.* She hurried down the hall behind the stairs and found Jane and the others in the back sitting room.

Their collective gaze went from the adjoining room, where the sound of the bell (not her ears after all) seemed to be coming from, to her, then back again.

"So who's ringing the bell?" she felt safe to ask since they were obviously hearing it too.

Jane quickly marched through the dining room, past the gateleg table, and unlocked and tugged open the door that led outside. The ringing stopped abruptly. Aileen peeked around her. The old iron bell sat silent and still atop the tall wooden stand where it was mounted halfway between the house and the kitchen.

"Well I don't know who would—" Jane started to say when the faint chords of the pianoforte drifted in from the other side of the house. Her eyes went wide. *"There's someone in the house!"* She rushed back to the others and quickly hustled everyone out onto the back porch.

The music floated dimly onto the porch where they were now standing. The tentative strands resolved into what sounded like Beethoven's "Moonlight Sonata."

"Wait a minute, what about our pocketbooks?" cried one of the older ladies.

Jane looked less than enthusiastic about going back in. Aileen followed behind her as she reluctantly reentered the house. She jumped when she realized Aileen was with her, then seemed grateful for her presence.

They crept towards the parlor and the eerie music where the purses lay piled up.

Jane stepped through the doorway, then Aileen, and the music fell silent.

Just as she had expected, there was no one in the room. The bench in front of the pianoforte was as empty as it had been earlier when they had first toured the room.

The blood drained from Jane's face. Without a word, she turned on her heel. Aileen could barely keep up with her as she flew back through the house. Realizing they had forgotten the pocketbooks again, Aileen reversed course and made her way back through the hall, past the stairs, and over to the front door. She stooped down and gathered up the purses.

She had just turned back around, her arms full, when she saw her.

She was standing in the middle of the staircase where it angled upwards to the nursery on the top floor, looking down at her with a positively delighted expression on her face. Even without the pallor of death on her skin, Aileen recognized her. It was the ghost-girl thing from the night of the storm. Only now she didn't look hideous; she looked . . . *cute*.

And that was somehow worse.

Aileen fled back to the safety of the porch nearly as fast as Jane had.

Jane managed to keep it all lighthearted, saying "the ghosts are in a playful mood today" but Aileen could tell she was shook up by the experience.

She wondered if she would stay on full-time now.

Chapter 12

Aileen needed a drink, or two, or five. She picked up her cell phone and called Colleen on her way home. She got no response on her cell, so she tried her landline at her apartment and got her on the third ring.

"Hey can you meet me at the Pearl?"

"Uh, yeah, what's up? Is something wrong?"

"No. Yes." Aileen sighed. "I'll explain when I get there."

"Is it something to do with what happened the other night?"

She had, of course, filled Colleen in on everything that happened to her the night of the ghost walk. After seeing her almost dive to her death, Colleen had witnessed enough firsthand to believe her beyond a shadow of a doubt, and Aileen had held nothing back.

"Yeah, I'll tell you about it when I get there. Oh, and if you get there before me, order me something strong, okay?"

"You got it."

Six o'clock was a slow time with most people still eating dinner or getting ready to go out for the evening, and there were only a few people sitting at the bar when Aileen arrived. She was a little earlier than she had told Colleen, so she ordered a fruity drink called a Midori Sunrise advertised on one of those little pop-up displays, and sat down in one of the booths along the back to wait.

She hadn't been sitting there long when her cell went off. She looked at the caller-ID. It was Colleen, calling from her house phone, so not on her way yet.

"Where are you?" Colleen asked as soon as she picked up.

"I'm here, waiting on you."

"Sorry. I'm leaving right now. I just had an idea, though. Why don't I get Bobby to join us? You haven't met him yet, and he's dying to meet you. I've told him all about you."

Aileen had counted on being able to talk to Colleen about what had happened at Rose Wood, but she knew she couldn't say no. She could tell Colleen was excited about her finally meeting Bobby. According to Colleen, he was drop-dead gorgeous, and she probably wanted to show him off.

"Sure," she said. "The more the merrier."

She hung up and finished her drink. She couldn't stand the thought of another sticky sweet drink. Besides, she hadn't quite achieved the level of buzz she had anticipated, so this time she ordered a double vodka straight up on the rocks. She drank half of it in one swallow, wiping her mouth with the back of her hand. The alcohol burned nicely in her stomach. That should do it.

By the time she drained her glass, more people were starting to trickle in, and the room had begun to have a warm, fuzzy glow to it. This was what she needed. Just like Josh, she needed to *forget*. None of it mattered. Not the least, little, *bit*. She didn't have to *do* this anymore. She could just quit too. She could just forget about whatever had happened to cause that sweet, cute, *angel of a child* to die and refuse to leave the land of the living. Aileen choked back tears as she remembered the infectious smile she had beamed at her from the stairs, as if delighted she'd come to play, and realized she was well on her way to being half-lit.

"Don't cry lil' lady. It can't be all that bad, can it?" said a voice at her elbow.

Aileen took a napkin and wiped her eyes. Geez, she was acting like one of those overly sentimental boozers. The next thing you know, she would be hugging everyone in sight and telling them she loved them.

"Here, let me git you another drink, you look like you could use one." He signaled the waitress and sat down across from her without waiting to be invited. And she let him because he was quite good-looking she saw as she squinted across at him. She might just have a little someone of her own to show off. She smiled at him and he smiled back. He really wasn't her type, but handsome nonetheless, with reddish hair cut in a crew cut and tight-fitting jeans. A little more redneck than she liked, but beggars couldn't be choosers.

The waitress returned with their drinks: two shots and beers to chase it with. Aileen picked up one of the shot glasses and gulped all of it down in one swallow then slammed the shot glass down.

"HOT damn!" he shouted, and did the same, slamming his glass down too. "WhooooEE!" he whooped, and they both dissolved into laughter. She nearly slid out of her side of the booth onto the floor, still laughing.

He grabbed her elbow and helped her up. Just then a song she liked started up from the jukebox in the corner, and she wrapped her arms around him, swaying into him. "Wanna dance, cowboy?" she murmured, seductively she hoped, and he pulled her onto the crowded dance floor. *Wow. Where had all the people come from, and where the hell was Colleen?*

He was a great dancer, moving easily from the fast beat to the slower number that followed. She let herself melt into him, letting him lead her, and pretty soon they were nearly doing their own version of dirty dancing, only slower. When the people around her began to whistle and one guy called out "Get a room!" she disentangled herself, and staggered towards the restroom.

Everything had begun a slow spin and she was starting to feel a little off.

The silence of the bathroom rang in her ears after the noisy dance floor. She splashed a little water on her face, and then touched up the makeup she had just ruined. "Damn," she exclaimed as she dropped the wand to her lip-gloss. She looked at it lying in the dirty sink and knew there was no way she would ever use it again, and left it there.

She went into one of the stalls and put her head down and took slow easy breaths until the room stopped spinning so much and her stomach settled down. She didn't know how long she sat there, but it didn't seem like too long before she felt a little better. She had gotten too hot, and she should have eaten something. She vowed to do that immediately, and emerged from the stall.

She stared in disbelief at the mirror above the sink.

Scrawled across her reflection, written in the unmistakable red of her lip-gloss, was the word *Beware*. Just the one word, spelled out across the mirror in uneven letters.

She stepped closer and looked down, and there was the lip-gloss wand lying in the bottom of the sink. Someone could have written it while she had been in the stall, but she was sure she hadn't heard anyone else come in.

The door swished open and another woman entered the bathroom. Aileen grabbed the door before it could swing shut and ran right into Billy Bob standing outside the restroom where he had apparently been waiting.

"Thought I was gonna have to come in after you. Thought you might of fell in," he said, grinning.

So, so funny, she hadn't heard that *one before.* She smiled weakly back at him and before she could protest, he pulled her hard up against him, and she did mean hard up against him—she could feel every part of him—and kissed her. She wasn't really in the mood anymore, but he was a pretty good kisser, at least until he tried to shove his tongue down her throat while simultaneously jamming his hand up her shirt. She tried to pull back, and he clamped a hand across the back of her head and forcefully held her in place while he basically assaulted her.

She wrenched away and his hand caught on a piece of her hair and she felt it rip. "*Ow*," she cried, "You pulled my hair!"

"*I* didn't pull your hair, *you* pulled your hair."

Aileen stared at him in disbelief and turned to walk away, back to the booth, and to look for Colleen. He grabbed her arm and jerked her back. They were still down the hall by the restrooms so there was no one to see her, or help her, as he dragged her up against him. He covered her mouth with his again, stifling her cries, and slowly started moving with her towards the rear exit door. The word *Beware* scrawled across the mirror flashed through her mind, and she began to struggle harder.

He had almost made it to the exit when she forced herself to stop fighting him. She let herself go limp, and right when he gave a huge lunge and practically lifted her off the floor and out the door, she reached down the one free hand she had and grabbed a piece of skin at the top of his leg beside his groin and gave a viscous twist, pinching him as hard as she could. She felt a nail break against his too-tight jeans, and he gave a squeal worthy of a little girl as he flung her from him.

She wasted no time and stumbled down the hall and out into the bar, nearly slamming into a waitress with a tray of drinks in her haste to get the hell away from him. She fell out into the night air and stumbled around the corner towards the parking lot and straight into the man coming around the side.

Aileen shrieked and beat against the chest and arms that held her until she finally realized that the voice saying "Easy! Easy!" wasn't the same guy trying to drag her off to sure rape and murder, but someone else. She collapsed against his chest, and the culmination of everything that had happened to her since the night of the storm and her inebriated state combined with her scene with the redneck, caused her to do something she hadn't done in public since she was a child, and she began to cry. Silent tears ran down her cheeks as she sagged against him.

"Hey," he said, pulling back slightly. "Are you all right?"

"I'm sorry," she said, sniffing and wiping ineffectually at the wet spot her tears had left on his shirt.

"What's wrong? Was someone bothering you?" His kind expression caused fresh tears to fill her eyes.

"It's okay. I'm fine now. Thank you." She wiped her eyes. "I'm sorry," she said again and turned, trying to get her bearings on where she had left her car, and promptly lost her balance. She flailed her arms, trying to recover, then went down hard on her side, painfully twisting her ankle.

"Fuck!" she cried in mortification and pain.

The stranger, whoever he was, began to chuckle, and then to laugh out loud as she looked up at him incredulously through her tears.

"Here," he said, bending down, and before she realized what was happening, he had slid an arm under her legs and scooped her up. "I don't think you're in any condition to drive." He carried her protesting across the parking lot.

They stopped beside a black Audi parked under a light, and he put her down long enough to hit the button on his key ring to unlock the doors, then helped her into the passenger seat.

He started the car and cranked up the heater. She absorbed the warmth gratefully, inhaling the aroma of new car and leather. He was right; she had drunk too much. As if the thought had triggered something, she felt her nausea rise again and she fought against it, lowering the window on her side. The cold air helped a bit, and after a minute she felt well enough to talk.

"If you could just give me a ride home, I can come and get my car tomorrow."

"Okay."

He drove considerately, following her directions through the streets, and she was grateful as she tried not to urp all over his beautiful car

When they finally arrived in front of her apartment building, she quickly opened her door. "Thank you so much. I really appreciate it," she said, and stepped out. As soon as her full weight came down on her left foot, sharp pain lanced through her ankle. She winced and held onto the door to keep from falling.

He cut off the car and came around to help her. Once again, he lifted her with no apparent effort, and carried her to her door. She was sober enough now to appreciate the tantalizing warm male scent of him mixed with the light trace of cologne. And when he placed her on the sofa to inspect her ankle, she realized he was easily the best-looking man she had ever seen. She stared at him unabashedly, barely feeling the pain as he gently rotated her foot. His hair was jet-black and matched the liquid ebony of his deep-set eyes. *Bedroom eyes, that's what they were.* They had an exotic cast to them that matched his golden skin. He was like Johnny Depp mixed with Keanu Reeves and Timothy Olyphant all rolled into one, only better. He looked up at her questioningly and caught her staring at him slack-mouthed. He smiled a slow smile, and she felt her stomach give a little flip. She managed to close her mouth and smiled back at him.

He leaned forward ever so slowly and brought his mouth up to hers. He kissed her softly at first, and then he deepened the kiss, and if she hadn't already been sitting she would have swooned. She had heard the expression "going weak in the knees" before, but she had never felt anything like it until that moment. He deepened the kiss even further, and Aileen felt a languidness come over her and all she wanted to do was to lie back on the couch and relinquish herself to him.

Her phone rang.

Damn. He pulled away, and she sat up. She was willing to ignore it, but he was already up and across the room examining her CD and DVD collection. Knowing it had to be Colleen, she picked up. "Hello?"

"Hey. I finally made it, where the hell are you?"

"Hey Colleen." Aileen glanced over at the man. He looked up and met her eyes, and straightened to a standing position. He walked over by the door and hovered there, still staring at her. "I was there. I'm at home now. Listen I have to go. I'll explain later."

"Fine. I'm going home."

She hung up the phone and stood up, trying not to put any weight on her foot. "Do you have to go?"

"Yeah. I think your ankle will be fine. It's probably just a sprain." He pulled the door open.

"Wait! I don't even know your name. I'm Aileen."

He paused at the door.

"Todd, my name's Todd," he said, and then left, pulling the door shut behind him.

She hobbled into the bathroom and ran a steaming hot bath while she dug out her cell phone and checked it. Three calls and three voice messages from Colleen earlier. She pressed the sequence of buttons to call up her voice mail.

Colleen's slightly distorted voice filled her ear. "You WON'T believe it. I have a flat tire! And I can't reach Bobby for shit! I'm on the side of the road waiting for the flippin auto club. I don't know how long this is gonna take—I'll try to make it as soon as I can—I'll have to call you back." Aileen pressed seven to delete and moved on to the second message. Colleen sounded beyond frustrated this time. "I'm still waiting. I can't believe this. I can't seem to reach anyone tonight. Bobby was supposed to meet us there, and I still can't reach him, and I can't even ask you if you see him because *you're not picking up your phone!*" Aileen pressed seven to delete and listened to the final message, recorded nearly an hour and a half later. Colleen sounded tired this time, her voice defeated. "Well, the auto club people finally showed up and changed the tire. I'm on my way."

She debated about calling her back right then, but she still didn't feel good and all she wanted was a nice hot bath and some sleep. She decided to call her in the morning when she felt better.

Chapter 13

She didn't feel much better in the morning, but at least Colleen was in a good mood when she finally got a hold of her.

"Where *were* you last night?" Colleen asked.

"I was there—waiting on you. Getting spectacularly drunk and having a wonderful time up until I was mauled by a marauding cowboy."

"Oh my *God*." Colleen began to laugh helplessly. "I'm sorry I missed it."

"I'm fine thank you."

Colleen laughed harder. "I'm *sorry*. I didn't have such a great night myself," she said, sobering somewhat.

Aileen knew she wasn't talking about her flat tire. "Is everything okay now?"

"Yeah." Colleen lowered her voice. "He's here now." In the background Aileen heard the faint electronic notes of a cell phone.

They promised to get together and catch up soon, and then Aileen let her go. It was clear the only thing

Colleen had on her mind was Bobby. She thought about her own drop-dead gorgeous man from the night before and couldn't say she blamed her.

She halfway expected Todd to show back up at some point, but by the time she had showered, she had talked herself out of getting her hopes up. He was just a stranger giving her a lift, nothing more. For all she knew, he had a girlfriend.

She looked around at her gloomy apartment and decided to go out. Her ankle was feeling better and she needed to do some shopping. And then she wasn't sure what she was going to do. For now, she'd just be like Scarlet O'Hara and "think about that tomorrow".

It wasn't until she saw her empty parking space that she remembered she had left her car at the bar the night before.

She called Colleen and got a ride over to her car, giving her an abbreviated version of what happened at Rose Wood. After Colleen dropped her off, she ran a few errands, and then stopped at the mall on impulse. It wouldn't hurt to make a *little* effort, just in case he did come back.

She tried on several uninspired pants and shirt outfits, then finally chose a creamy beige sweater dress that stopped mid-thigh, and a pair of knee-high chocolate suede boots.

On the way out of the mall, she caught sight of her scraggly half-grown-out hair in the reflection of a salon mirror and veered inside. She really couldn't afford it, but she couldn't seem to stop herself. What was the point of a new outfit if her hair was going to look like that?

She had her hair—no sign of gray yet, thank God—highlighted and cut into multiple long layers. She drew in her breath when the beautician turned her around to see. It was worth it. It was worth every penny and more. The ashy brown drabness had been replaced with honey strands that flattered and brightened her skin tone, and the long layers had been curled into thick sexy waves.

Delighted, she tipped the stylist a ridiculous amount, and walked out of the mall. She wasn't even sure where she left her car, and didn't even care. She was in a better mood than she had been in since the strike. She was alive. She looked good, and she felt good—well reasonably good, her ankle was starting to protest all the walking. A guy in a truck gave a low whistle of appreciation as he passed, and she smiled broadly. Life was good. Life was for the living.

Her good mood lasted all the way through the grocery store where she picked up candles, chocolates, gourmet coffee, wine, flowers, and way more food than she needed. And then she threw in a movie, too. She would need something to occupy herself with—*while she waited on him.* STOP IT, she screamed silently at herself. She needed to get a grip. Just because she had felt something with him that she had never felt before didn't mean he felt the same for her.

After getting home and putting everything away, she gave the apartment a good once-over. She opened all the curtains and raised the blinds to let the last of the afternoon light in. She put the wine on ice, and clicked on the stereo.

She danced around the best she could with her bad ankle, enjoying the music while she dusted, then swept and vacuumed, loaded the dishwasher, and emptied the trash. She arranged the flowers in a vase on the bar, and later when it began to get dark, she kept all the lights off and lit a large cherry candle in the kitchen, and three smaller blackberry ones on the coffee and end tables.

She went to get cleaned up. She showered off, careful not to disturb her new hairdo, brushed her teeth, and applied a little makeup. Even though she had nowhere to go and nobody to show it off to—*the story of my life*, she mused—she decided to wear her new dress. The soft material fit her perfectly, emphasizing her curves without clinging, and the short length showed off her legs. She spritzed on the lighter scent of Channel 19 she preferred, fluffed her hair, and pulled on the dark suede boots. She zipped them up and stood before the full-length mirror mounted on the back of her bedroom door. Well, it was as good as it was going to get. She wished Todd could see her now. She could just imagine what kind of ridiculous falling down drunken impression she had given him the night before.

Back in the living room it was a little too dark, so she clicked on a small accent lamp in the corner. The music she had left on was starting to grate on her nerves. She spun the knob, searching until she found a classical station, and adjusted the volume.

After wrestling the cork out of the Pinot Grigio she had chosen, she poured herself a large glass, grabbed one of the candles and a small throw off the couch, braced herself for the cold, and went out on the balcony. It was cold, but not frigid. There was virtually no wind, which helped, and with the blanket draped around her shoulders she felt almost comfortable. She sipped her wine and looked at the night sky. The soothing strands of Pachelbel's "Canon" drifted out and seemed to match the majesticness of the constellations above her. She settled back into the patio chair to listen, and watched the flicker of the candle and the stars, and drank her wine.

She relaxed further into the chair and leaned her head back, resting her eyes for a minute, and let her mind wander. When she was a child, she and her brother, Shane, used to stargaze all the time. He had a fat red telescope that he would drag out into the yard, and he would tune in the moon and Mars, and one time even the rings of Saturn. Those nights had seemed like magic, standing in the cold night air, held by gravity on the spinning ball of the earth under the steady beam of countless stars.

The scent of blackberries from the candle wafted over, and her mind wandered some more, and she thought back to picking wild blackberries with her mother, trying mostly in vain to find any that had ripened and not been eaten yet by the deer and the birds. Her eyes flickered once more to the stars above her. She dimly registered the song had changed and now sounded like "Moonlight Sonata," then her eyes closed again, and she slowly drifted off.

The girl picked another fat purple berry and bit into it. She was just reaching over the edge of the bank for more when a sound from behind startled her. She whirled around. Her eyes widened and she dropped the basket, spilling berries on the ground.

The sky changed. The clouds rolled back in and with them came the rumble of something else. The earth gave a tremor, then a vibration, and then bucked hard and slammed back down in a clap of thunder.

Aileen jerked awake. Someone was knocking insistently. She staggered up out of the chair and hurried inside. Thankfully the banging stopped when she began unlocking and unchaining the door because her head was starting to pound again. She barely had the door cracked when the man from the night before, *Todd,* pushed it the rest of the way open and stepped inside.

"Are you okay? I saw you out on the balcony and—" he stopped in mid-sentence as he took in her new appearance. His eyebrows went up. "Wow, you look h—" he stopped again. "You look great."

"Thank you."

"I saw your candle on the balcony when I pulled in, and I was worried you had fallen asleep in the cold."

"Well, actually I did. I guess I was more tired than I realized. It was a good thing you woke me, I'm freezing." She shivered and looked around for her throw blanket.

"Here," he said and grabbed it from the end of the couch where she had tossed it. He wrapped it and his arms around her. He held her that way for a moment, and then released her. She had not realized how tall he was. He didn't exactly tower over her, but he was at least six foot one or so. And looking at him now as he perched on the edge of the sofa, she saw he was older than she had first thought. He was probably closer to thirty-five. He wore a faded pair of blue jeans and a T-shirt under a black leather jacket. She was by no means a virgin, and had been in several brief relationships in college, but she had never dated anyone so *masculine*. He exuded testosterone in his current five o'clock shadow and in the shape of his body. This was not, and probably never had been, some skinny kid. This was a real man, and she had never been more attracted to anyone in her life.

"I actually came by to see how you were doing. How's your ankle?" he asked.

"Better." She stuck out her booted foot and wiggled it. "It was bothering me a little earlier, but it's okay now."

"Good. So do you feel well enough to go out?"

"Sure. What did you have in mind?" Her dirty gyrations with the cowboy popped into her head like a nasty rerun. "I don't know if I'm up to dancing."

"No, I was thinking we could get a bite to eat? Nothing fancy. Unless you've already eaten?"

"No, that'd be great. Let me get my coat."

Aileen was glad she had worn her new outfit when fifteen minutes later, they walked into the little diner and several men and one woman eyed them appreciatively as they crossed over to an empty booth in the corner.

They both ordered tuna melts and iced tea. She was starving, and her headache was getting worse by the minute, probably the result of her not having eaten anything since the slice of cake she had grabbed with her Frappuccino earlier at the mall.

They chatted a little as they waited on their food. They mostly made small talk, neither one of them willing to delve too deep yet. They were like two socialites from a different era determined not to make the faux pas of asking what one did for a living. They kept it on the surface, and that was fine with her. She wanted to get to know him, and for him to get to know her, before she had to decide exactly how much she wanted to tell him about her work and her recent experiences.

She glanced around the diner as they ate. It was just the kind of place she liked, low-key and homey with real food like meat and potatoes and pie. There was an assortment of desserts on display inside a glass case on the counter: chocolate cake, coconut cake, cheesecake, as well as pie—egg custard, peach, and one that looked like blueberry or maybe blackberry.

The fragment of dream came back to her. *Blackberries*. The girl had been picking berries and something or someone had frightened her. Aileen forced herself to take another bite of her sandwich and tried not to lose her appetite.

An older couple in their late sixties or early seventies came in and sat down in the booth beside them. The waitress came over after a minute, and they both ordered coffee and pie—blackberry pie. Aileen almost choked and pushed her plate away.

"You okay? Is your food all right?"

"Yeah, I'm fine. I've just got a bit of a headache. I shouldn't have drank that wine earlier," she said, then immediately regretted it. Both times when he met her, she had been drinking. She didn't want him to think she was an alcoholic. Although everything that had been happening to her lately was enough to drive anyone to drink.

The waitress brought over the older couple's pie. Aileen could see the little seeds as the man cut into his and brought a purple glistening bite up to his mouth. She wrenched her gaze away.

Todd had finished eating and was gazing at her in concern. He wiped his mouth with a napkin then signaled for the check. "Let's get out of here."

She slipped into her coat gratefully. She was afraid the floor would start bucking any minute like it had during her vision at Rose Wood. The few bites of tuna she had eaten felt like a greasy lump in her stomach.

By the time the got back to her apartment, she was feeling worse. Her stomach seemed to be holding out for now, but her head was killing her and her ankle was hurting again. She needed something better than Tylenol or aspirin. She went immediately down the hall and into the bathroom where she knew she had left her last few remaining pain pills. She fumbled for the bottle and dropped it.

"Here. I got it," Todd said, picking it up. He turned it around and read the label. "What are you taking these for?"

"It was just . . . I was hit by lightning." She took the bottle from him and headed back to the kitchen for a drink to take it with.

"What? You were hit by lightning?" He came into the kitchen behind her. "Here, let me do that," he said, taking the juice out of her hand. "Go. Sit down, and I'll bring it to you."

She didn't argue. She went into the living room and sank down on the couch. Todd brought her the juice, and she quickly fished one of the pills out and took it with a swallow of the juice. She sat back on the couch and took a deep breath.

Todd sat down beside her. "Tell me."

She filled him in about her lightning strike, and nothing else. "I got caught in a storm. My car wouldn't start so I started walking and the next thing you know I'm waking up on the ground about ten feet away." She shrugged her shoulders.

"My *God*, that must have been horrible. How bad were you hurt?"

"I had some burns and a few other temporary symptoms. Nothing too bad, but now I get headaches." *And visions, and I'm seeing ghosts.*

"Well, I'm glad you're okay now." He moved off the couch. "Maybe you should lie down."

"NO, don't go." She didn't want the night to end this way.

He hesitated. "Please stay for a while," she said. "I'm feeling better already." And she was. She could already feel the renewing effects of the pain medication.

He sat back down, and she left him flipping through the channels on the TV while she went to get out of her dress and boots. She quickly changed into a camisole top and low-slung pair of pajama pants. They were tight and sexy and had little white lambs all over them.

"Oh my, aren't you cute," he said, smiling, when she came back into the living room. "How about one of these?" He tossed a handful of movies down.

She picked up the DVDs and chose the one she hadn't seen yet.

If they were going to watch a movie, then they needed popcorn. She headed into the kitchen, and dug out a large bowl and a box of microwavable popcorn. While it was popping, she grabbed a couple of cans of soda and some napkins. The microwave dinged, and she dumped the popcorn into the bowl and started towards the living room.

"Oh come on," he said, coming into the kitchen. "Where's the butter?"

She laughed, delighted he was making himself at home, as he opened the fridge and got the butter.

She grabbed a ramekin out of the cabinet and watched in amusement while he heated the butter and poured a ridiculous amount of it over the popcorn, then liberally coated it with salt.

They set the bowl on the coffee table and took turns grabbing handfuls as they watched the movie. Little by little, she relaxed in his company. She felt comfortable with him, and later when they finished with the popcorn, it seemed completely natural for him to pile up some pillows on one end of the couch and lie over, pulling her down with him. She waited on him to make his move but hoped he didn't. She already felt bad about her urge to sleep with him the night before when she hadn't even known his name. To her relief, he merely kissed her once then settled back to finish the movie.

She stifled a yawn. She really was tired. Sometime near the end of the movie, she gave up trying to keep her eyes open and promptly fell asleep. And stepped right back into the dream she had been having earlier.

The same girl with the light brown skin reaching for the berries. The same shock and surprise on her pretty face that quickly turns to fear and then to horror as she drops the basket and flies back over the edge into the air and down to the jagged rocks below. And then she was running, breath rasping in her throat, legs pumping, a voice calling behind her as she stumbled along the twisting mud-filled path into the cave. The voice echoed behind her again, and she was slowing, the ground moving beneath her feet. Rocks and sediment rained down on her, larger boulders thundering around her . . .

Aileen cried out and jerked awake.

"What's wrong? What is it?" Todd asked, sitting up on the couch beside her.

"I'm sorry." Aileen shook her head, trying to clear it. "I was having a dream."

He looked at her in concern. "Sounded more like a nightmare to me."

"Yeah, I've been having a lot of them lately."

"You're having nightmares? From the lightning strike?"

"You wouldn't believe me if I told you."

"You might be surprised." He reached over and brushed the hair out of her face.

Catching hold of her chin, he kissed her lightly on the mouth. "Are you sure you don't want to talk about it?"

She shook her head again. "I just need some sleep."

"You're sure?" he asked again, standing up to leave.

She nodded and he gave her another quick kiss, fixed the door to lock behind him, and left.

Chapter 14

About 7:00 a.m. she gave up on getting any more sleep and got up and made a pot of coffee.

Her life was a mess. Some people would think she had it together—a place of her own, a career. But the truth was, she was nearly thirty years old and had a tiny one-bedroom apartment she could barely afford and a job she had taken by default. She still didn't know what she was going to tell Todd. Before, she had been embarrassed about what she did for a living because she didn't really believe, and now she was embarrassed because she *did* believe. It was ridiculous. And that's what he would think of her, that she was ridiculous, or crazy, or both.

Part of her marveled at what all her visions and dreams and encounters truly meant. That people, or some form of them, went on after death. That the fleeting life they lived was not the end, but a transition to something more complex and enduring than the earthly mind could ever comprehend. But with that knowledge came a price. For where there was light, there was darkness, and limitless possibilities brought forth the potential for chaos, evil, and madness.

She didn't know how much further she wanted to take this, or if she had a choice. It was her job and she no longer had to feel like a fraud, but confronting the dead remnants of living people caught in some time warp of misery day in and day out for the rest of her life, or until she did go crazy, sounded like a living hell to her.

Her mind kept coming back to Ed. He had not had a nightmare encounter. His had been full of hope and love and reassurance. Proof that his beloved daughter was not gone from him forever. Maybe some good could come out of it. She owed that much to him.

Filled with a disquieting sense of inevitableness, she dumped out her now cold coffee and poured a fresh cup. She went into the living room where her computer was set up and switched it on. She sipped her coffee while it booted up.

She owed Ed her latest investigation, and while she didn't feel ready to deal with the ghost of the girl she had seen at Rose Wood, she could at least do a passable report on the "crybaby" bridge that had started the whole thing.

For the rest of the morning she sat and worked, researching and writing her section. Since she had not actually heard a crying baby, or seen the mother's ghostly figure, she had to resort to focusing on the history and pervasiveness of the Crybaby Bridge legend throughout the southern states. She concluded with what actual facts she could find on the site she had visited (precious few), attached a grainy black-and-white picture of the old rusty Tugaloo River bridge along with several new ones, then sent it off to Ed. She would hear from him later about any revisions she might need to make.

She hung around her apartment that night and the next two nights hoping Todd would stop by again. Normally, she wouldn't dream of sitting around waiting on a man, not even one as handsome as Todd, but she didn't feel like she had a choice. They had not exchanged phone numbers and he had no way to reach her.

By the end of the week when he still had not shown, the excitement and promise of a new relationship had faded, and she basically gave up. It was pretty much back to the same old, same old after that. She got up. She wrote a little. She visited possible future sites to use for her section. She shopped. She ate. She slept. Boring, and that was just the way she was wanted it, if scary ghostly encounters and bad dreams were her only other options. There was one good thing she had noticed. Some of the effects of her lightning strike had begun to disappear. She had gone out on several occasions, even to a church out in the country where she had stood right beside a graveyard, and not once had she had any kind of paranormal encounter. The only thing she had noticed was a continuing connection to the girl from Rose Wood. She found herself plagued with rose-like coincidences. The smell of roses, a waitress named Rose, and just the day before, the ghost-girl's face had momentarily filled her rear-view mirror causing her heart to nearly stop. Even if she could deny the rest as merely things she had only noticed because she was looking for them, there had been no denying the girl's face with her dark blue eyes staring intently back at her. She suspected that when she had touched the lock of hair, that she was almost certain had belonged to the girl, she had strengthened whatever bond she seemed to have with her. But whatever tenuous thread that remained could be blocked out, if not entirely severed, if she concentrated hard enough on not thinking about anything to do with her, the girl picking berries, or Rose Wood in general.

She thought she had succeeded until the following Sunday night when she had another dream. She had gone to the flea market that morning, and stopping to look at a selection of baskets, she had inadvertently encountered a display of homemade preserves, primarily made up of blackberry, of course. And it seemed that everywhere she turned, someone had a picture of a rose, or a carving, or a glass figurine. She couldn't get away from things that reminded her of Rose Wood. She tried to put it all out of her mind, but even the radio was against her and had been playing "Moonlight Sonata" *again* as she was leaving.

That night, her mind kept trying to skip back to Rose Wood like a scratched record. Her last thought before finally falling asleep sometime before dawn was that she had forgotten to ask Jane who the cute little boy in the picture had been. She faded down,

down into sleep, down into the years past, down into Rose Wood.

He rolled his wooden car disconsolately across the floor. He liked his other one better, but brother had broken it. He wished he had someone to play with. He got up from the floor and holding onto the rail with one hand and his car with the other, he climbed down the stairs ... carefully, like Mammy always told him.

Maybe this time they would play with him. Maybe this time they would be nice. He reached up and knocked softly on the door. When there was no response, he screwed up his courage and knocked harder, hurting his hand. He rubbed his knuckles and waited. The door was wrenched open. Good. It was his older brother, the one who played with him that time he got his new telescope from Santa.

"Hey James, you wanna play something?" he piped out.

"What? No, not right now."

"Can I come in?" he quickly asked before James could shut the door.

"NO! Now go away and quit bothering us!" his brother shouted, and slammed the door in his face.

He stumbled back. Why did they hate him so? He loved them. He loved everybody. He began to cry. He shuffled down the hall, tears running down his face. Crying harder, he climbed the stairs again and curled up in a chair in the farthest corner.

"Charlie?" His sister's voice called to him from below. "Charrrlieeeee..." He raised his tear-streaked face.

She appeared above the stairs. "Hey Charlie Boy."

"Hey Emma," he said in a small voice.

"You wanna go catch some lightning bugs?" she asked, walking over and grinning down at him.

He beamed a watery smile up at her and climbed down from the chair.

Together they walked down the wooden steps.

"We can make a lantern with them," Emma said.

"And then we'll let them go, right?"

"Of course. We'll take good care of them."

He ran ahead to wrestle open the front door. Happy now, he grabbed Emma's hand, and they ran out into the waning sunset.

Aileen gasped and sat up in bed. Her face was wet; she had been crying in her sleep. Wiping her eyes, she looked around at the clock. 10:45. She had practically slept the morning away. She shut her eyes tight and another tear leaked out. She knew exactly who the little boy was. He was the boy in the picture that she had seen on the wall at Rose Wood. And she recognized the girl too, despite the fact that she had appeared older this time. The ghost-girl's name was Emma, and she had been his sister.

Someone knocked on the door. *Oh shit.* It was nearly lunchtime and she wasn't even dressed. And her face was probably a splotchy mess. Whoever it was knocked again, harder. She grabbed a brush and scraped it through her hair.

Still wiping her eyes, she checked the peephole. It was Todd, and she looked like hell. Sighing in resignation, she opened the door and waited on him to throw up his hand and cry out in disgust.

"You've been crying."

She met his eyes and saw he genuinely seemed concerned and not the least bit grossed out by her slovenly appearance. She shut the door and he followed her into the kitchen. He watched her while she got a glass of water.

"I'm sorry I haven't been by. I've been working a lot, trying to get caught up. I should have gotten your number and called—what?" he asked as he took in her expression.

"I'm not crying because of *you*," she said, aghast.

"What? No, I didn't think—"

"I'm sorry. What I mean is, it's about something else. Something you wouldn't even believe."

"Like I said before, why don't you try me? You might be surprised."

She shook her head. She barely knew him. He hadn't been around for weeks. Did he think she was just going to pour her heart out to him? And no matter what he said, she had felt sure for a minute there that he had assumed she had been crying over him.

"Get your coat and I'll prove it to you."

"What? I'm not even dressed." Let alone her matted hair and undoubtedly wretched face. Had the man lost his mind?

"Well, throw something on. It'll be better if I show you."

What would be better if he showed her? "Come on," he said, grabbing her arm and propelling her towards her bedroom. "Get dressed and there's something I want to show you, and then I'll take you to lunch. You'll feel better, I promise."

She didn't much like being manhandled, even by him, even if he was probably right. She made him wait a good half hour while she showered off and dressed.

In the parking lot out front, Todd hit the button on his key ring and unlocked the car. She stepped forward and reached for the door handle, but Todd beat her to it and opened the door for her. *Oh my, a girl could get used to that,* she thought, climbing in. This was more like it.

He refused to answer any of her questions, repeating only that it would be better if he showed her. He stopped briefly at a small bookstore, telling her to wait in the car. He came back out after only a few minutes and they were off again. On the outskirts of downtown, he spotted a Books-A-Million, and pulled in. He must have thought he had a better chance at finding whatever book he was looking for, because this time he took her in with him.

He pulled her through the store, avoiding the customer service booth, scanning the shelves himself. He stopped and hesitated after going up and down the aisles several times. He seemed to be leaning toward the customer service counter after all when he spotted the discount section along the back. She stood back a little ways while he walked around searching through all the different books stacked and piled up on the tables.

She walked over to see the book he had just picked up. "Did you find it?"

His voice sounded strained. "Oh I found it all right."

She read the title of the book he held in his hand. *In the Dark Night*. Todd flipped it over and showed her the picture on the back flap. It was unmistakably Todd, only younger and, if possible, even more devastatingly handsome than he was now. His name under About the Author was listed as R.T. Black, obviously a pseudonym.

"You published a book!" She glanced up at his face and tried to decipher his expression. A small pulse beat in his temple and a faint tinge of red colored his already swarthy complexion. She took another look at the book and spotted the green sticker in the corner discounting the book down to five dollars and ninety-nine cents. Oh, he was *embarrassed*. He had brought her out to find his book and show it off to her, and the only place he had been able to find it was in the discount section for a lousy five ninety-nine. Her heart moved for him.

"Oh Todd, I had no idea you were a writer." She smiled up at him and clasped the book to her chest. She didn't know exactly why he felt his book would help her, but there was no way she was leaving without it.

"I'm going to buy it," she said.

Todd seemed about to protest but then didn't. He followed her silently towards the checkout counter. He lagged behind the closer they got to the register, and figuring he was afraid of being recognized buying his own book out of the discount section, she offered to meet him outside. Agreeing, he gave her a grateful look and slipped out the door.

Back in the car Todd remained subdued. All of his earlier excitement had vanished, and she was determined to get it back. He had written a book. And had it published. That was no small feat as far as she was concerned.

This called for a change of plans.

"Hey, why don't we go out to lunch another day? I've got a better idea. Pull in there." She pointed at a Whole Foods Market.

He shot her a quizzical look, but didn't argue.

He lucked out and got a space near the front just as someone was leaving, and she had her door open before he had the car stopped good. "I'll be right back," she said, and hurried into the store.

She grabbed a basket, and went straight to the refrigerated beer and wine section in the back. She chose a bottle of Veuve Clicquot, one of the better champagnes they carried. She winced at the price. At fifty bucks it wasn't incredibly expensive as far as good champagne went, but it was more than her measly budget could really afford. Trying not to think about how much everything was going to cost, she grabbed a marbled chunk of blue cheese, a nice slab of Brie, some grapes, and a crusty loaf of French bread. In the deli, she chose a rotisserie chicken and a pound of pasta salad, and rounded everything off with a fresh baked raspberry tart. On impulse she snagged an arrangement of cut flowers on the way to the checkout counter.

Todd jumped out of the car when she came out and helped her place everything in the trunk. He said nothing about her purchases, but the corner of his mouth was starting to turn up a little.

She was grinning broadly as they carried everything in. This was going to be fun. She was surprised and pleased to find out he was a writer, and her opinion of him had risen significantly. And from what little she could tell about the book from her cursory inspection while she had waited in line, it had something to do with the supernatural. If he was ready to share his life with her, then she was willing to try and share her life and recent experiences with him. Especially now that she knew he wrote about the paranormal too.

Todd dropped the last bag on the table. On impulse, she stepped closer and threw her arms around him. He stiffened for a moment, then relaxed into her and hugged her back. She gave him a squeeze and a quick kiss on the mouth before letting go.

"What's all this for?" he asked as she stuck the champagne in an ice bucket and started unpacking the food.

"We're celebrating."

Todd stayed back out of her way, grinning now. It was one of the odd unseasonably warm days the south sometimes enjoyed, so she opened the sliding glass doors to the balcony and arranged everything along with plates and silverware on the outside table. She found a vase and arranged the flowers, then turned on the stereo. Something was missing. She ran back in and grabbed two candles and a lighter.

Todd pulled her chair out, then sat down across from her and lit the candles. She went to pour them both a glass of champagne and realized they hadn't opened it.

"Wait, let me." He pulled the dripping bottle out of the ice water and peeled the foil off. Stepping back, he gripped the bottle in both hands and pushed up on the cork with his thumbs. "Look out," he said, and she ducked just as it came out with a loud *pop* and flew through the air and over the balcony.

"Ow!" they heard from below. Aileen and Todd's eyes went wide, and they ran to the edge and looked down. One of her neighbors, a divorcee who lived one floor up, stood rubbing the top of his head.

"Oh! I'm sorry Mr. Pritchard! We're just having a little celebration," she called down to him.

Mr. Pritchard glared up at her then flapped his hand and walked off, still rubbing his head and muttering something unintelligible.

Choking back laughter, they sat back down. Todd poured the champagne, and she raised her glass.

"To your book."

His face broke into a smile and he clicked his glass to hers. They both took a polite sip, staring at each other across the rim of their champagne flutes. Then, simultaneously, they each drained their glass. She held back a little burp of air from the bubbles while Todd gave a discreet belch into his napkin. For some reason this struck both of them as funny, and they started laughing again.

They munched on all the food while they sipped their champagne. She was hungry and loaded up her plate and Todd's, glad to see he had a good appetite and seemed to be enjoying himself. They talked about his book, and she found out he had published his one and only book five years previously but hadn't published since. She decided not to let that deter her or him from what she saw as an extraordinary accomplishment.

"You did it once, you can do it again," she said matter-of-factly around a bite of raspberry tart.

Todd cut himself a second piece, and took a large bite. "This is good," he said when he could speak again.

"I *know*."

She filled their glasses with the last of the bubbly, and went in to get his book. Coming back out, she saw again how devastatingly handsome he really was. Even in the middle of winter his skin appeared tan as if he had some kind of exotic blood in him. His eyes were so dark they looked black as he watched her walking towards him across the balcony. When he looked at her like that, his expression serious and almost . . . *hard,* she was made aware again of how much of a man he was. A man in every sense of the word, whom she barely knew. And she was alone with him. *Dangerous,* her mind whispered, and she felt a shiver of desire despite, or maybe because, of it.

Todd's book was about the haunting of the Guise family in Arnett, Pennsylvania, with firsthand accounts from the daughter, Virginia. After finishing their feast, they had moved back inside, and she had made a pot of the gourmet coffee she had purchased but not yet opened. And now they sat sipping the fragrant brew while she skimmed though the book and read certain passages aloud. Todd didn't seem to mind expounding on his writing, and as he explained and elaborated on his book, she was drawn in and intrigued by the events leading up to that last awful night.

"How did you know Virginia?"

"We lived next door to them. My father moved there a few months before the Guises moved in, and I was staying with him at the time. I got to know Ginny and ended up spending a lot of time over at her house. What I didn't witness myself, I heard about from her. We were close."

"You were lovers, you mean?"

"Yes. But it was more than that. I knew what was happening to her and she was so frightened. I wanted to help her, only I didn't know how."

She flipped to a page of Ginny's writing. "How did you manage to get all of this written in her own words?"

"She gave me her diary the day before. She said if anything happened to her she wanted everyone to know the truth."

"It was like she knew."

"But she couldn't have."

No, she couldn't have. There was no doubt that her father had attacked her. He had left enough evidence to paint a bloody picture of what had gone on that night. Her father, who had been nothing but devoted to her, her mother, and her little brother, who rarely raised his voice, and took his family to church every Sunday, had shot her brother in the head while he slept. Then he had strangled her mother when she came running down the hall, shot Ginny while she undoubtedly screamed over her body, and rounded the evening off by blowing his own brains out.

"But Ginny didn't die right away."

A spasm of pain crossed his features. "No, she lingered until the next day when she regained consciousness."

Ginny had lingered until she had woken up the next day and realized her entire family was dead and she was a paraplegic. It had all been too much and she had suffered a heart attack and died. And Todd had been there when it happened.

"And she didn't say anything before she passed away?"

"Actually, she did. Her last words to me were 'It wasn't Daddy. It wasn't him.'"

"And do you think she was right?"

"Hell yes I do, he had to have been possessed. I knew Jake Guise and he would have *never*—" his voice broke off.

She could see the faint sheen of tears in his eyes and knew what it had cost him to dredge up everything again. He was doing it for her, and she owed him the same in return.

"I wasn't completely honest with you before," she said.

He took a deep breath. "You mean about the lightning strike and the nightmares?"

"Yeah, I've had some other side effects I didn't mention."

He regarded her steadily. "Some paranormal side effects?"

"Yes."

She told him everything.

Chapter 15

The next morning, doubting she would see Todd again so soon since he hadn't left until well after midnight, Aileen tried to get caught up on all of the dirty clothes and towels spilling out of her hamper. Her apartment didn't have its own washer and dryer connections and she had to carry her laundry to the on-site laundromat adjacent to her building. She ruminated on everything they had talked about the night before as she lugged baskets to and fro, barely noticing what she was doing, working on autopilot. That afternoon, she was surprised to realize she had finished the last load. And she was no closer to figuring out what she was going to do with her life.

Later on, bored and tired of sitting around the apartment, she called Colleen at work. It was close to time for her to get off, and she thought she might drive over and hang out with her for a while at her place. But when Mackenzie finally picked up the phone at the office, she learned Colleen had called in sick that morning. She tried Colleen's home phone and then her cell, and after getting no response on either one, she finally sent her a text and headed on over.

By coincidence Todd was staying with a friend of his who lived in the same apartment building as Colleen, and she looked for his car as she pulled in, but didn't see it. From what he had told her, his friend worked the night shift and because of that, Todd tried to stay gone as much as possible in order to not disturb his erratic sleep schedule. Todd was probably out getting something to eat or researching the new book he was writing. After exhausting themselves talking about his previous book and her current problems, they had talked only briefly about his new book, a collection of gravestone art and history he was amassing and thinking of publishing as a coffee-table book. She made a mental note to ask him more about it the next time she saw him.

Colleen's apartment was on the ground floor, and she picked her way around scattered toys and bicycles as she made her way around to her door. Unless she was gone with Bobby, she was there because her car was parked out front. Aileen knocked and waited. She waited a couple of minutes and knocked again. The door next to Colleen's opened and an elderly woman with curlers in her hair stuck her head out, looked as if she wanted to say something, then thought better of it and went back inside.

Aileen banged on the door and yelled, "Colleen, it's ME." She was almost certain she was in there, and now she was starting to get a little worried. She banged again. "Colleen!"

She was just about to give up when she heard the faint jingle of her unchaining the door. It cracked open, and Aileen slipped inside. It was just as she had feared; Colleen was either sick or in one of her funks. All the curtains were still closed; dishes, trash, and overflowing ashtrays littered her normally immaculate apartment, and she could see her unmade bed through the open bedroom door.

Colleen glowered at her from across the room. Her tangled hair hung lankly around her face, and a black band ran across the top of her head where her roots were starting to show.

"Shit, Aileen."

Damn. She was mad. "I tried to call you, and I texted you."

"I was a*sleep!*" Colleen grabbed a pack of Marlboros off the bar that divided the kitchen from the dining room area, and thumped one out. She was wearing an old stained T-shirt and this plus the fact that she lit up standing right beside Aileen made her instantly on guard. No matter how many times she told her she didn't mind, Colleen had always refused to smoke around her. She would only take small quick puffs standing over an ashtray beside her open kitchen window if Aileen was present. She had only seen her this bad on one other occasion when they had first met, and it hadn't been pretty. She had seen a side of Colleen she had hoped to never see again. She had thought at the time that Colleen's attitude had been a defense mechanism and that she was possibly jealous or insecure, and had made a special effort to befriend her. And she had never regretted it until that moment. She felt a cough coming on from Colleen's cigarette and took a step back.

"What the fuck, Aileen?" Colleen took a deep drag of her cigarette and blew a long plume of smoke in her face.

Aileen felt an instant urge to slap her and worked to control herself. *What the hell was wrong with her?*

"I'm sorry. I was worried because I called work and they said you took a sick day," she bit out, taking another step back and waving her hand around to clear the smoke.

"Well, SOMETIMES you just need to give me my SPACE," Colleen said, and stomped into the kitchen.

Oh that was rich, implying she was needy and pathetic. It was time for her to go. She turned around and started for the door when Colleen's voice from the other end of the kitchen stopped her.

"I think he's seeing someone else."

She turned around and saw that Colleen was crying, where she had moved over by the window after all.

She crossed the linoleum floor and wrapped her arms around her, hugging her tight. Although she felt like her mother certainly loved her, she had not been a very demonstrative parent and now hugs and other intimacies between friends did not come easily for her, and she broke it off after a second. She climbed up on a bar stool, her usual place when she came to visit, and gave Colleen time to compose herself. Colleen could at times be a little too emotional when she drank (and she had been drinking, Aileen had smelled it when she hugged her) and as much as she sympathized with her, she knew better than to let her get mired down in self-pity.

"What the hell did he do?" If she read the situation right, now was not the time to boost her up with reassurances of Bobby's virtues, but a time to engage in some sisterly male-bashing.

"Hell." Colleen stubbed out her cigarette and immediately lit another one. "You want a glass of tea?"

"Sure."

Colleen filled a glass with ice. "I can't prove anything. But he gets calls sometimes, and I don't know whom he's talking to. And he gets pissed if I question him, you know? He hardly ever leaves his phone lying around for me to go through it. And he leaves, and I don't know where he goes. Last night he was gone until nearly one o'clock!"

Aileen took a drink of her tea. "Is he living here?"

"More or less."

"So my Mom once knew this woman who called a private detective about those lie detector tests?" she said carefully, "and he told her if she was that sure he was lying then she didn't need the test."

"I know," Colleen whispered, looking down.

"We could follow him."

Colleen's head snapped back up. "*Could* we? You would go with me?" Colleen was smiling now, her eyes shining with either relief or malice, she wasn't sure which, but it was better than the crying.

"Of course, you let me know when, and we'll go. We can take my car if you want so he won't know it's you."

"All right!"

"Where's he at?" From what little Colleen had told her, she knew Bobby did some kind of contract web designing or something and worked his own hours.

"Who knows?"

"Well, from now on, instead of sitting around here being upset, the next time he's gone like that you call me and we'll go do something."

"Okay."

The mood considerably lighter now, she was able to tell her a little bit more about Todd.

"Does he have a friend?" Colleen asked.

She laughed. "I don't know, *maybe*."

"Did you sleep with him?"

"No! I barely know him!" She kept quiet about the first night when she had wanted nothing more than that and hadn't even known his name.

They talked a little bit more, catching up on things, including her most recent encounter at Rose Wood and continuing problems. Colleen thought she should capitalize on the whole thing and write a more in-depth story for Ed. "You could do a feature article. I know he would do it."

"I don't know. I don't think I want to do this anymore, Colleen."

"It doesn't sound like you have a choice. Might as well make a living at it."

"I know. I could sure use the money."

"Well, I'd loan you some, but I'm all tapped out. Bobby hits me up for money every time you turn around. I'm about to get tired of it, too."

Aileen stood up. "No, don't worry about me, I'm fine. And I'm sorry about Bobby."

Colleen shrugged. "Maybe I'm wrong."

Chapter 16

Her almost argument with Colleen seemed to set the tone for the rest of the week, and things just went downhill after that. And to make matters worse, Friday was Valentine's Day. And she hated Valentine's Day. The only good thing that happened was she got to see Todd again on Wednesday when he took her to lunch. They were at an awkward phase in their relationship—if you could call it that—at least as far as the silly holiday was concerned. She didn't know if they qualified as "sweethearts" and she wasn't sure if he would acknowledge her or not, and how she would feel if he didn't. So she made no mention of it during their lunch, preferring to stick primarily with his new book idea and her ongoing saga of dissatisfaction and now trepidation with her job.

Todd leaned forward and grasped her hand in his. "But Aileen, you went into this job of yours, this career, in order to promote the reasonable, logical, *scientific* study for evidence of the afterlife. Life after death. And now you've done it."

"I haven't done anything. I can't *prove* anything."

"But *you* know, Aileen. *You* know." He let go of her hand and sat back in his chair, the muscles of his flat stomach and thighs flexing slightly.

Oh God he was so handsome, she thought. Not only was she falling in lust with him, she was in danger of falling in love with him. She pulled her thoughts away from the sexy perfection of his anatomy and tried to focus on the subject at hand.

"But things are different now. Before, it was just a theory. And now it's a reality and it scares the hell out of me. I'm sorry to bring it up again, but look what happened to Ginny?"

"That's different. Have you felt at any point like you were in danger, that someone or something was malevolent towards you?"

She thought about it. It was true that the initial sight of Emma had frightened her, but ever since, she had gotten the impression she was trying to tell her something or show her something, not hurt her.

"No. But I don't even know what happened. I mean, I really don't know anything. First I saw Emma, and then I started having these dreams. I had another one last night. And I have no idea how her little brother, the girl picking berries, or the woman I saw crying, tie into it all."

"Well, that's what you need to find out. There must be a reason all of this is happening to you. Maybe you just need to let things take their course and see this thing through."

"I don't know. Maybe. It's true I can't keep going on like I have been."

"It's make or break time, baby."

She thought about what he said several times over the next couple of weeks.

That night when she went to bed, she had the dream she had told Todd about again. It was like she was there, but nobody could see her. It started with the same distant clanking of the bell.

The bell rang and echoed, reaching far across the now empty fields. The men were grouped around the house in twos and threes. A dirty burlap sack covered the girl's body, the ends of it trailing on the ground as the two men carried her up and onto the porch.

"Nooo! You get that off my baby!" shrieked the black woman who had just come out of the house. She ripped the dirty sack off the girl and screamed again, this time long and horrible, and fell to her knees. Her scream became a high thin wail at the sight of her daughter's broken body, and she threw herself across her, keening and rocking against her.

"My God man, what were you thinking?" The woman who had been screaming her own grief on the hilltop now carried a clean soft quilt over to the grieving mother. She bent down and pressed it into her hands.

The black woman clutched at the blanket and began tucking it around the girl, crooning softly to her, tears streaming in a steady trail down her shocked face. "Oh Ms. 'Lizbeth, I done told her not to go near that bank. I told her not to pick berries there, but she said it was the only place where there were any left. Oh Jesus, my baby." She broke down again, sobbing wretchedly.

Elizabeth laid her hand on her shoulder, and she managed to look up from her grief. "Did they find Miss Emma?" *she choked out.*

Elizabeth shook her head silently.

"Oh no, Ms. 'Lizbeth! Where could she be? What done happened to our girls?" *The dead girl's mother began to wail again, breaking down into sobs as she held her baby girl for the last time.*

Elizabeth's eyes, looking out over all the faces grouped around them, and the fields and river beyond, were blank and dry as if her very soul had been ripped out along with her earlier cries of grief and sorrow.

Someone, somewhere, began to ring the bell again as the men prepared to search once more for Emma. Clang, clang, Clang, clang. Clang—

Aileen jerked awake, breathing hard. *Not again.* She drew in a ragged breath and looked at the clock. 4:15. Only forty-five minutes since the last time she had woken from the same dream. She flopped back down on the pillow. She couldn't stand it anymore. She had to find out what happened. Emma wasn't resting so she wasn't going to let her rest either. She turned over, hoping for a few more hours of sleep.

But it wasn't to be, and the next night wasn't any better. Every time she fell asleep, she dreamed the same thing and jerked awake at the same exact spot. It was driving her crazy, and by Friday her nerves were a jangled mess. If the lack of sleep weren't bad enough, now she was having trouble with her car. It refused to start, and she had to get a jump-start from Mr. Pritchard, the only neighbor around, and have a new battery installed, further depleting her bank account. And then to top things off, there was a mix-up with payroll and her check had been printed out instead of direct deposited, and she had to drive over to get it.

The first thing that greeted her when she walked into the reception area was a large bouquet of bright red roses. Colleen was away from her desk, but even without asking her, Aileen knew they had to be from Bobby. She leaned over and started to sniff the flowers out of instinct, then pulled back. She had smelled enough roses lately to last a lifetime.

She walked down the hall to the tiny area in the back of the copy room that had been designated hers when she had taken the job. She found her check lying on her desk. She grabbed it and some other mail and memos and headed back out. She had kind of been hoping there would be flowers waiting for her too. She hadn't received anything at her apartment yet. She doubted Todd would send them to her job since he knew she mostly worked from home, but she had told him she was coming in to pick up her check, and she had hoped a little bit in the back of her mind that he was only trying to surprise her.

Colleen still wasn't at her desk, and she didn't have time to look for her. She hurried on out the door and headed for the bank.

She made it just in time before they closed, deposited her check, then gassed up her car and headed home. Maybe Todd would come by that night.

But he didn't. She killed as much time as she could straightening up her apartment and taking a long hot bath. She put on a pair of soft gray pants and a white shirt so she would be dressed in case Todd did come by, but comfortable in the meantime, fluffed up her hair, and gave her lips a dash of gloss.

At a quarter to eight, he still hadn't shown up. There had been no flowers delivered, no card, and no phone call. And there was no way he didn't realize what day it was, not with all the ads on the television, radio, and the Internet. But why should he do anything? It was true that they had been seeing a lot of each other, but they still hadn't slept together, and they were nowhere near a committed relationship. But still, it would have been nice. This was why she hated Valentine's Day. With her inability to establish a lasting relationship, she invariably got left out while all the other girls received flowers, candy, and jewelry, or got taken out for the evening.

Whatever, she thought, and tried to put the whole stupid day out of her mind. It was too early to go to bed, and she was too keyed up to watch television, so she switched on her computer and began checking her e-mail. She made a few notes on what little she had found out so far about Rose Wood—just in case she did decide to do an article on it—and on impulse began a new online journal program for her thoughts and feelings about her experiences so far since her lightning strike when it had all began. She worked for an hour or so, listing her paranormal experiences in chronological order with their approximate dates, trying to get down details before she forgot them.

By ten o'clock she was starting to feel tired. She shut down her computer, ate a bowl of cereal, and fell asleep while watching a rerun of Seinfeld.

She was just getting to the end of the same dream she seemed destined to live through every single time she closed her eyes when someone hammering on the door jerked her awake. Who in the world? Todd? This late?

She peered through the peephole and got an eye full of nothing but bright yellow. The yellow moved back, and Todd's mildly distorted face appeared. She unlocked and opened the door.

He held out a large bouquet of sunshine yellow tulips. "These are for you. I hope you like them. I know they're a little unusual for Valentine's Day, but I didn't think you would appreciate roses."

Aileen laughed. "No, you're right. These are perfect. They're beautiful. Thank you Todd."

"I'm sorry I'm so late. I meant to be here earlier, but something came up and I couldn't get away."

She didn't care how late he was. He was there and that's all that mattered. She gave the flowers, which seemed to actually have a scent unlike most hothouse flowers, an appreciative sniff and placed them in the center of the kitchen table.

"I brought this, too." He held out a bottle of wine. "I thought we could have some."

He went to work opening it while she got down the wine glasses. The cork finally popped out with a *thook,* and he filled their glasses.

Todd swirled his wine around, then raised his glass.

"To you, Aileen."

"To us," she said, and clinked her glass to his.

She watched him carefully but so saw no hint of disagreement with her not-so-subtle establishment of them as a couple. If anything, he seemed to be in total agreement with her, pulling her into his arms and kissing her thoroughly. His mouth tasted sweet like wine, and just as intoxicating.

She turned on some low music, and he took her back in his arms, and they danced slowly, enjoying the wine and each other until she finally felt the time was right and led him to her bedroom.

Chapter 17

The next day, she glided about the apartment in the afterglow of Todd's lovemaking. She felt a low thump of desire deep in her belly every time she thought about his mouth and hands and body on hers the night before. It had been everything she had imagined and more. After making love, twice, they had fallen asleep together, and then around twelve forty-five he had got up and left. She didn't mind. Although well on their way to a real relationship, she was in no hurry to share her morning routine and all its embarrassing necessities with him just yet.

But she did want to share with Colleen. She went into the kitchen and grabbed her cordless and dialed Colleen's number. After getting no answer on her landline or her cell phone, she left a message for her to call and hung the phone up. Thinking she might have a text from Colleen, she went back into the living room to retrieve her cell phone from where she had dropped it in her bag. She dug it out, then slowly straightened to a standing position, her eyes taking in the glow of the flat-screen monitor.

Her computer was on.

That was odd. She distinctly remembered shutting it down the night before. And she was sure it had been off when she had come through earlier because she had been thinking she should switch it on and get it going in case she needed it. And now it was back on, booted up and ready to go, little icons waiting across the blue expanse of the deep-sea background. Must have had a glitch and turned itself on.

She didn't think too much about it until later when she shut it down to go do some errands. She was just putting on her coat when she heard the click and unmistakable sound of the computer starting up. She considered for a minute that she might have clicked Restart instead of Shut Down, but immediately rejected the idea since it had been at least ten minutes since she had turned it off. Wonderful. Now her computer was screwing up and she would probably have to buy a new one. She waited on it impatiently to come all the way up so she could shut it down again. This time after it finished, she reached around behind it and flipped the switch on the back to the "off" position. She picked her coat back up again, grabbed her purse, and heard it start up again behind her.

"Dammit!" She turned around again in exasperation. Maybe somebody was trying to hack in? She would have to pull the plug.

She went through the whole process again, gave it time to click all the way off, and then jerked the cord out of the outlet. And just to be on the safe side, she pulled the Ethernet cord out of her modem box, too.

She started out the door, trying to come to terms with yet another problem to contend with.

The computer clicked to life behind her.

She whirled around. The lights on the tower glowed blue then began to flicker as the computer began initializing. Her eyes traced the cord from where it came out of the back of the computer to the floor where it now lay. Her heart started galloping. This couldn't be happening. The screen flickered and resolved itself with a jerk into the familiar ocean scene. She walked slowly towards the glowing screen. The tower lights began to flash again with some internal process, and after a second the picture changed to the open folder where she had placed the digital pictures she had taken at Rose Wood—the pictures she had uploaded but never finished looking at. She stepped closer. One side of the yellow brick house and part of a magnolia tree filled the screen. Almost afraid to touch it, she reached for the mouse. Suddenly the little arrow beneath it flashed and clicked as if some unseen hand were advancing to the next photo. Pictures popped up on the screen, much quicker than they ever had before, faster and faster, clicking and blurring together until suddenly they stopped. She was looking at the last picture she had taken right before she left that day. She had snapped it on impulse, stopping her car halfway down the drive and clicking a shot of the house and immediate yard before continuing on down and out the gates. Looking at it now, she couldn't see anything unusual about it. She was still studying it when the unseen hand acted again and clicked the zoom button. The picture zoomed in on one of the upstairs windows once, twice, and then BAM the ghost-girl's face popped up, taking up the entire screen with her fierce glare. For a second, she looked just as horrific as she had the first time Aileen saw her, causing her to jump and cry out. Then she blended and sharpened into the young lady she had seen in her dream. Emma looked straight at her, her gaze dead on her, *following* her with her inky blue eyes as Aileen backed away. The scene from *The Ring* where the inhuman girl slithers out of the television set crawled into her mind, and she was one second from screaming when the screen went blank.

The computer sat powerless, dark, and silent.

She stood shaking from head to toe, her breath hitching in and out of her chest.

She fled the apartment.

All her errands completely forgotten, she drove around, basically in circles, trying to get her head together. If bad dreams and visions weren't enough, now it was invading her real life. Nowhere was safe.

She couldn't go on like this. She made an illegal U-turn and got on the interstate. She could make it to Andersonville, and the public library there, by noon. It was time for some answers.

Chapter 18

She found the public library easily enough on the corner of South and Main in the old downtown section. It was actually called the Andersonville Carnegie Library she saw as she drove by on her way to park around the back.

It looked nothing like any library she had ever seen. A thick green lawn reached all the way down to the road, suitable more for a house than a public library. The building itself was beautiful, made out of yellow and red brick with ornate features, including a pair of entrance columns, pediments, scrollwork, stained-glass arched windows, and a copper roof crowned with a dome.

The building was built in 1905 using the French Beaux-Arts style of neoclassical architecture, which explained its opulent style, she found out by reading several plaques on the wall just inside the entrance. The library had been renovated in 1985, but she could still smell a dusty hint of age as she entered the main room.

The library closed early on Saturday, and as a result, most of the computers were full and there was a small line waiting to be checked out at the circulation desk. Aileen decided to see what she could find out on her own while she waited for the line to die down. She jumped on the first available online catalog and started looking for anything on the Gage family.

She found a few books that briefly mentioned Senator Gage and his political part in the succession of South Carolina, and a large photo book titled *Historic Homes in the Antebellum South* that featured a two-page article on Rose Wood. But she was just killing time. Whatever had happened all those years ago had faded into the past and had not made the history books. What she really needed was to see copies of old newspapers and for that she was going to need help.

She waited until there was no one else in line and approached the librarian hesitantly. She had not really thought this thing through. She didn't even know what year to start looking or if they still had newspapers from back then.

The lady behind the desk looked older now that she saw her up close. She was tiny, so thin that her face had kept its shape and her chin was tight, giving the appearance of being younger than she probably was. Only the deep lines that ran across her forehead and down her chiseled cheekbones gave it away. Her white-blond hair was cut in a short pixy-like cut, and her equally tiny, ever so slightly pointed ears made her look like a little elf. She must have been spectacular when she was young.

"I'm looking for information on . . . something that may have happened a long time ago. Do you have copies of old newspapers here?"

"Yes, we do. What year were you looking for?"

"I'm not sure exactly."

"Well, what are you researching?"

Aileen hesitated, still trying to think of how to word it so she wouldn't sound like she was crazy. "Possibly an old murder. Two girls. I'm not sure what year."

"The murder of two girls? You're going to have to be more specific than that."

Aileen took a deep breath and glanced over her shoulder. A line was starting to form behind her.

"Just a minute," said the elfin librarian, then called back over her shoulder, "Tina, could you take over? I need to help this lady here with some newspapers." She waited until Tina came out of the room behind her and began helping the other patrons before gesturing for Aileen to follow her.

"The periodicals we have are kept out in the main room if they're current, and down in the basement if they're archived." She opened the door at the end of the hall, and they emerged into a stairwell. She kept talking as they climbed down the worn steps. "Some of them are still hard copies, but the older ones are on microfilm. We're trying to digitize them and hope to offer them online at some point." At the bottom she pulled a set of keys out of her pocket, unlocked the door directly in front of them, and pushed it open. She flipped on the lights.

A deep room with a short ceiling reached out in front of them. The hooded lights that hung down continued across the entire room, but only the first half or so had been filled with shelves and equipment. Small work areas with microfilm machines were arranged around the room in sections. Newspapers were bound in oversized hard covers and stacked beside a long table for easy viewing, and rows of filing cabinets lined the walls.

Aileen followed her over to the first drawer. "It would certainly help if you knew what year. There's just too many to look through," she said, indicating the long row.

Aileen thought back on what little she knew about the plantation, and what she had discerned from her dreams. She started to say "Around the civil war?" and caught herself. The woman, *Elizabeth*, that she had seen crying on the hilltop and again in the dream with the girl's body, had not been wearing the type of dress normally worn back then. It hadn't been like the old-fashioned hoop dresses the women had worn in the Old South, or like the one on display at Rose Wood. The woman in her dreams or visions or whatever they were, had been the best dressed and it was clear she was the lady of the house, but her dress had been in a completely different style. So not during the Civil War era. She tried to picture her again. Her dress had looked looser and kind of flat with a low waistline. All of this went through her mind in only seconds.

"Maybe the twenties?"

The librarian's eyebrows went up. "Well! We only have back to 1981 stored here. For that you would have to try the archives in Columbia."

Her heart sank.

"Where was it at? Was it well publicized?"

"I'm not sure. I just kind of ran across the whole thing myself. I'm Aileen, by the way," she said, and held out her hand.

"Diana." They shook hands.

"I know it happened at Rose Wood Plantation. There was a black girl, a daughter of one of the servants, who died or was murdered, and a missing girl that may have been murdered also."

From Diana's openmouthed intake of breath, she knew something in her memory had been triggered. "Ohh," she said. "The Rose Wood Plantation. Yes."

"What? What do you remember?"

"There's always talk, you know," she said after a second. Now that Diana knew what it was about, she seemed in danger of clamming up.

"What, were there rumors?"

"If you don't mind my asking, why are you so interested in something that happened so long ago?"

The moment of truth. She could tell her the truth, which she'd never believe, or she could give some version of it.

"I work for *Southern Aurora* magazine. I ran across Rose Wood a while back and . . . got interested. I would really appreciate any help you can give me."

"Are you going to write about it?"

"Honestly? I don't know."

"I don't see how I can help you. My parents talked about something that happened there, but I don't really remember anything."

Aileen didn't think that was true, not by a long shot. She tried again, appealing to her as directly and honestly as possible. "Please. This isn't just some story to me."

Diana regarded her for a moment, then said, "I can tell you this much. It was in the twenties. Probably the early twenties. And that's all I can really remember." She paused and Aileen waited, sensing she had something more she wanted to say, and out it came. "There are some people in this town that might not appreciate a story about Rose Wood. We take care of our own here and we'd hate to see Mr. Gage upset. If it wasn't for him we wouldn't even have Rose Wood as a tourist attraction, and then I don't know what would have come of our little town." Diana said this all quietly, never losing the friendly tone in her voice, but there was no doubt of the underlying steel in her words. Aileen started to say that certain people would consider rumors of an old murder mystery conducive to attracting tourist, when she thought about what she had just said. *Mr. Gage.* Pieces of Jane's monolog from the day she had visited Rose Wood came back to her. She had said something about the last living descendant. Her mind reran the night of the storm at Rose Wood and she saw again the bent figure of the old man who had called the ambulance for her. She wondered . . .

"Do you have a picture of him?" Seeing the expression on Diana's face, she hastily added, "I'm not really here about a story."

Diana now looked not only puzzled but suspicious, as well.

Aileen stepped closer. "I think I might have met him. I was there for an investigation, but not about Rose Wood. I was checking out a haunted bridge—"

"Crybaby Bridge?"

"Yes. And I got caught in a bad storm. I had to walk, and I made it all the way to the house, and then I was struck by lightning."

Diana's eyes went wide.

"I think Mr. Gage might have been the one who called the ambulance for me."

Diana was still staring at her wide-eyed with bewilderment, but the suspicion was gone at least.

Aileen decided to go for broke. Like Todd said, it was make or break time. She looked around the room, making sure they were still alone. She lowered her voice, and Diana leaned in closer to listen. "I've been having these weird dreams. Bad dreams. Nightmares. And it's got something to do with what happened at Rose Wood." Diana still looked less than convinced. "I think I'm being haunted!" she blurted out.

"Oh! Well, why didn't you say so!" exclaimed Diana. Apparently a reporter there to do a story on an old murder mystery invoked way more hostility than someone who simply claimed to be seeing dead people. She put on the glasses that had been hanging around her neck on a chain and marched briskly down the row of file cabinets and started pulling out drawers.

After only a few false starts, Diana had the correct edition she was looking for up on one of the machines.

It was a piece on the reopening of Rose Wood to the public after the restoration. The accompanying picture showed the last living descendant of the Gage family cutting a ribbon strung across the two front porch columns. It was a younger version of Mr. Gage than the one she remembered leaning over her that night, but she could still tell it was him.

"That's Timothy Gage. Is it the same man?" Diana asked.

"Yes." Aileen turned to her. "Do you know anything about a relative named Emma, or Elizabeth?"

Diana shook her head. "I really don't know any details, but I know who would. I have a friend who works down at the archives. Hang on a minute and I'll give her a call. They really like it if you have an appointment, but I'll see what I can do." She stepped over and pulled out her cell phone. She held the phone out in front of her and walked around the room until she found a better signal, and started dialing.

Aileen looked again at the picture of Mr. Gage. She read the paragraph beneath: *Ribbon Cutting Ceremony marks the opening of historical Rose Wood Plantation to the public.* Of course he wouldn't want there to be stories about Rose Wood. It was the home of his ancestors and he wouldn't want their reputations tarnished.

"Okay," Diana said, coming back over, "what they mostly have are collections of *The Gazette* from the colonial period, but she says they do have some of a local newspaper from around the twenties. Her name is Clara and she said she'll be there today until five."

Aileen thanked her, and quickly stood up to leave. Now that she knew where she might find the answers she wanted, she was anxious to be on her way.

"Oh, and you might try Edith over at the museum, too. I know she has a display of Senator Gage and a few things donated from the family, as well."

"Okay. Thanks again," she said, and left.

Chapter 19

The South Carolina Archives was a whole different ballgame than the musty basement of the Carnegie Library. With the help of her GPS, Aileen made it to the modern-looking building at around one o'clock and it took her until nearly one thirty to park, gain entrance to the building, and get directed to the right floor. The lobby registration desk was located just inside the main foyer, and she had to fill out a form giving her name, address, subject of research—that was a tough one; she finally put *missing person search*—and purpose of research—that was easy enough; she just wrote *work related*. After being given an identification number for future visits, she was then handed a list of rules and regulations and pointed to the locker room where all of her belongings were to be left. Cameras were allowed to be used with permission, but since she had run out of her apartment in such a hurry, she hadn't brought one with her. She put away her purse and coat and was directed to the second floor, where she was greeted by another list of posted rules reminding patrons that researchers were *not allowed to take anything out of the room and were* subject to a search of briefcases, knapsacks, purses, books, and papers before entering or leaving.

At the reference desk, she was told that Diana's friend Clara had stepped away but would be back any minute. She was sent into the microfilm reading room to wait, where she half-expected to be strip-searched at any second.

The microfilm readers were only half filled, so she wouldn't have any trouble getting a spot, and she was happy to see another smaller room on the right contained a microfilm copy machine.

Not wanting to just sit and do nothing, she went back out into the research room. She wandered around the shelves and tables and found the microfilm cabinets beside the public access computers. She flipped through the microfilm List Notebook on top marked *Church, Newspaper, Private Records* but mostly found only parish registers and county and municipal records.

She didn't know what she would really find anyway. Some old news about a missing local girl? And since the other girl's death might have been considered an accident, she wasn't sure if she would find anything about her at all. But if she did find something, it would mean that her dreams were real, flashbacks to something that really happened, and not that she was going crazy or having some kind of sensory side effect from the strike causing her to hallucinate.

She had just decided to try an online catalogue when a thin woman of about fifty with salt-and-pepper hair wound into a bun approached her.

Aileen smiled and held out her hand. "You must be Clara. Thank you for helping me on such short notice."

They shook hands, and Aileen explained that she was looking for any old newspapers from the Andersonville area.

"We have quite a few old Colonial newspapers for South Carolina, as well as an extensive collection of *The Charleston Post and Courier,* but only a few from Andersonville county. What year are you looking for?"

"Somewhere between say, 1920 and 1927."

"I'll see what I can find."

Aileen amused herself while she waited doing various searches on the online catalogue.

In no time it seemed, Clara was back with several rolls of microfilm in her hand.

"I brought copies of *The Tribune* to start. It's the most comprehensive collection we have during that time period."

Clara helped Aileen get the first one started, and then she left her to it.

For the next couple of hours, she sat fascinated, scanning and studying the tattered newspaper copies, starting in June of 1920 and working forwards. The twenties had been a time of change, socially and politically, as World War I ended and people began to live life to the fullest. Women were released from the tight confines of previous fashion and allowed to vote for the first time. Jazz, blues, and the onset of the "Roaring Twenties" swept the country, barely pausing for prohibition to move into clandestine speakeasies. The stock market soared—everyone knew how that had turned out—and manufacturers began mass production of consumer goods. The first radio station opened in Pittsburgh, the *Mark of Zorro* starring Douglas Fairbanks was playing in theatres, and Babe Ruth and Shoeless Joe Jackson made their mark on baseball. She saw evidence of it all as she pored over the old stories and ads and read the equivalent of today's entertainment sections.

Small-town notices like "Horse Strayed or Stolen" and "Public Accountant" were intermixed with advertisements for anything from Reymer's Fresh Cigars, to Beiget Shoes, to Lux Flakes. The Hershey candy bar and a pack of Wrigley's Doublemint gum was still only 5 cents, and Jell-O, *America's Most Famous Dessert in pure fruit flavors,* sold for a mere 10 cents a box.

Among these were other disturbing ads like the one she found halfway through an August 1924 edition. This one took up an entire page and announced a Ku Klux Klan State Demonstration being held at the county fairgrounds Saturday and Sunday, Sept. 3rd and 4th. A parade, lectures, religious services, band concerts, and a fireworks display were advertised.

She quickly skipped past that page and continued scanning as fast as she could. She was running out of time and really didn't want to have to drive back down another day.

She still hadn't found anything by the time she hit 1927. It wasn't a complete collection and she was afraid that what she was looking for might have been in one of the missing papers. She started seeing stories on Charles Lindberg and his first solo crossing of the Atlantic and was about to give it up as a lost cause when she hit on an article on the Great Mississippi Flood that mentioned *other disasters like the 1919 Andersonville County earthquake.*

She had not gone back far enough.

After finding Clara and getting the correct microfilm for 1919, she started scanning the headlines for major stories and quickly found an article on the quake:

Andersonville County Earthquake

Thirty-three years after the 1886 Charleston earthquake, another strong earthquake occurred in South Carolina. The quake happened on August 1, at 2:26 p.m. near the town of Andersonville with an estimated magnitude of 5.7. Shock waves moved out from the northern part of South Carolina into Georgia and North Carolina. Although the damage was minimal, this signifies that large earthquakes can still strike the Southern region.

She reversed the microfilm, started at the beginning, and began inspecting each page more carefully this time. She hit pay dirt on the second page of the August 3rd edition.

Search for Missing Girl

Mystery surrounds the disappearance of 14-year-old Emma Gage, the great-granddaughter of Senator Walter Gage, most noted for his support of the succession of South Carolina before the Civil War. She's been missing from her home at Rose Wood Plantation since Saturday afternoon. Efforts are being made by local law enforcement officials to trace and locate the girl. Several hundred people have been searching the property and surrounding area. Further complicating matters, police and searchers are dealing with property damage, diverted rivers, and rockslides following in the wake of the August 1st earthquake.

The photo underneath was provided courtesy of *Andersonville Graded School* and showed a group of boys and girls sitting and standing on the steps of a brick building. A woman wearing a long dress stood to the side of them. A chalkboard slat sat propped in the lap of a girl sitting on the bottom step, but the picture was too indistinct for her to read the teacher's name. She looked for Emma and found her smiling enigmatically from the middle row.

A little further, and she found a follow-up story buried on the back page of the August 10th edition.

Andersonville County Girl Still Missing

Police are planning to scale back their search for 14-year-old Emma Gage, who went missing from outside her home at Rose Wood Plantation over a week ago. Search teams have spent several days searching the plantation and surrounding terrain but have yet to find any sign of the girl. In a related matter, the body of another girl from Rose Wood, Leona Cole, who went missing on the same day, was found last Sunday at the bottom of a ravine following the earthquake on August 1st. Authorities suspect the girl may have fallen due to the subsequent aftershocks and speculate something similar may have happened to young Emma Gage, although her body has not been found to confirm or deny this.

Aileen kept scanning the papers, looking for anything else, until Clara called out a ten-minute warning that they were closing, but she found no further mention of Emma's disappearance.

She quickly gathered up the microfilm, and after enlisting Clara's help again, managed to copy each article before leaving as they were locking the doors.

Chapter 20

The museum that Diana had mentioned was closed on Sunday, so she spent the day working. She scanned the newspaper articles she had copied and added them to the growing collection of pictures and information she had acquired on Rose Wood, made an entry in her online journal, and began writing the article she had tentatively started for Ed.

This was more than her usual short section and she tried to be as in depth as possible. She began with her earlier career and skepticism, followed with the lightning strike and accounts of similar near-death experiences, then recounted her ensuing paranormal encounters, dreams, and the vision she'd had at Rose Wood. And since she wasn't sure what it all meant, she theorized what possible causes Emma might have for continuing to inhabit the earth. The words just seemed to flow, thoughts and conjectures linking in her mind effortlessly and flying off her fingertips onto the page. She knew it was some of the best writing she had ever done.

By that afternoon she was exhausted, her eyes tired and strained from looking at the computer too long. She decided to stop for the day. She plugged in the new

USB flash drive she had bought on her way home the night before, backed everything up, and shut down the computer. She'd had no further encounters with Emma, probably because she was finally doing what she wanted, and this time it stayed shut down.

After eating a light dinner, she debated about calling Todd. But she hadn't heard from him since they had slept together and she didn't want to be the first to call. She watched a little television, and then decided to go to bed early and take advantage of Emma's absence and get caught up on her sleep. She had a big day ahead of her tomorrow. She needed to go in and speak with Ed and she wanted to go visit the museum.

Colleen was just stepping out for an early lunch when Aileen got to the office the next day, and she decided to join her before speaking with Ed. In truth she was dreading it. She was going to have to ask for an advance and she wasn't sure how he would react. After the fiasco of Crystal Edward's show, and the drama of her being hit by lightning, she was afraid this would push him over the edge.

After getting their food, they settled down into a booth. Aileen took a bite of her lettuce and tomato on wheat.

"I don't see how you can eat that," Colleen said, taking a big bite of her Cheeseburger.

"I'm trying to lose weight."

Colleen didn't argue with her and say the usual "You're not fat!" that most people would, and she loved her for it. Colleen understood. She put down her cheeseburger and eyed her appraisingly. "You do look like you've lost some."

"I have. I decided to take advantage of the weight I lost after I was in the hospital, and I went on a diet. Sort of." She had never been one to eat on a strict schedule and now with everything that had been going on, and the added incentive of an attractive man's attention, her meals had become more hit or miss than ever and she had finally lost most of the weight she had put on since college.

"Maybe I need to go on a diet," Colleen said, pausing before taking another bite.

"No you don't. And I really mean that."

Colleen put her burger down and stared pensively out the window.

"Listen. Whatever's going on with Bobby is not your fault. Whatever he's going through, he's just going to have to figure it out for himself, and if he doesn't have sense enough to choose you and hold on to you then he's an idiot, right?

"I mean," she said, continuing, "Who the hell is he anyway? Some guy who's broke all the time and who doesn't even have a real job?"

"He's not that bad," Colleen said, and Aileen thought she might have gone too far, but it worked and Colleen resumed eating.

"So what are you here to talk to Ed about? Are you going to do the feature after all?" Colleen asked, taking a long drink of her soda.

"Yeah, I think so. I mean, I'm committed to this now. I want to know what happened."

"What else have you found out?"

Aileen filled Colleen in on her trip to the archives.

"So this really happened. All the stuff in your dreams and all."

"Yeah, you don't know the half of it."

"So what do you think happened to Emma?"

"I don't know, but I have a feeling she's going to make sure I find out."

Ed was in his office when they got back, and she waited for him to get off the phone before stepping in.

"Aileen! Good of you to stop by."

The words were said pleasantly enough, but she definitely detected sarcasm. This was going to be harder than she thought.

"Did you get my piece on the Crybaby Bridge? I sent it to you."

"Yeah, I got it. What can I do for you?"

She hardly knew where to begin. So much had happened. So much had changed. Taking a deep breath, she plunged into the main reason she was there. "I need to get an advance."

Ed took off his glasses and pinched the bridge of his nose.

"And I may need a little extra time for something I'm working on."

Ed glared at her. "Look, if you expect to get paid, then I need you to do your job. To the best of your ability, anyway."

She didn't appreciate that last part. Did he think she was just some kind of slacker trying to feed off of him?

She glared right back at him. She had never once asked for time off, other than when she was in the hospital, and she had never complained to him about her paltry paycheck or asked for a raise, let alone an advance. And she had always tried to do a good job. Well, most of the time. What more did he want from her? But she knew what he wanted. Like everyone else he just wanted a little hope. That he would see his daughter again. That one day there would be more than the everyday struggle to exist that passed for their lives.

A draft was coming in from the hallway, and she got up and pushed the door shut before speaking. "I'm just asking for my regular paycheck a little early." She felt the cold air again. She looked over at the window, but it was closed. Maybe the heat had just kicked on and hadn't begun to warm up yet.

Ed sighed deeply. "You need to make a decision about this job. I told you before, if you don't want to do this anymore, I can assign someone else to your section."

"It's not that." She smelled flowers. And there were no flowers in Ed's office. But not roses, this time she smelled . . . honeysuckles? It seemed to be wafting in with the frigid cold she was feeling.

She was just about to speak when she caught movement out of the corner of her eye. She looked quickly to the side but saw nothing but Ed's coat rack and a standing lamp in the corner. She smelled the sweet smell again, and a vision suddenly filled her mind: his daughter, Regina, when she was little, holding a clump of honeysuckle while she pulled out one of the delicate strands from the middle of a blossom and sucked the tiny droplet of honey off the end. She remembered doing the same thing when she was a child. There was just that one flash of her in her head, and then it was gone.

"Out with it. What's going on? Aileen? What is it?" Ed asked, sitting up straighter.

A shape wavered behind him, becoming clearer by the second. She stared in wonder as Regina slowly appeared. She looked much as she must have right before she was killed in the car wreck. She swayed and shimmered like she was having trouble staying materialized. Her mouth was moving, but Aileen couldn't make out what she was saying.

Ed spun around to see what she was looking at, but it was apparent he wasn't seeing her.

"It's Regina," she breathed.

His face went white. *"Is this some kind of a joke?"*

"She's trying to say something." She tried to read her lips. She seemed to be saying the same thing over and over. It looked like ... "don't something on the something." Don't leap? (lead? lean?) Yes, don't lean on the ... but she couldn't get the rest.

Aileen was suddenly hit by a blast of ice-cold air. Her hair blew sideways, and Ed jerked back, slamming his hand down on his desk to keep his papers from blowing away. "What the—"

One more vivid scene hit her, and then Regina was gone as if that final burst had taken all her energy. But it was enough for her to know what she had said. It made no sense, but she was sure she had it right because she had heard her voice say it clear as day.

"Did you and Regina ever watch movies together?" Because that was what she had seen—Regina and Ed sitting on the couch sharing a bag of M&M's.

Ed stared at her in wild-eyed shock. "Yes, why? *What? What did she say?*"

"She said 'Don't lean on the transit.' Just 'Don't lean on the transit.' Does that mean anything to you?"

Ed's eyes got even wider, and he wheezed out an amazed laugh as he took in her words. The term obviously meant something significant to him. He gave another openmouthed guffaw and then collapsed back in his chair.

"My God," he said, still reeling from what she'd said. His mouth hung open slightly, an expression of awe on his face.

"What does it mean?"

"It means . . ." He laughed softly to himself. "A transit is a tool they use to make a three-dimensional map of an archeological site. It takes a long time to set up." He shook his head, smiling. "She yelled it out during *The Raiders of the Lost Ark* in the scene with Harrison Ford. Of course I didn't get it and she had to explain it to me. It's kind of an inside joke."

Aileen was grinning now too. She had a feeling this one moment had just made it all worth it for Ed. And for her. She felt unexpected tears prick her eyes.

"Is she still here?" he asked, looking around.

"No. I'm sorry, she's gone now."

She leaned forward. "Something happened to me, Ed, when I was struck by lightning. I seem to have gained some kind of connection. It's not there all the time now, it's beginning to fade, but it has something to do with where I was hit that night. At Rose Wood."

"Rose Wood Plantation?"

"You've heard of it?"

He nodded, still looking stunned. "Of course. Years ago before Regina passed away, we stopped by and toured the house."

"I've been having dreams. About the family that lived there in 1919. I'm being contacted for a reason, and I need to find out what happened and why this girl won't rest."

"My God, this is incredible. I'll help you all I can, Aileen. I still can't believe it," he said, giving a shake of his head. "I can start by running that piece you did when you first started working here on the old Buford Hospital. We can run that again. We had a lot of good responses from it. And I can give you your regular pay until we sort this out. I'll let payroll know."

"Thank you, Ed." She got up to leave.

At the door she looked back. Ed was smiling down at a picture of Regina, and she caught a last glimmer of her standing slightly to the side of him, her hand lifted as if resting on his shoulder.

Chapter 21

Two and a half hours later, after a quick stop at a rest area and a candy bar, she wedged her car into one of the parallel parking spaces in front of the museum. The street and buildings lining it reminded her of those mill towns you used to see all the time before textiles went out. The old brick two-story building looked more like a storefront than a museum, with inlaid arched windows set across the top and an awning above the doorway.

A bell attached to the top of the door jingled as she walked in. The floors were hardwood, and glass cases, shelves, and displays crowded the space. It smelled like a museum should smell: old, musty, and woodsy.

Pictures, framed documents, quilts, and other various artifacts hung on the walls. It was dim even with the light coming in from the front, and small accent lights and wrought-iron light fixtures lit the displays.

In the middle of the floor there was a small open space with an old-fashioned oil lamp on a post standing beside two park benches set back to back. She wasn't sure if it was meant as a resting place for visitors or not.

She decided to look around a bit before trying to find Diana's friend Edith. Along one wall, glass curio cabinets were filled with all sorts of military memorabilia. Swords, knives, guns, grenades, hats, purple hearts, bronze stars, flags, and meal cans (now called mess kits) were arranged neatly on the shelves. Old uniforms and other historical clothing hung in an open wardrobe.

The sheer volume of the historical material was overwhelming, and she wanted to come back on another day when she had more time. There was an entire wood-paneled wall containing nothing but barbed wire, saws, skeleton keys, tools, and other farming implements hanging beside a Coco Cola calendar from 1942. A small alcove held a wooden plow, a saddle, a metal washtub, and an old milk can. A display case contained silver tea sets and trays and other treasures and mementoes. Another locked glass case contained a collection of antique pottery of local historic value. And in the corner there was a telephone operator's booth, complete with wires hanging out for plugging in calls.

She wandered through the rooms for a while before she went to look for Edith. She found her near the front, manning the entryway. Edith, a tall woman of indeterminate age, listened while she explained who she was and what she was looking for, then directed her to a narrow set of stairs down a short hallway near the back exit. Edith returned to the front, and Aileen went down alone. The steps led down into another smaller area that must have originally been part of the basement.

The ceiling here was lower, and it was cooler. A set of closed, locked doors probably led to storage and office space. A large bookcase filled with rare volumes taken from the first county library in 1809, antique children's books, and late 19th century cookbooks took up one wall. A corner cupboard that seemed to be an artifact itself, made in 1709, stood catty-corner. An exhibit on a raised platform cordoned off by velvet ropes took up the rest of the remaining space.

She walked over. According to a small white sign posted, State Senator Walter Gage originally owned the large scuffed up desk that sat on display. Ahh, now she was getting somewhere. A large oil painting of the Senator handing the reins from his horse to a small black boy was positioned in front of the exhibit on a standing easel on the right-hand side, and a large copy of some sort of signed document was displayed on the wall to the left.

There were a few other paintings, but nothing that could really help her. She turned to leave and noticed a small display case she had missed tucked into the corner.

She stepped closer. The case contained mementos and pictures of the Gage family at Rose Wood Plantation. There was a family Bible and a full-size head and shoulders bust of the Senator, but what interested her the most was the collection of pictures in the back. They were simply labeled "1900–1930". A few were fanned out almost haphazardly, but she could see more in a box behind them.

She could hardly contain her excitement as she rushed back up the stairs. Edith was talking to a young couple beside one of the military cases, and she had to wait several interminable minutes before she could get her attention.

"Those pictures down there, in the case in the back? Could I look at them?"

"Oh, those in the box? That's a work in progress. We just recently acquired some of them. I'm sorry but we don't allow anyone to handle them."

"Please, if I could just get a better look at them. I don't have to actually touch them. You could do it for me."

"You say Diana sent you?"

"Yes ma'am."

"Well all right, but just for a few minutes and I'll have to bring them up here."

"Thank you." She stepped back meekly to let her by.

A few minutes later, Edith came back up with the box of photos and beckoned for Aileen. She propped them on a sloping glass-topped table displaying a fringed flag from 1861. The standing table, similar to a drafting table, worked perfect for displaying the pictures. Edith pulled the first couple of photos out and positioned them carefully across the angled glass.

The first two were snapshots of oil paintings done before 1900. One was the same painting Aileen had seen on the mansion wall of the Senator and Mrs. Gage, and the other was a not-so-flattering portrait of a young Louisa in a pale yellow dress with puffed sleeves.

"You see this one here," Edith said, pointing to the portrait. "Back then, the portraits were frequently done by just filling in the face. The artist sometimes completed a generic body and background before the actual sitting in order to save time."

That would explain the slightly odd angle of the face and the color distortions.

Edith laid out another one. "And this is a mourning picture embroidered on silk. Notice the weeping willow and tombstone."

Aileen examined the simple depiction of a willow tree and headstone. This was the kind of stuff Todd would be interested in. The snapshot of the picture looked as if it had been taken in the master bedroom. She'd been so preoccupied with the larger mourning portrait that she hadn't even noticed it when she was there.

The next picture Edith removed from the box was a wedding photo. Aileen instantly recognized the woman she had seen in her dreams—*Ms. 'Lizbeth*. Aileen reached out and carefully flipped the picture over. Someone had written on the back, *Mary Elizabeth and David Gage—1904*. Emma and Charlie's parents.

She laid that one down and picked up another one. Edith didn't seem to mind. She was preoccupied with a couple that had just come in that was looking at the pottery display. "Let me go see if they need any help. I'll be right back."

Aileen continued placing pictures across the glass, including one of Charlie. It was so similar to the one she had seen on the wall at Rose Wood that had so captivated her that she knew it had to have been taken at the same time. He was still smiling impishly, but his head was turned a little to the side and his hair was sticking up even more in the back. Smiling, she put it down and picked up another one. This one was also Charlie, and it wiped the smile from her face. He was older in the photo and any trace of childish innocence had disappeared, leaving behind the shattered, sullen boy that stared back at her from the photo. She turned it over. *1927 – 14 years old.* Eight years after Emma's disappearance. She grimaced in pity for him. With his beloved sister gone, and his mother undoubtedly destroyed, he had probably been left at the mercy of his horrid older brothers.

The next picture was larger, more professional, and she tried not to damage the already frayed edges as she lifted it out.

Her breath caught.

It was Emma, as she had never seen her. *She was lovely.* The picture had to have been taken right before she died, and you could see the beautiful woman she would have become. Her thick wavy hair was caught up in some kind of up-do and curling tendrils escaped alongside her face. She was smiling softly and a small cleft dimpled her cheek. The picture was from the waist up. She was wearing a white lace high-necked dress that contrasted prettily with her rich olive skin and dark hair. But what got Aileen the most was that she was so *real*. So there. So alive. The light from the flash when the picture was taken shone on the planes of her face and was clearly reflected in her eyes. Aileen felt like she was going to cry for the girl who had once truly existed, if only for a while.

She had seen enough. She pulled the rest of the remaining photos out of the box and quickly went through them, barely even looking. She went to put them all back when one of them slipped out and fell to the floor just as Edith walked back over. Aileen hissed between her teeth and stooped to pick it up. Thankfully it didn't seem to be damaged. She held it by the corner and gave it a little shake and blew on it before handing it to Edith to put in the box with the others. To her credit, Edith said nothing, but she doubted she would be whipping out pictures for anyone else anytime soon.

"Wait," Aileen said as her brain finally registered what her eyes had looked at but had not truly seen. She leaned over and took another look at the picture. She had mistaken it for just another obscure relative at first glance but now she could see the familiarity. The photo she was looking at of an almost unrecognizable Charlie in adulthood merged in her mind with the picture of Mr. Gage at the ribbon cutting ceremony, and she knew they were one and the same. She tried to do some fast calculations in her mind. But that would make him . . . ninety-seven! She flipped the picture over and written on the back clear as day was *Timothy Charles Gage*. She had been so stupid. She had not even entertained the idea that the boy might still be *alive*. She had not thought it was possible. Now that she was looking for it, she could see it clearly. He was already developing the hard flinty stare and slight sneer she had seen in the newspaper photo from 1980. For God's sake, Jane had mentioned it during the tour of the house. She had not just said the last living descendant, she had said the last living descendant *to have actually lived in the house.*

"Who is this?" she asked Edith to be sure.

Edith reached for the photo. "Why, that's Mr. Gage. Not so old here," she said, turning the picture over. "It doesn't say what age, but he looks like he might be in his late thirties."

"And he's still alive."

"Oh yes. He even comes in here every so often. Or he used to before he got to be so old. He must be—"

"Ninety-seven."

"Yes, that sounds about right."

Her mind was whirling with so much at once that she almost forgot to thank Edith before she went to put the box away.

She left the museum in a daze.

Her cell phone rang just as she was getting in her car. She looked at the caller-Id. It was Todd. Her mind still churning, she picked up. "Hey."

"Hey! Where are you?"

"I just left the museum. You wouldn't believe what I found out. I don't know how I could have missed it. It was right there in front of my face. I don't know, with the lightning strike and all, I guess I just wasn't really looking for it at first. I was trying hard *not* to look, you know." She realized she was babbling and forced herself to stop.

"What? What did you find out?"

"The old man, old man Gage, who called the ambulance for me. He's the little boy! He's still alive!"

"What? But that would make him like..."

"Ninety-seven!"

"Wow! That's unbelievable. That's great, Aileen."

Todd sounded just as excited about it as she was. He knew what this meant. After all this time, she still had a witness to what had happened all those years ago, and maybe now she could get some answers.

"I have to go see him."

"When? Where? Where does he live?"

"I don't know. I'll have to find out." A thought occurred to her. "I could ask Carter at Rose Wood. He seems to be pretty much the head honcho down there. I met him when I was there before. You want to go with me? We could go tomorrow."

"Um, well, I would but I planned on going down to Redhill like you recommended and getting some pictures of the gravestones."

She considered going with him instead, but couldn't stand the thought of putting her visit off.

"You go ahead," he said. "And tomorrow night we'll have dinner and you can tell me all about it. I'll come over and we can do some work together. How about that?"

"Okay. Sounds good."

Chapter 22

Aileen was so excited about the little boy still being alive and her impending visit that she could barely sleep that night. She tossed and turned until some time in the early morning before finally falling asleep. She managed a few hours, and then she was up getting her shower.

She dressed to see Carter with extra care. A little harmless flirting might help the situation. After all, he was a man. And he might not be so willing to hand out ol' Mr. Gage's personal address. She had to find a way to get him to talk, and it was going to be bad enough that she might have to tell him more than the lame excuse she had planned, which was that she wanted to thank the man in person for calling the ambulance for her.

She put on a pair of tight jeans she hadn't been able to wear for some time and a push-up bra under a low-cut shirt. Not wanting to wear heels, she settled for her new suede boots. She styled her hair with the blow dryer then did her makeup, taking special pains with it. A light spritz of perfume and she was ready to go.

She was out of the apartment and on her way by ten thirty.

She made good time and turned into the plantation gates at a quarter past noon. From what she had gathered from the contact information on the website, Carter served not only as the constable but also as the park manager. He would know how to find Charlie.

There was no sign of him when she parked and got out of her car. She made her way around to the front of the house.

The front door was locked, but she could hear the murmur of voices inside. She checked her watch. Jane, if she still worked there, would be finishing up a tour.

She walked around to the back to wait.

The door to the little wooden building she had seen Carter come out of before stood open, and she stepped inside. She blinked her eyes to adjust them from the glare outside. She had been right about it being the kitchen.

Cast-iron pots and pans and stacks of wood sat on the hearth of a huge deep fireplace that took up one entire wall. A scarred wooden table was pushed against the window and served as a counter top and held a rusty meat grinder along with bowls, a rolling pin, and other cooking utensils. Baskets filled with various produce were stacked under the table, but upon closer inspection, she saw that all the fruits and vegetables were clever fakes, except for a pile of gourds in the corner.

A closed door led to what was probably Carter's office. Killing time until the tour was over and she could find out where he was, she signed the guest book sitting on top of a wooden stand by the door, and then leafed through a stack of brochures.

After a while she heard voices again, and Jane and a small group of people came in.

"Oh hi," said Jane, seeing Aileen.

"Hi. I was just looking for Carter?"

"Oh, okay. Hang on a minute." Pulling out a ring of keys, Jane unlocked the door to the office and went inside. She came back out a few seconds later with a stack of papers. After giving everyone what looked like a handout on the different flags of South Carolina, the tour was over and everyone left except for Aileen and Jane.

"You're looking for Carter?"

"Yeah, is he around?" She hoped she wasn't going to have to explain herself.

Thankfully, Jane asked no questions. "Carter's off today. But you could try him at his house. He lives on the property. He's basically our security when no one's here at night."

I bet he is, she thought, remembering the large gun he wore on his side.

"Here, I'll show you." Walking outside, Jane pointed down to where the drive continued on around and branched off to the right leading away from the house.

Aileen thanked her, got in her car, and drove slowly down the gravel drive.

Carter lived in a small frame house at the end near the main road. A small truck with *South Carolina*

Parks printed on the side was parked out front, but no one came to the door when she knocked.

She shaded her eyes and looked back up the drive. She could just see the edge of one pale yellow chimney sticking up above the trees. What must it be like for Carter, living on the property beside the big house? A place only allowed brief visits by others. She imagined it must be exhilarating and rewarding to be able to walk through the rooms, sit on the front porch, or explore the grounds whenever he wanted. Did he imagine a grander, more expansive style of living than the restricted and confined homes and apartments now inhabited by most of society?

Her cell phone rang, sounding abnormally loud in the stillness. She jerked it out of her pocket and quickly silenced it. It was Todd, and she let it go over to voice mail.

She walked back towards her car. She hated to just leave after driving all the way down. She would just have to find something to do and hope he came back soon. She had just decided to head into town for some lunch when she heard the sound of a motorcycle coming down the road. The loud roar of the bike downshifted and became a throaty purr as it turned in. The wheels of the Harley bit into the gravel. She stepped back out of the way. It was Carter, and he wasn't wearing a helmet. He kicked his legs out and came to a stop, dropping his feet to the ground. He still hadn't gotten a haircut. His hair hung well over his collar now.

He climbed off the bike. "Hey."

"Hey," she said, walking over and checking him out at the same time. This time he was wearing civilian clothes—jeans and a black leather jacket—instead of his uniform. He really wasn't bad-looking, she thought. Tall, not as good-looking as Todd, but ruggedly appealing nonetheless. She sucked in her stomach and stuck her shoulders back.

She wasn't sure if he recognized her, he probably saw so many people. "I'm Aileen, we met a while back when I came for a tour?"

"Sure, I remember you. What can I do for you?"

"Um," was all she managed before she lost her nerve. She wasn't so good at this. Then she saw his eyes shift down, traveling the length of her body. *Oh, Okay.* She smiled at him, amused, when his eyes finally came back up again. He smiled back, and then the moment passed. But they had definitely had a moment.

"I was hoping to talk with you for a while. I spoke to Jane, and she said you were off today."

"Yeah, actually I just came back for my wallet. I thought I'd go for ride while the weather's good." He walked over to the truck, reached in, and retrieved the wallet.

She followed him over. "I just need a few minutes of your time. I won't keep you."

He turned back to her. "If you need information on the house, I can send it to you if you want. My office number and e-mail are on the website."

"No, I'm really only looking for an address. For Mr. Gage? I'm sure you don't normally give out private information, but—"

Carter's brow wrinkled. "Old man Gage? Why would you want his address?"

"It's kind of a long story." She paused. "I didn't say anything about it when I was here before, but a couple of months ago he helped me and I never got a chance to thank him. I was hoping you could tell me where he lives."

"You met him?"

"Yeah, well, not exactly. Like I said, it's a long story."

"Okay, well how about this. You go for a ride with me, and then I'll hear your story."

What! Was he *serious*? Oh, he *was*. "Come on," he said, walking back to his bike and beckoning.

"I don't think so."

"Come on, we'll just go for a quick ride. I even have a sissy bar if you need it." He strode over and grabbed the bar from beside the house, quickly attached it, and patted the seat. "Let's go."

"Fine," she said, laughing nervously. She retrieved her sunglasses from the car and reluctantly let him coax her onto the bike. It wasn't the first time she had ridden. She had gone through a very brief Harley craze when she was a teenager, but that had been a long time ago. She hoped this was going to be worth it.

He started the bike and it roared to life. He backed them up and then pulled forward to the edge of the driveway. "You can grab hold of my waist if you need to!" he shouted back at her. He accelerated onto the road, and she shifted forward and wrapped her arms around him. She held on tight as took off. Encouraged, he throttled down even harder, and then they were flying. They roared down a long straight away and then turned onto another smaller back road, and he let off after that. After her initial fear and discomfort passed, she began to enjoy the ride. She leaned back. It was a spectacularly beautiful day for the time of the year. The sun was shining and it felt almost like spring. She had been afraid that she would get cold, but the jacket she had worn protected her just enough. They wound down around the country roads, enjoying the sun and the scenery. They barely passed any houses and except for the little bit of asphalt left on the old road, and the fact that they were on a Harley instead of a horse, they could have been a hundred years in the past. She never wanted it to stop. All thoughts of visiting Charlie left her head and she just enjoyed the day.

Carter drove them in a long, roundabout loop back into town. They rumbled along through Andersonville, occasionally stopping for a red light. It was a slow time, after lunch and before dinner, and the streets were almost deserted. They passed another Harley coming the other way and she thought they weren't going to acknowledge each other, then they each lifted a finger in silent greeting. Carter roared by and swung wide into a parking lot. He rolled into a parking space and killed the motor.

They were at some kind of Mexican restaurant.

"I thought we'd grab a bite. I haven't eaten, have you?"

"No." Now that he mentioned it, she was starving.

She tried to finger-comb her hair on the way in. Now she knew why woman who rode motorcycles always wore their hair up. She had forgotten about that. Thankfully the place was almost empty. Only one other couple sat in a booth along the back.

A pretty Latino woman took their order. Carter ordered a burrito, and she ordered the same.

"You can have a drink if you want," he said.

"Okay." She turned to the waitress. "I'll take a margarita."

"And I'll have a Coke."

"Just a Coke?"

"Yeah, I'm on duty later. But you go ahead."

Carter didn't seem in a hurry to bring up why she was there, so she didn't mention it. She asked him how he ended up at Rose Wood and found out he had quite an extensive background. Not only did he have a Bachelor's Degree in History, he had a Master's in Historical Administration, too. He had started out as an intern at a museum and had worked his way up from preservation specialist to park interpreter to manager.

Their food and drinks came at the same time, and they dug in. She took a long drink of her margarita. It was perfect, icy-cold and salty. The burritos were good too, served with a bed of shredded lettuce, tomatoes, sour cream, and guacamole, and covered in cheese and a thick, spicy sauce.

They ate for a while, and then she continued their earlier conversation. "So how did you end up in South

Carolina?" She could tell by his accent, or lack of accent, that he wasn't from there.

"Oh, I've worked all over the place. I saw the job, put in for it, and got it."

She finished her drink while he told her about all his previous jobs. He had worked in archives in Alaska, on exhibits in Wyoming, in collections in Pennsylvania, as a preservation specialist in Michigan, and then as an intern at Redhill plantation.

"Wait," she said, interrupting him. "You worked at Redhill?"

"Yeah, I was an interpretive ranger."

"I've been there." She might as well stop avoiding the issue. "For work. I did a story on it. I write a paranormal section for *Southern Aurora* magazine out of Atlanta. That's where I live."

"Oh?" he said, taking a drink of his soda.

Well that didn't seem to faze him.

"That's how I encountered Mr. Gage. I was out on another assignment a couple of months ago, and I got caught out in a storm and ended up at Rose Wood. I know this is going to be hard to believe, but I was struck by lightning."

"That was you?" he exclaimed.

"Yes. And I wanted to thank Mr. Gage. He was the one who called the ambulance, you see."

"Well I'm glad you're okay. How bad were you hurt?"

Before she had to answer, the waitress came over and set down the bill and picked up their dirty plates. After she was gone, he crossed his arms and rested his elbows on the table. "You want to tell me the real reason you want to talk to him?"

Oh, he was too smart by far.

She just shook her head. Some other people had just come in and sat down not far from them, and there was no way she was going into it right then.

Carter sighed. "Okay. You ready?"

He gave her another long extended drive on the way back, and it felt like they had been riding forever when they pulled up in his yard. She got her bag out of her car and followed him inside.

She used his bathroom and tried unsuccessfully to comb the snarls out of her hair. She did the best she could, then touched up her smeared makeup. She looked at her watch. It was getting late and she had a long drive home. She would have to wait until tomorrow to go see Charlie.

She found Carter waiting for her in the kitchen, propped against the counter with his arms folded.

"Do you have any aspirin?" She was starting to get a headache from drinking one drink and then stopping. She pulled out a chair from his kitchen table and sat down.

Silently he got the aspirin and poured her a glass of water. He placed them in front of her then sat down across from her.

"Out with it."

"Fine." She popped two aspirin in her mouth and washed them down with half the water. "I was a paranormal investigator who didn't believe in ghosts. Then I was struck by lightning. I starting seeing ghosts, and

Mr. Gage's sister started haunting me. And now I do believe in ghosts. End of story. Except I don't know what the hell she wants."

Carter stared at her through narrowed eyes from across the table.

"You don't have to believe me."

"Who says I don't believe you?"

"You don't think I'm crazy?"

"No, I don't," he said, then added under his breath, "Not yet anyway."

"What was that?"

He slouched back in his chair. "Let's just say you're not the first to have strange experiences around here."

"What are you talking about?"

"You first," he said, smiling.

Aileen gave a little laugh and told him everything again, but slower this time and with all the details.

He sighed long and hard when she finished, considering everything she had told him.

"Now you," she said, giving him her best *I mean business* look. "Out with it."

"Let's just say I know what this place can do to you. Some things are just best left alone. Maybe it isn't for us to know." He straightened back up. "I can give you Mr. Gage's address, but I don't know how far you really want to take this. You may never figure out what happened."

"But Carter, this isn't like that." She thought again about Todd's Ginny and what had happened to her. But this was different. "I just want to know what really happened to her. I just want closure like she does.

I mean, fourteen-year-old girls don't just disappear into thin air. Something happened to her. Her brother deserves to know what happened to her."

"Are you sure you can handle this?"

"Yes, because I didn't believe for so long, don't you see? I'm looking at this from the most rational point of view. I'm not going to be drawn in and go crazy or something if that's what you're worried about." At least she hoped not. "I've been training for this, for *years*."

He said nothing for several long moments, looking off to the side.

"Three people before me have died in this house, you know," he said conversationally.

Aileen gasped.

He turned to face her. "The park manager before me committed suicide in this house, and then Julie one of the tour guides who lived here was murdered by her husband before he killed himself. I was living somewhere else at the time, but I was on duty that night and I heard the shots."

A shiver ran down her back. They had died right there in the house where she was sitting. She looked around fearfully. He had said the park manager before him. Was something affecting Carter too? She was suddenly a little afraid for him living there all alone. His life didn't seem so idyllic now. Maybe he was afraid *he* would go crazy.

"That's not going to happen to me," she said. "You of all people know how many people have died on this property over the years. Who knows how many spirits are floating around out here. Who knows what kind of presence the people in this house may have encountered. The only connection I have is with Emma. She's not trying to hurt me."

"Let's hope not."

Yeah, let's hope not, she said to herself.

PART THREE

Love Is But A Dream

Through the clear mirror of our eyes,
Through the soft sigh of kiss to kiss,
Desolate winds assail with cries
The shadowy garden where love is.
~ James Joyce

Chapter 23

The two aspirin she had taken were wearing off by the time she made it home. All the driving, not to mention the margarita at lunch, had left her tired and headachy. She still hadn't called Todd back and was just debating on canceling with him when she spotted his car parked in front of her building.

She found him sitting on the steps leading up to her apartment. "Hey! Have you been waiting long?"

He followed her silently in. She snuck a look at her watch. It was nearly eight thirty—a little late for dinner maybe, but they hadn't said an exact time, had they? She went into the bedroom and threw her bag down on the bed.

Coming back out, she caught sight of Todd's face and faltered. He was still standing by the door, and she could tell by the set expression on his face that he was upset—really upset. His eyes raked her from head to toe, taking in everything.

"Where have you been?" he asked, his soft voice belying the angry look on his face.

"I went to Rose Wood to get Mr. Gage's address," she said, matching his tone with a "*duh*" one of her own.

"And did you get what you wanted?" His black eyes seemed to drill a hole in her.

She waited a beat, resenting the way he had worded it. "I got the address if that's what you're asking," she answered evenly.

"You haven't been to see the old man yet?"

"Noo, not yet. I thought I'd go tomorrow."

"So you've been with Carter this whole time?" He looked her up and down again, and she resisted the urge to adjust her shirt over her cleavage.

"Look, I'm sorry. I should have called."

"And what the hell happened to your hair?"

She reached up and started to smooth down her hair then dropped her hand. This was getting ridiculous.

"We took a ride on his motorcycle."

"You WHAT?"

"Yeah," she said. Where *exactly* was he going with this? "We rode into town and had a bite to eat." *What of it?* hung unsaid in the air between them.

"WE were supposed to get something to eat."

"I know," she said, relenting somewhat. She stepped closer to him. "Look, I'm sorry I didn't call."

He leaned over and gave a sniff. "Have you been *drinking?*"

She inhaled sharply. "I had one drink, hours ago," she said, unable to keep the defensiveness out of her voice.

"Right. One drink. Hours ago. And just what did you do with all the other hours, *Aileen?*" he asked, looking at her in open disgust.

Her eyes went wide. *Oh my God,* he did *not.* This was too much.

"*Get out.*"

"What?"

"*Get out of my apartment!*"

His face twisted into an ugly sneer. "I'm sorry. Pardon me for being a little upset that my girlfriend spent all day with another man."

"NOW." She stared him down, inches from his face. How *dare* he?

He stared back at her in silent condemnation for another moment, and then walked out, slamming the door behind him.

She barely slept at all that night, thanks to Todd. She got up at eight, exhausted and in a bad mood. She didn't know what to think about him now. Part of what she liked about him was his intensity, and when he had called her "my girlfriend" a part of her had rejoiced. It figured. She would have liked to have been very happy about that. But she really didn't know him all that well, when it came right down to it. She pictured them as a couple and suppressed a pang of hurt. She had thought they were on their way to something special and it hurt that he had not realized that and given her the benefit of doubt. She wanted him to put her on a pedestal, not treat her like a bimbo.

She had gotten used to having him around, to having someone to talk to, someone to encourage her. And she liked the perspective he gave to her work. To be honest with herself, she had begun to rely on him.

She spooned coffee into a filter, filled the carafe with water, poured it in, and slammed it back into place.

Despite what he thought, she was *not* promiscuous. She didn't know what kind of women he was used to seeing, but she wasn't like that and she wouldn't stand to be insulted that way. It was better it ended now before she grew even more attached.

She grabbed her bag and started stuffing things into it. She would go ahead with her visit to Charlie, and to hell with it. She didn't need him.

No, she didn't need him, but she had wanted him. It had been more than physical. She had started to feel connected to him in a way that she never had with anyone else. She thought about their lovemaking and pushed it away, only for it to be replaced by how good his arms had felt around her that first night when they had fallen asleep together on the sofa. She was tired of being alone. A tear slid down her cheek, and she wiped it angrily away.

While on one level she understood why he had gotten jealous, and was more than a little gratified by it, what she hadn't liked had been the embarrassment of it. She had felt a little like an errant teenager being drilled by her father, and a little like ... well, like a bimbo!

But that's how you were acting, her conscience whispered to her. Now she was second-guessing herself! It was true that she had dressed up for Carter, and that she had taken it to a more personal level by going on the ride and out to lunch with him even though she was seeing Todd. And it was true that she had more or less blown off dinner with Todd, but that didn't mean . . . Oh hell, she was in the wrong. She was totally and absolutely in the wrong. She dropped down on the couch and put her head in her hands. She had deliberately flirted with Carter to get what she wanted. No wonder Todd had thought the worst. She had ignored his calls and then shown up late with her hair all mussed up, smelling like liquor.

She thought about calling him and trying to make up, but decided against it. He might have had reason to be jealous, but she still didn't like the way he had handled it. He had not really given her a chance to explain. It wasn't like she had been dishonest or anything. If he didn't realize that she had morals and standards, then that was his fault for not getting to know her better. If he had known her at all, he wouldn't have assumed the worst. Just like something her grandmother had once said to her: Always have faith in the ones you love.

Chapter 24

Todd called once before she left then again on her way to where Mr. Gage lived. She didn't pick up. She wasn't in the mood to deal with him yet. She was anxious to talk to Mr. Gage, whom she still thought of as Emma's little brother, Charlie. That was her main priority.

She'd popped the address she had gotten from Carter into the GPS, and she found the house easily enough. From what little she had inadvertently picked up about architecture researching Rose Wood, it looked as if it had been built around the 1940s. It was a pretty house, painted white with red shutters and trim.

She drove up the driveway and parked. A black iron fence surrounded the house with a gate that opened onto a small path leading up to the front porch. She noticed there were no rose bushes. She grabbed her purse and marched determinedly through the open gate and up the path. Feeling like Emma was there with her giving her courage, she climbed the steps and rapped on the door.

She knocked again, banging hard this time. She heard a faint muffled sound from within. He was home, and she was not going away. She hammered again and called out "Mr. Gage!"

Just when she started to knock again, the door opened and the bent form of Mr. Gage—Charlie—appeared in the doorway. "If you're selling something, I'm not buying," he said in a querulous voice.

"No, I'm not selling anything, Mr. Gage. I just wanted to talk with you for a few minutes if I could?"

He surveyed her skeptically. Aileen noticed in amusement that his hair still stuck out on the back of his head in the same spot.

"What are you smiling about?" he suddenly barked at her in a surprisingly loud voice. "And what do you want?"

He didn't scare her a bit, but for his benefit, she sobered her expression.

"I hope you don't mind, but I got your address from Carter, the park manager. I don't know if you remember me or not, but you called the ambulance for me over at Rose Wood?"

At her mention of Rose Wood he gave an almost imperceptible flinch. The sweet little boy with the long lost grin she had seen in the picture flashed through her mind. She worked to keep her face neutral to hide the pity she was feeling. She could only imagine what kind of pain he associated with his childhood home, a place and time she couldn't even imagine growing up in.

"The night of the storm," he said.

"Yes." She blinked at him, unsure how she wanted to continue. Wanting to ease him into it, she began with, "I wanted to thank you for calling the ambulance for me. Thank you so much."

He nodded. "Glad to do it. Now you've said your piece. Good Day." Having summarily dismissed her, he turned away and began to close the door.

Without hesitation Aileen stuck her foot in the door and stopped it from closing. It bounced off her shoe and he reared back in surprise.

"I'm sorry, but we need to talk, Charlie Boy. It's about your sister," she said, keeping her foot firmly in place.

To say he was thrown was an understatement. His face immediately went blank with shock, the color seeping out of it right before her eyes.

"What did you call me?"

"That's what she called you, wasn't it? Charlie? Charlie Boy?" She felt like she was being too cruel, taunting him like she was, but she had to get through to him.

He stood swaying in front of her, his eyes on some faraway place. Then he turned and walked silently away, leaving the door ajar.

She followed him inside. She found him at the back of the house in a smallish room he had made into a sort of library. As well as several bookcases filled with books of all kinds, there was quite a collection of pictures arranged on the shelves and across the mantle of the fireplace. The bare hardwood floor was made cozy by the thick rug in front of the hearth and the chair that had been placed in front of it, where Charlie now sat, staring at the low-burning fire with watery eyes.

She eased into the room. The boy, now an old man, looked up at her approach. "There's a chair in the kitchen."

She eased back out. She found the dining room, but the chairs were too heavy and cumbersome. She located the kitchen and had just grabbed a smaller chair when she heard a car door outside. Setting it back down, she made her way to the front of the house and peeked out the window. She could see a truck parked in the driveway behind her car, but there was no sign of the driver.

She went back to the kitchen, and a moment later, there was a knock at the back door. She glanced towards the library but didn't see bothering him with it. Hoping it wasn't some family member who would question her business there, she opened the door.

"Hi, how ya doing? Here you go," said the man standing there. He handed her a small box.

She took it automatically. He was striding back to his truck before she had a chance to say anything. She looked down at the box. She was actually holding a divided aluminum plate with a flat paper lid. Charlie got Meals on Wheels. Throwing up her hand at the departing man, she closed the door.

She set the plate down on the counter. Was that all he had to eat? Pulling open the refrigerator, she found several other unopened containers just like it. She pried the lid off of one and saw it contained one single size can of beans and franks, a corn muffin, a small container of fruit cocktail, and a carton of milk. Not very much and not very appetizing. Another one looked only slightly better with some kind of mystery meat patty covered in gravy, cabbage, a biscuit, and a small butterscotch pudding.

Charlie's faint voice called out, "Miss!"

She hastily grabbed the chair and carried it back to the library and set it down beside Charlie with a thump.

"No one's called me that in years. What do you know about my sister?" he bit out with no preamble.

He regarded her shrewdly. However feeble his body might be, his mind was still sharp. She had gotten in the door, but he would suffer no fools gladly. She wondered if he had ever turned that formidable demeanor on his brothers.

"I know you loved her. And that she loved you."

"What do you know? How could you know anything?" he snapped.

"Charlie—"

"Stop calling me that."

"Charlie, I'm here because Emma sent me."

He jerked as if slapped. "What kind of nonsense is this?"

"After I was struck by lightning at your house, Emma started contacting me."

"My sister is *dead. She's not contacting anyone!*" Charlie struggled out of his chair. He was shaking all over, and she could see from the way his clothes hung on him that he was too thin. He loomed over her, his face a seething mixture of anger and outrage.

She remained seated with difficulty. She knew his reaction stemmed from what he perceived as her intention to somehow exploit his childhood tragedy but that underneath it was the wound of his loss of Emma. She made placating gestures with her hands. "Please, Charlie—Mr. Gage—hear me out. Please. I didn't mean to upset you. Just five minutes, okay? Please." He was still standing over her, but the strength seemed to have gone out of him. He dropped heavily into the chair, facing the fire. His breathing was so fast and shallow that she was beginning to wonder if she had made a grave mistake.

He leaned his head back and closed his eyes.

"Mr. Gage? Are you okay? Do you need some water?"

He nodded weakly. She jumped up and hurried into the kitchen.

As soon as she stepped into the room, she was assaulted by the thick odor of roses. The room positively reeked of it. The stench of it was so strong it smelled putrid. She gagged and covered her nose and mouth with her hand.

Trying to ignore the smell, she removed her hand and spoke to the room at large, "Don't worry, Emma, I got this."

She searched around until she found a glass and filled it with water. She took the drink to Charlie and then returned to the kitchen.

The smell had begun to fade, and by the time she had searched the cupboards and a freezer she found in an adjoining pantry, it had disappeared all together. She found a can of coffee and got that started first. She debated about whether or not to cook the slice of country ham she found in the freezer, but there was nothing else so she defrosted it in the ancient microwave in the corner. She took the last six eggs and cracked them in a bowl, added a little milk and some salt and pepper, and whisked them up. After frying the ham and dividing it into two plates, she started some toast in the equally ancient looking toaster, and scrambled the eggs.

She took the plates filled with food and set them on the table in the dining room, then went and got utensils, cups, a small container of milk, and the cracked sugar bowl.

Going back to where Charlie waited, she stood in the doorway until she got his attention. He appeared to have dozed off. He blinked and focused in on her.

"Come on," she said, motioning towards the dining room. "I made dinner."

She left him there, hoping he would follow, and went to look for jelly. She found a slightly circumspect jar of homemade preserves on the back shelf of the pantry and brought it and the coffee pot to the table, where Charlie was easing himself into a chair. For such an incredibly old man, he seemed to get around pretty good.

She filled both cups with coffee and sat down. "I know it's not really dinner, it's really breakfast for dinner, but that's all there was."

"Now listen," he said, again in a surprisingly strong, rather loud voice, "if I'm going to break bread with you, I would at least like to know who the hell you are."

"Oh, I am so sorry. I haven't properly introduced myself, have I?" She looked down at them both sitting there having a meal together and laughed ruefully at the absurdness of it.

She held out her hand. "I'm Aileen Whitney."

He shook her hand, his own still firm despite his age. "I guess you know who I am."

"I'm sorry, Mr. Gage. Let me explain why I'm here."

"You can call me Charlie."

"Huh? Oh, okay . . . Charlie." That disconcerted her for a moment and she busied herself fixing her coffee.

"I'm not supposed to have this, you know," he said, cutting a healthy slice of his ham.

"Oh, well, you only live once," she blurted and then could have kicked herself.

"That's right. You might have to worry about it," He pointed his fork at her, "but at my age, I might as well eat any ol' thing I want. At least that's what I keep telling my doctor."

"What about this jam?" She held up the jar. "Is it still good?"

He peered at it. "Should be. I got it from Sadie last summer, I believe."

"Sadie?" she asked, straining and popping the lid open.

"My old mammy's girl. She and her granddaughter Kendra come by to check on me once in a while."

Charlie finished off his eggs while she spread what tuned out to be excellent peach preserves on their toast.

"Charlie, that night I was struck by lightning I did see Emma." She watched his face, but other than making a "Hmph" noise, he didn't seem in danger of getting upset again. "I've been having dreams. And visions. About you and Emma and what happened to her."

Charlie had stopped eating and was looking at her intently. "Nobody knows what happened to Emma."

"Do you know what happened to her?" She met his piercing gaze.

He looked away and started fiddling with his cup.

"What is it?" she asked.

He looked at her then looked away again.

"You have to tell me, Charlie. Emma is contacting me for a reason. I think she's trying to tell me what happened to her. Why is that, Charlie? What do you have to do with it?"

He closed his eyes for a moment.

"TELL ME."

"It was my fault," he finally said in a low voice.

"*How* was it your fault?" She reached over and grasped his hand, half-expecting him to pull away, but he merely squeezed back. She let go, and he sat back and wiped his hand over his face wearily.

"I ran her off. I was being your classic pesky little brother and I ran her off."

"What do you mean?"

"The weather was bad that day. We had just had an earthquake, did you know that?"

She nodded.

"I still remember how it felt. I was sitting on the floor listening to the radio we had just gotten when I felt the floor move. Like being on an elevator." He shook his head at the memory. "The aftershocks weren't too bad, but us kids were supposed to stay in that day because of the flooding and the rockslides and all."

"And then what happened?"

"Oh, I kept bugging her, knocking on her door and wanting her to play with me until finally she went outside to get away from me for a while, I guess."

She waited on him to finish. "And?" she finally prompted him.

"And I never saw her again."

He looked at her with such naked grief and remorse that she had to look away. She gazed down at her half-empty plate. "I'm sorry."

"You say you've seen things in your so-called visions. What did you see?"

"Not much. I saw a black girl picking berries."

"Leona, Sadie's older sister. She went missing at the same time."

"Only they found her." He nodded. "I saw you when you were little." He seemed surprised at that. "That's when I heard Emma call you Charlie Boy. You were going out to catch lightning bugs."

He looked off to the side, remembering. Smiling slightly, he said, "We used to make a lantern with them," at the same time she said, "You used to make a lantern with them."

They both laughed. And it felt good, if bittersweet.

After they finished eating, Charlie settled himself back by the fire, and she went to clean up the kitchen.

When she rejoined him, she found him standing in front of the pictures lined up on the mantle.

"I like that one," she said, pointing at another lovely portrait of Emma that must have been taken on the same day as the one she had found at the museum.

"Yes," Charlie said, picking up the picture. "That's how I remember her."

Most of the small framed photographs on the mantle were of Emma. Aileen walked around the room and looked at all the pictures scattered about on the tables and bookshelves. There were more of Emma and Charlie, several of Elizabeth and David, some taken with the children and some separately when they were older, and pictures of a heavy black woman wearing a uniform dress and two beautiful caramel-colored girls. Aileen recognized the oldest girl, Leona, from her dream. There were no pictures of his brothers.

"That's Sadie," Charlie said, pointing to the younger girl. "She's the only one left. From the old house."

"What about your brothers?"

He shook his head. "They're both gone now. Not that we ever saw each other much."

"You weren't close after you grew up?"

"No," he said, a resigned look on his face. "We didn't get along."

"And how did they react to Emma's disappearance and Leona's death? Did anyone question them to see if they knew anything?"

He didn't answer, but she could see him thinking back. He gave his head a shake, and for just a second she saw a flicker of shame.

"They blamed you."

"Oh yes." He didn't have to say any more than that. She could imagine the rest. They had blamed him, and then he had spent the rest of his life doing the same thing.

"You know, whatever happened to her, it wasn't your fault."

"If I hadn't kept bothering her that morning she wouldn't have gone outside. Emma was always so nice to me, not like James and Joseph. But I guess everyone has their limits." He shuffled back towards his chair, still talking. "I just kept bugging her till she got tired of it and ran outside, and then ... and then she was gone," he said, throwing up his hands.

"I'm sorry," she said again, sadness welling up in her for the little boy who hadn't meant any harm.

Charlie sank down into his chair, and she turned back to the pictures.

Closely examining the ones of Elizabeth, Aileen noticed she was wearing a silver locket in many of the earlier photos. It was similar to the one she had been wearing the night of the storm but larger, more ornate with some kind of etched flower design. She picked up a later picture of Elizabeth after Emma's disappearance that looked like a snapshot that had been blown up. A long streak of white ran down the length of her dark hair.

"Your mother's hair turned white," she said, turning around and holding out the picture to him.

His hand trembled slightly as he took it from her. "That streak showed up nearly overnight. Just a few years later, her hair was completely white. It wasn't just her hair that changed. My sister's disappearance nearly destroyed her. She was never the same again."

Aileen rested her hand on his shoulder for a moment, then took the picture and placed it back with the others.

She visited with him a little longer, and they talked about Emma and other unrelated subjects.

Sadie and Kendra were coming the next day to check on him and do some shopping, so she felt reasonably secure in leaving him.

She promised to come and visit with him again one day to talk some more, and left for another long drive home.

Chapter 25

It was a relief getting back to Atlanta, but she still didn't want to go to her apartment. She felt drained and stressed out at the same time from her visit with Charlie and her confrontation with Todd the night before. She was still ignoring his calls and wouldn't put it past him to be waiting on her again.

She drove to Colleen's. Out in the parking lot she texted her, *U busy? Want sum company?* Colleen must have had her cell beside her, because she texted right back, *Sure come on.*

Colleen opened the door as soon as she knocked. "That was quick!"

"I need a drink. And I don't care what anyone thinks about it."

"Whoa, who's gonna care? Todd? What's going on, you two fighting?"

Aileen dropped her bag on the bar and started rummaging through the kitchen cabinets. "What do you have? Do we need to run to the store?"

"Here, sweetie, I got you." Colleen opened up the freezer and pulled out a large icy-cold bottle of coconut rum.

"Oooh that looks good."

"I thought so. I haven't tried it yet." Colleen grabbed a jug of pineapple juice out of the fridge and mixed them two tall drinks over ice, heavy on the rum.

Aileen took a long thirsty drink of hers, and Colleen did the same.

"Thanks, I really needed this." She killed off the rest of her drink, and Colleen made her another one.

"Now that we've got that taken care of, what's going on?"

"We had a fight. Last night."

"About what?"

Aileen told her all about it. About going to see Carter and going for a ride with him and having a margarita at lunch. About getting home late and what Todd had thought.

"Well, did he actually accuse you of sleeping with him?"

"Basically. I mean there I was. I wore my white shirt, the new one you said you liked?" Colleen nodded. She knew which one she was talking about. She had called it "sexy". "And I had on my tight jeans and my hair was all messed up from the ride. And I smelled like booze!"

"Yeah, guess I can see that," Colleen mused. She grinned at her. "What kind of shoes where you wearing?"

"Uh, my new boots."

"Pants tucked in or out?"

"In, dammit," Aileen said, laughing.

"Uh-huh. Well, did it work?"

"What? You're as bad as Todd! And *yes it did*, thank you. I got the old guy's address and I've already been to see him. All *without* sleeping with Carter, I might add."

"Well *I* know that. I never thought you did. And he shouldn't have, either."

"But still."

"Still," Colleen agreed. They both sat sipping in silence for a minute.

"You gonna talk to him?" Colleen asked.

"Yeah, I guess. You still having trouble with Bobby?"

"Yeah. With us it's always about him. I wish he was as jealous of me as Todd is of you."

"I don't know about that."

Colleen moved over by the window to have a smoke, and Aileen heard about her latest issues with Bobby.

After agreeing to give Colleen a call the next day to let her know how it went, she headed for her apartment.

Her nerves had settled down a bit from her visit with Colleen and now she found herself a little disappointed when Todd wasn't waiting for her. He had overreacted, but she could sort of see why.

She checked her cell phone. The last time he had called had been that morning when she was on her way to Charlie's and he hadn't left a message. Now he probably wouldn't ever call again. Trying to convince herself that she didn't care, she went into her apartment.

It was about an hour later, after a much-needed hot bath, when she heard it. It sounded like . . . someone skinning a cat, or Todd *serenading her?*

She ran out on the balcony. It was Todd all right, and he was down on one knee, singing his heart out in all of his tone-deaf glory.

Peering down in disbelief, she didn't recognize the song, but he was yowling something about *"... You CAME along, and STOLE my heart when you entered my life. OOOooooh I neeed you ..."*

People were raising windows and sliding doors open all around the complex. "What the hell?" she heard someone exclaim. Sheila, two apartments over, smiled down at Todd. She flicked a glance at Aileen, and she could just *feel* what she was thinking: *He can sing to me anytime.*

"Todd, stop it!" she shouted down.

He just kept right on screeching, *"Since theeen I've never looked backkk, it's almost like living a dreamm, ooooooh I got youuu ..."*

"Todd, STOP!" She left the balcony and ran through the apartment and down the stairs. She burst out onto the spot of grass where Todd still knelt and grabbed his arm, toppling him over and thankfully putting a stop to his caterwauling.

"Fine!" she said. "Just don't sing!"

Ignoring the burst of applause and Todd's enthusiastic bowing, she stomped back up to her apartment, leaving him to follow.

Not knowing whether to be mad or happy, she paced around the room. Todd came through the doorway and stopped. He dug a piece of paper out of his pocket, smoothed it out, and began to read:

"*HOW* DO I LOVE THEE." Aileen choked out a laugh. "LET me count the ways. I love thee to the *depth* and *breadth* and *height* my soul can reach—" She burst into full out laughter. "—when feeling out of sight for the ends of being and ideal Grace." He raised his voice, "I LOVE THEE TO THE LEVEL OF—", which set her off again, and she fell on the sofa. "Stop! No more!" she wheezed, giggling and wiping at her eyes. "Seriously."

He helped her off the couch and pulled her to him. "Hey," he said, tilting her chin up. "I'm sorry." He dropped his head and kissed her. Her mind and senses were whirling from his romantic display and the feel of him pressed up against her. Her heart, not to mention her body, was thrilled, even if her mind wasn't so sure.

She pulled back and held him at arm's length. "Nothing happened with Carter you know." She held his gaze.

He had the good grace to look contrite. "I know, Aileen. I know you're not like . . . some women."

She wondered whom he had been about to say, but let it go.

"You forgive me?" he asked, and crushed her to him. Her kissed her again, deeper this time, and began to move with her down the hall towards the bedroom.

Well, she guessed she did forgive him.

Afterwards she showered off and threw on some clothes while Todd ran down to the car for something.

He was back a few minutes later with two grocery bags. He started piling things out by the stove.

"What you got there?" she asked.

"I, my dear lady, am going to cook for you."

It was hard to believe she had been so miserable before compared to how happy she was right then. She opened the wine he had brought, and they sipped it while he cooked. After a bit, he turned on a radio station playing Andrea Bocelli's "Con Te Partiro" and grabbed her and swung her around the kitchen as he sang along, not even coming close to getting the words right. She couldn't remember when she had laughed so much and had such a good time.

The meal was superb: pasta and meatballs made with sausage, simmered in tomato sauce; and garlic bread he made himself with French bread, olive oil, and fresh garlic. He had even picked up Tiramisu for their dessert.

They were both stuffed by the time they finished eating, and they decided to wait a bit on dessert. Aileen cleared the table while he got his laptop.

She switched on her computer. She was tired, albeit pleasantly so, and didn't feel like working, but Todd seemed eager and she didn't want to disappoint him.

She went to get the picture she had gotten from Charlie before she left. She had promised to scan it and return it right away.

Todd was on the phone when she came back in the room. His back was to her, and she caught "I appreciate it. I think you'll be very happy with it. If it does as well as the last . . ." before he turned around, smiled at her, and moved off into the dining room. "Right

Of course. Whatever you can do." He stepped into the kitchen, still talking.

A few minutes later he came back out "grinning like a 'possum," as her mother liked to say. He picked her up and spun her around. "They like the book proposal!"

"Are you serious!"

"We're negotiating the contract right now."

"Oh, that's wonderful. I'm so happy for you." And she was, at least his career was going somewhere even if hers wasn't.

They talked a little bit about his book deal, and then he refused to discuss it anymore. She showed him the picture of Emma and Charlie, and he watched while she scanned and saved it in the folder with her other pictures and newspaper articles.

She had just started to tell him about her visit with Charlie when he stopped her. "Hold on." He pulled his cell phone out of his back pocket and put it in the bag he had brought his laptop in, fiddled around for a minute, then withdrew his hand. "Okay." He usually kept his phone turned down when he was with her and he must have forgotten to lower the volume.

She went to begin again, and her cell went off. She picked it up and looked at it—Colleen. She put it back down without taking it.

"I know why Emma won't rest now. She can't rest knowing Charlie blames himself."

"What did he have to do with it? What did he tell you?"

She told him everything that Charlie had told her—that there had been aftershocks, and Emma had left the house, and Charlie felt responsible. Todd listened attentively, asking relevant questions and adding his perspective.

"So you see, he thinks that Leona was killed when an aftershock caused her to fall. And he thinks something similar happened to Emma, only they never found her body. In his mind, if he hadn't caused her to go outside then she would have been safe."

"But you don't buy it?"

"No. In my dream, I clearly saw someone push Leona over the edge, someone she was scared of. And that someone chased Emma and ultimately killed her too. This was no accident and Timothy Charles Gage was in no way responsible." A familiar scent wafted by. She raised her head. "Do you smell that?"

"Smell what?"

"Roses." The smell was distinct for a second then grew fainter.

Todd looked around in alarm, his eyes wide.

She shook her head. "It's gone now. Emma's trying to tell me I'm right. I know it."

She got up and fixed them both bowls of the Tiramisu. Taking a bite, she sat down at the table where he had set up his laptop. "Show me some of the gravestone art you found. You still haven't shown me any of the pictures you took."

"At least tell me this. What are you going to do next?"

She had been thinking about that. "I'm going to go visit Sadie. Other than Charlie, she is the only person still alive who lived in the house. She may know something without even realizing it."

She scooted her chair closer. "Now let me see some of that headstone art you've been telling me about." She leaned over and looked at his laptop. It was still sitting on the password screen, and he quickly typed it in. He tapped on the correct folder and turned the laptop around for her to see.

He got up and went down the hall to the bathroom while she looked through the different examples of cemetery sculpture and funerary art he had collected. There were weeping angels; long-dead children; doves; lambs; all sorts of flowers, including roses; skulls; as well as the now familiar weeping willow. She didn't see any of the graves from Redhill. None of the surrounding area in any of the shots looked like the graveyard there. They must have been placed in a separate folder.

She had just started looking on the desktop when her phone rang. This time it was her landline, and it was Colleen again. Probably having trouble with Bobby. As much as she wanted to help her, it had been a long day and she was dog-tired. She was ready to fall into bed and do nothing but sleep.

Todd returned from the bathroom, and she tried unsuccessfully to stifle a yawn.

He looked at her in amusement. "I need to let you get some sleep."

He packed up despite her protests, told her to get some rest, and left.

Chapter 26

The next morning, Colleen had already called twice by the time she showered and made it into the living room.

The phone rang again for the third time, and she picked up. "Hey."

"It's about time! I've been calling you since last night. Why didn't you answer?"

"I'm sorry. Todd came over, and we got to talking and . . . one thing led to another . . . and he ended up staying late."

There was a pause on the other end of the line, and then Colleen said, "I was going to ask how it went with you and *Todd,* but I guess you made up if *one thing led to another.*"

Aileen gave a laugh, ignoring Colleen's attitude. "Oh yeah, we definitely made up. And you won't believe what he did when he showed up. He *cooked* for me, can you believe it?"

Colleen was quiet for so long this time that Aileen was beginning to think they had been cut off, then she asked, "Was this the first time you slept together?"

"Uh . . . no, but it felt like the first time!" she replied, attempting a joke, but it fell flat.

She waited on Colleen to say something like "You go girl!" but there was some distortions on the line, a hard click, and then they were disconnected.

She sat without moving.

Right before the line went dead, she could have sworn she heard Colleen hiss something in the background, something that sounded just like "*slut.*"

She was still mulling over the strange call when Colleen suddenly showed up about twenty minutes later. There had been a lot of interference on the line. Her voice had been distorted. That couldn't possibly have been what she said.

"Here." Colleen handed her a Styrofoam cup. "It's hot tea."

"Thank you, that's very thoughtful of you." Maybe she felt bad about her little burst of irritation earlier.

Colleen shook her head impatiently. "It's just a stupid cup of tea, Aileen."

Maybe not. She took the lid off her tea and blew on the hot liquid. She sipped on it while she waited her out.

"Mind if I smoke?"

She was surprised but tried not to show it. "Go ahead." She walked over and slid the balcony door open for ventilation. Colleen sat down on the couch and lit up.

Aileen drank some more of her tea, then couldn't stand it any longer. "So what happened earlier? On the phone?"

"Oh, I've been having trouble with my cell," Colleen said with a wave of her hand.

She was lying. Colleen sat on the end of the sofa, her face averted with her legs crossed, puffing and blowing the smoke towards the open door.

She finally turned to face her, and Aileen saw her eyes were red and puffy. "Bobby asked me to marry him."

WHAT? If that were the case, then why did she look like she had been crying?

"What's the matter, aren't you happy for me?"

Aileen tried to gather herself. "Of course. I'm just surprised, that's all."

"It's not all about you, you know, Aileen." Colleen was swinging her leg madly now, her mouth a narrow slit as she drew angrily on her cigarette.

She didn't know what to say to that. What was *with* her?

"I mean, you didn't like me dating him from the beginning did you?"

"That's not true! I had my misgivings, same as you. You said he always borrowed money off of you." She caught site of the small diamond on Colleen's finger. "He gave you a ring?"

"This morning." With a slight smirk, Colleen held up her hand. "So what's *Todd* given *you*?"

Aileen couldn't help it. She hadn't been there for Colleen, but she was tired of her attitude, which seemed out of proportion. "So how did he pay for it?" she asked.

Colleen gasped as if slapped. "You see, that's what I'm talking about! You're right! I had to buy my own damn ring, are you satisfied?"

Instantly Aileen felt bad. Whatever was going on with Colleen and Bobby, she wasn't helping by antagonizing her.

Colleen stood up. "I came over here because I wanted to make up, and I wanted to tell you about my engagement, but I guess I made a mistake."

Make up? Had they had a fight?

"Wait. Colleen!" But she was gone, already out the door and descending the stairs.

What the hell had just happened?

She tried to puzzle it out as she drove to the post office and mailed Charlie's picture back. Colleen had obviously had some kind of trouble with Bobby and had tried repeatedly to call her. Yet now she was suddenly engaged. It seemed like bad timing. Unless it had been a tactic on Bobby's part for whatever he had done, which explained Colleen's crying.

She had just gotten home when she felt the first inclination that something wasn't right.

A wave of heat flashed over her, and just like that, she was nauseous.

She was going to be sick.

She doubled over, moaning. *Oh no*. More than anything she hated to be sick to her stomach.

Bent over, she hurried to the bedroom and lay down on her side. She tried to lie as still as possible but the nausea only worsened and soon she was up, lurching to the bathroom.

She threw up violently. But instead of making her feel better, she felt worse.

Every time she moved her head she felt dizzy. She felt so miserable she sat on the floor and cried. She blinked and tried to focus her eyes, but her vision only partially cleared. *Oh God.* Her arms and legs were tingling and itching, and she felt like she was breaking out in hives. She was hideously sick to her stomach. She felt it coming again and was sick over and over until she was only heaving wretchedly.

Breathing raggedly, she stood up on shaky legs. She grabbed a washcloth and wiped her mouth. Her face was gray and drawn in the mirror, her lips bloodless. She splashed water on her face, brushed her teeth, and stumbled back to the bed.

She had to get up two more times over the next couple of hours, each time after she had broken down and drank some water, before the vomiting finally stopped. And that's when the diarrhea began. Her stomach gave a last cramp sometime later, and she fell into a miserable, exhausted sleep.

She still didn't feel right when she was finally able to get out of bed the next day. She hurt all over and she had a nasty headache. The horrible nausea was gone for the most part, but she kept getting dizzy, and she was so woozy she could barely sit up.

That afternoon she was able to keep down some saltines, so she heated up some of Todd's leftover pasta and ate it thinking it might make her feel better. She thought it worked for a while, but then she started to feel queasy. *Oh no not again.* She lay down on the couch and tried to will her stomach to keep the food down. Almost like before, the nausea came on fast, and she was running for the bathroom.

Later, spent, she brushed her teeth once again and cursed herself for eating the spaghetti. She should have made some broth. And come to think of it, maybe that was what had made her ill in the first place. Maybe she had food poisoning from bad meat or something. The thought of it sent her stomach rolling again and she groaned. Incredibly, her body seemed to want to vomit *again*.

Afterwards, her muscles sore from heaving, she knew she had to be dehydrated. When she stood up and almost fell down, she realized it was time for help. Despite their problems, it was Colleen she wanted. Not her mother, who would make a big deal out of it and take too long, and not Todd, whom she didn't want seeing her this way.

Weakly, she made her way over to the phone and dialed Colleen's number.

Colleen picked right up. "Colleen," she tried to say, but her voice was little more than a whisper. She tried again, "*Colleen*."

"What? What's wrong?" She had her attention now.

"I'm sick. I am so sick," she croaked. "I've been throwing up all night and all day."

"I'm on my way! I'll be right there!"

The phone crashed down and Aileen collapsed on the sofa. She lay there, panting and weak, and waited on Colleen.

By the time she showed up, Aileen was feeling a little silly for being so dramatic.

Colleen held a cup of something under her lips. "Here." Aileen screwed up her nose and tried to turn away. "Yes!" Colleen said. "You have to drink this. It has ginger in it to stop you from getting sick." Aileen managed a few sips until Colleen was satisfied.

Colleen felt her forehead. "You don't feel like you're running a fever. Drink some more. You need liquids. Do you think you should go to the hospital?"

Aileen shook her head, and took another dutiful drink. "No. I feel a little better now. I'm sorry I overreacted. I know I'm being a big baby."

"Don't be silly, you would do the same for me." Colleen busied herself straightening up the coffee table.

"Well, thank you. And I'm sorry I wasn't there for you when you needed me."

Colleen looked up at her and grinned. "It's okay. I'm getting married, remember?"

Aileen managed a weak laugh. "That's right."

"Now let's get you settled down," Colleen said, and just like before, she pulled back the covers and helped Aileen into bed.

Sometime later she realized Colleen was still there when she tiptoed into the bedroom to check on her. "What's your password? I need to check my e-mail," she whispered. Aileen gave it to her and then fell back asleep to the faint sound of her clicking and typing.

She woke up some time in the middle of the night. Her nausea had passed, and she was wide-awake. She sat up slowly, afraid any sudden movement would cause her to start heaving again, but her stomach finally seemed to have settled.

She padded into the living room and found Colleen gone, the computer off. There was a note on the kitchen counter by the phone: *Call me if you need anything!*

She poured a big glass of the ginger ale Colleen had brought over and carried it to the couch. She picked up the remote and flipped on the TV. *Whatever Happened to Baby Jane* was playing on TCM. Normally she loved movies from the thirties and forties, especially anything with Betty Davis or Joan Crawford, but this time it didn't hold her attention; she had seen it too many times. She scrolled through the channels and landed on *Silent Running*, a rare find, and lay there watching Bruce Dern fight for the last trees in a ruined future until she fell back asleep to the flicker of the television screen.

Chapter 27

Aileen jerked awake. The TV station was going off the air. The American flag she remembered from her childhood had come on and the national anthem was playing. It sounded just like she remembered it. Wait, did they still do that? Snow filled the screen and static noise emanated from the speakers.

She reached over and picked up the remote off the coffee table and punched in the number for TCM.

They were showing *The Grapes of Wrath* with Henry Fonda. She went to lay back when the movie suddenly switched to some forensics show. She hit the Prev button and switched it back to TCM.

She had no sooner gotten comfortable when it did it again. It kept landing on the same show that she now saw was *Forensics Hours*. Sighing in irritation, she decided to go to bed and try changing the batteries in the morning. She pointed the remote and pressed the Off button. The TV went dead.

The screen stayed blank for only a second before switching back on again. *"Thirty-year-old Tonya Hensley..."*

She considered pulling the plug, but she was starting to suspect it wouldn't do any good. She focused in on the show. *"They had only been married a year when she began first experiencing health problems. She was plagued by sudden bouts of nausea and diarrhea, unexplained hives and rashes, blurred vision, headaches, as well as other symptoms. At first, family and friends say her husband took good care of her, and other than her mysterious illness, they seemed like any other newly married couple. But as time went on, the couple began to have problems."*

Sudden bouts of nausea. Hives and rashes.

She turned the volume up. *"By September Tonya's symptoms started to worsen. She began to experience new and more alarming symptoms such as heart palpitations, disorientation, and a strange metallic taste in her mouth. One week later she decided to act. She had her neighbor drive her to the local ER, where she demanded a blood test for poisoning. The results came back positive for arsenic, and the police were called."*

She clicked the television off. It clicked back on.

"The results were undeniable. She had been deliberately poisoned either in her food or her drink by someone close to her."

She stood up and hit the Power button on the front of the TV. It turned off, then came back on.

She hit the Power button again and mercifully it stayed off.

She went into the kitchen and pulled open the refrigerator. Todd's pasta and Colleen's ginger ale stared back at her. Who the hell would want to *poison* her? She heard the television click on once again.

She spun around. *What was Emma trying to tell her?* She could hear the narrator again, and then the voice of the woman, "*If it hadn't been for my neighbor insisting that I go to the ER, I would never have been tested and I would have died. I still have a hard time believing that this happened to me. If you had told me that one day my husband would try to kill me, I would have never believed it. As far as I knew, he loved me and had no reason to want me dead.*"

No one had reason to poison *her*. Not Colleen, her best friend, and not Todd . . . but doubts were creeping in now. It had seemed to come on so suddenly. And her arms and legs, as well as part of her stomach, had broken out into a rash that was just now starting to fade.

The woman had gone to her local hospital. They made it sound so easy. "Sure," she said out loud, "I can just call up Steven and have him meet me at the hospital to see if there's a murder plot against me. No problem."

The TV clicked off.

She dumped out the bowl of leftover pasta and poured the rest of the ginger ale down the drain. Evidence or not, if she had been poisoned somehow, she didn't want to risk anyone else eating or drinking it.

Not sure how to get a hold of Steven, she ended up calling her mother who only agreed to help her after Aileen promised a more detailed explanation would soon be forthcoming. Less than ten minutes after she had woken her mother up, she was calling back.

"He's in the ER. He's still filling in for his father. He's there checking on a heart attack patient, only forty-nine years old, poor thing. It seems she was—"

"Mom!"

She managed to get off the phone and before she could change her mind, she dressed, grabbed her purse, and left for the hospital.

She almost turned around and went home, but Betty Jean had already told Steven she was coming. Aileen was to have him paged when she got there.

She went in the through the heavy automatic doors of the emergency room entrance. After telling the woman behind the check-in desk that she was there to see Steven and that he was expecting her, she sat down in one of the plastic chairs to wait.

Steven came down presently. She stood up and went to meet him. "Nice to see you again, Aileen." They shook hands. He extended an arm and led the way into a cubicle.

"What can I do for you?"

She stepped up and sat on the edge of the examining table. "I want you to test my blood."

His forehead wrinkled in confusion. "For what?"

"Poison."

His eyebrows shot up in surprise, but there was no sign of the skepticism she had seen at her mother's.

"What are the symptoms?"

She rattled them off. He gave no hint at what he was thinking until she said, "And I haven't had a strange taste, but I did break out into hives and I kept getting dizzy," and then his expression became serious.

"Nothing like metal? No metallic taste?"

"No."

"Let me look at your arms." He pulled up the sleeves of her shirt and examined the fading red bumps, then listened to her heart.

He stepped back out into the hall, and she heard him ordering some tests. A few minutes later a nurse came in and took her blood pressure and collected two vials of blood.

Steven stepped back in to talk with her. "I'm assuming you want to keep this hush-hush for now, or do you want to go ahead and involve the authorities?"

"Oh Lord no. I don't even know for sure if anyone really poisoned me. Maybe it was just food poisoning."

Steven shook his head. "From what you've told me, with the symptoms you've mentioned, I could explain some of it away, but not all of it. Your blood pressure is low, and I detected a faint disturbance in your heart rhythm. And cardiac arrhythmias can be a symptom of poisoning. Along with the rash."

"That's why I came in."

Steven was blunt. "Who do you think could have poisoned you? Who had access to your food and drink?"

Aileen looked back at him. He truly suspected what she couldn't wrap her head around, that she had been deliberately poisoned. "It would've had to have been either my boyfriend or my best friend."

He nodded, his face grim.

"Why?" he asked.

"I don't *know*. I don't know why—" she broke off. Colleen? No, why would she? Todd? You *don't really know him*, her mind warned. She shook her head and then thought about Todd, there at her apartment, there while they shared their work, there like he had been for *Ginny*.

"I'll put a rush on it," Steven said, pulling her out of her reverie.

Anxiety, exhaustion, and dread took their toll on her, and she only managed a few tortured hours of sleep after she got home. Bad dreams made her thrash in her bed, but they weren't visions, only the disjointed ramblings of her subconscious mind.

Chapter 28

She avoided Todd all the next day, only talking to him long enough to tell him she was sick and would call him later. She heard nothing from Colleen. That night, she turned down the ringer on her house phone, cut off her cell, and went to bed early.

Bright sunshine streamed in her windows the next morning. She opened the blinds and curtains and faced the fact that she had gotten carried away. In the clear light of day, her fears seemed ridiculous.

I mean come on, why would Todd need my story? He had his own book he was working on. Except she never seemed to see him do any actual work. And his editor had said they were going to publish his coffee-table book on cemetery art. *But even if they did, his book would probably only sell at Halloween.* She stifled the nasty little voice in her head. There had to be some other explanation. It was just too inconceivable. The test results would come back negative for any poison, or show that some other kind of contaminate had gotten in her food somehow. And then she would look like a fool, and Steven would be mad at her for making *him* look like a fool.

Either way it was done now, and she tried to put the whole thing out of her mind—the two miserable days of debilitating nausea, and her silly fear that someone could have actually done something so heinous to her.

Todd showed up unexpectedly right after lunch the next day. "Hey, did you try to call?" she asked, letting him in.

"No. I didn't want you to have the chance to put me off again."

"Oh. I'm sorry. I've just been so sick."

He put his arms around her and hugged her to him. "Are you okay? Are you feeling better?"

She hugged him back briefly and then pulled away. "Yes, much better now."

"Good. I was going to ask you if you wanted to work for a while, but maybe you just need to take it easy today." He gazed at her in concern.

Her enthusiasm at collaborating with him and finding out what happened to Emma had evaporated since being sick, and she didn't want to see, hear, or talk about anything to do with Rose Wood. "No, I'm okay. And I definitely don't feel like working." She looked around the apartment. "I need to get out of here and take my mind off of things. Let's do something completely unrelated, something silly, just for the fun of it."

They decided on the zoo. They drove down and spent the afternoon checking out all the cages and enclosures, admiring the sleek animals and feeding peanuts and crackers to the monkeys and goats. She kept the topic turned from anything to do with her job, or his new book, and he didn't seem to mind.

The sun was shining, and for a little while she tried to forget everything and just feel like a normal person out enjoying the day. Todd climbed up on a large stone statue of a turtle, and she snapped a picture of him with her cell, wishing she had brought her camera.

A little later when Todd began gnawing on one of the crackers they had bought for the animals, she laughed and suggested they go get something to eat.

They stopped at a barbecue shack just outside of Atlanta and ate chopped pork sandwiches with some of the best sauce she had ever tasted. She was going to have a soda, but Todd asked for a beer, so she had one too. They both declined a second one, and had Cokes instead. They finished up with sweet potato pie for Aileen and pecan for Todd. It was a nice day—a nice, blessedly uneventful day. The likelihood that someone had poisoned her now seemed so utterly remote as to border on the absurd.

When they got back to her apartment, Todd followed her up.

"You coming in?" she asked, unlocking the door.

"Nah." He looked at his watch. "I better go. You're probably tired, and besides, you need your rest for tomorrow."

"Tomorrow?"

Todd laughed. "For your visit with Sadie?"

"Oh, yeah." She had all but forgotten her tentative plans to visit her the next day. And he was right; she was tired, and she had another long drive ahead of her.

"You get some sleep." He started down the stairs, and she closed the door. She hadn't gotten more than two steps when she heard him knock. She turned back around and opened the door. Todd leaned in and kissed her. "Call me when you get home after your visit," he murmured, rubbing her cheek with his thumb.

"'kay," she said, and he was gone.

Chapter 29

She called Charlie and found out that Sadie lived in one of the renovated servant's quarters across from Rose Wood.

The small dirt drive was barely visible. If it hadn't been wintertime she would have never spotted it through the dense tangle of trees. Limbs scraped the sides of her car as she bumped up to a small wooden house badly in need of a paint job. Someone was home; a nondescript four-door car sat parked to the side of the old clapboard house and the front door was open, leaving only the screen door. She could hear the sound of someone's soap opera playing inside.

The immediate area in front of the porch was devoid of grass, and two chickens scratched and pecked at the dirt. She stepped warily around them and mounted the steps. She knocked and immediately heard the creak of movement within.

A light-skinned black girl appeared out the dimness and approached the doorway.

"Hi. I'm here to see Sadie? I'd like to talk to her about Char—Mr. Gage?"

The girl, who looked more like a young lady up close, just looked at her.

"Is she here? Could I speak with her?"

She cracked open the door. "How you know Charlie?"

That would be difficult to sum up through a screen door. "If you could just tell her I'm here. My name's Aileen Whitney."

An obstinate look settled on her face. "She taking a nap."

"Oh? Well, when she getting up?" she asked, unconsciously mimicking her.

Aileen had just opened her mouth to speak again, when a stout gray-haired woman came to the door. Sadie was now old and slightly hunched, but Aileen still recognized her from the picture at Charlie's. She stepped out onto the porch and, darting a quick look at Aileen, walked with difficulty over to one of the two rocking chairs and lowered herself into it. "Well, come on," she said.

Aileen crossed the porch and sat down in the other rocker. Even with virtually no wind, it was still chilly and she was grateful for the sun's warmth shining across the porch where they were sitting. She was just opening her mouth to try and explain why she was there when Sadie twisted around and yelled into the house, "Kendra! Go on and bring those beans out."

She turned back around and they exchanged smiles. "You say you here about Mr. Gage?"

"Yes ma'am. It's kind of a long story, if you've got time."

"Oh honey, I've got all the time in the world now that I'm on social security and don't have to work. It's just me and Kendra to take care of now. And sometimes Mr. Charlie."

Kendra came out holding three large bowls. Two held green beans and one was empty. She set the empty bowl on the porch and handed one of the filled bowls to Sadie, and one to Aileen. She was so surprised she nearly dropped it. Kendra snickered and went back into the house.

"I don't know how good these beans gonna be. Came from the supermarket. Must get 'em in from someplace. Lord knows where."

They sat in silence for a few minutes, snapping the ends off the beans and dropping them into the empty bowl.

"You the one got hit by lightning?"

Snap, drop. "Yes ma'am. That's how I met Charlie. He called the ambulance for me."

Sadie nodded, snapped a bean in two, and dropped it.

"I went to see him." Sadie didn't seem surprised. Charlie must have filled her in.

"I'm surprised you got in the door."

Aileen barked a laugh. "It wasn't easy."

Sadie chuckled. "He sure is different from when he was a boy. Course I was just a child myself back then. That was 1919, so I must've been . . ." She scrunched up her eyes, "about eight years old, but I remember it like it was yesterday. I guess things like that tend to stay with a person.

"It was Charlie that took it the hardest, even worse than his mama. He was always so close to Emma. He was never the same after that. It was like the light left the boy that day."

"I know everyone thinks that Leona and Emma died from the earthquake, and Charlie blames himself, but I know that's not what happened," Aileen said.

Sadie stopped snapping and gazed at her lap. "My mamaw from my father's side used to have the sight. Said it used to keep her up at night—all those bad dreams."

"I can relate."

Sadie turned her head and met Aileen's eyes. "What did you see?"

"I saw someone push your sister off the ravine above the river."

Sadie squeezed her eyes shut for a moment, then slowly nodded.

"Were you there that day? The day they brought her home?"

Still not speaking, Sadie nodded again. Even after all this time, it must still hurt to think about it.

Kendra came back out and handed them both a glass of iced tea. As Aileen thanked her and took hers, she realized with a little thrill that Kendra resembled Leona. She had the same chiseled beauty, and there was something about her eyes.

Aileen waited until Kendra had gone back into the house before speaking again. "I saw something else that day. I saw Emma running from someone. I think it must have been during one of the aftershocks. There were rocks falling all over the place. I think she ran into a cave."

"What you mean, a cave?"

"Well, it was dark, and like I said there were rocks. It looked like a cave from what I could tell."

"The only cave I know of was the one that led into the secret tunnel."

"The secret tunnel" seemed to vibrate in Aileen's head. "Did you say *tunnel*?"

"Yes, but we searched it."

"This is the first I heard of a tunnel."

"Well, it was supposed to be secret. Hardly anyone other than a few members of the immediate family knew about it."

"And you and your family."

"Of course."

Of course, the servants always knew everything.

"And you say it was searched? Because I think that was where Emma died."

Sadie shook her head. "I searched it myself with Ms. 'Lizbeth. It'd been there since the Civil War and with the earthquake and all we knew the tunnel was dangerous. Mr. Gage was nowhere to be found, and Ms. 'Lizbeth couldn't wait. I held the lantern while she searched for Miss Emma and Leona, but there was no sign of them. We barely made it back before the tunnel started coming down behind us."

"Could you tell me where it was at?"

"The entrance in the house was behind the wall of the closet under the stairs."

"And where did it come out at? Where was the cave entrance?"

"It was down by the river. But it'd be hard for me to explain where it was at, and I'm too old to go out there and show you."

"What about a picture by any chance?"

"Kendra! Bring out that old photo album!" The floor creaked over by the door where Kendra had been standing.

She came out and handed Sadie the album.

Sadie opened it up and started going through it page by page. About halfway through, she stopped and pointed at one of the pictures. She turned it around for Aileen to see. The picture was an early black-and-white snapshot taken down by the river. This wasn't a posed shot; this was an impromptu picture. Charlie cavorted over by the riverbank and Sadie stood with her head turned beside the willowy figure of her sister. Standing behind Leona was David Gage. He stood very close to her and while Leona was looking at the camera, he was looking at her. And behind him, Elizabeth was looking at *him*. The shot had captured the smoldering, proprietary way he was staring at Leona, and the disillusioned way his wife was staring at him. Behind them yawned the mouth of the cave.

"Your sister was very pretty."

"Yes, everyone thought so."

"Did David think so?"

Sadie looked at her sharply. "You caught that, too, huh?"

"Did he ... was he ...?"

"No. But we wondered at first, when she told Mama she was pregnant."

"She was pregnant!"

"Yes, only fifteen, and pregnant. Turns out it was this boy from down the road. He used to get dropped off every day to work in the fields. He showed up the day after she died, all tore up. Broke that boy's heart losing Leona and his baby. He left that day and we never saw him again."

Leona had been pregnant and there was a secret passageway. She couldn't believe it. She barely heard Sadie as they talked and looked at more pictures. Her mind kept coming back to the secret tunnel. It was possible that Emma's body had been moved before Elizabeth searched for it. From what her dreams had shown her, Leona had died on the rocks by the river, but Emma had died in that tunnel. She was sure of it.

Chapter 30

Energized by her visit with Sadie, some of her old drive to find out what happened to Emma, and to Leona, returned. She made a few notes that night after she got back from her visit, then started writing in earnest the next morning.

She worked on the piece for Ed that she had begun to call "Roses for Emma" (for want of a better title) for the rest of the morning, and was surprised to see if was nearly two o'clock when she finally wound down.

Todd gave his customary knock. She had halfway been expecting him all morning. As promised she had called him when she got back from Sadie's house the night before but had put off telling him any details, wanting to get off the phone and make notes before she forgot everything.

She let him in, and he greeted her with a hug.

He glanced over at the page she had left up on the screen. "Have you been working all day?"

"Since about nine." She walked over and closed out the page.

"Have you eaten?"

"No," she admitted.

"Well let's go. Let's get something to eat."

"Okay, just give me a minute to freshen up."

Todd was on her computer when she came back into the living room. "I hope you don't mind." He pulled a little blue flash drive out of the USB slot. "I was just trying to take care of a few things."

"No, that's fine. You ready?"

They took his car. He drove them over to the same diner they had eaten at when they first met. Again she was aware of the admiring glances sent their way as they got out of his car and made their way in. Most of the looks seemed to be aimed at Todd. He was unbelievably handsome, she thought, looking at his perfect profile. Idly she wondered how he could have possibly remained unattached.

They both ordered cheeseburgers and fries. She told him more about her visit with Sadie as they ate.

"And if I could just get into what's left of the passageway, I might be able . . ." He wasn't listening. She had been trying to look over it, but he had seemed distracted the whole time they had been there. Well no wonder, all she had talked about so far was herself.

"I'm sorry, Todd. I don't mean to monopolize the conversation." She grabbed his hand. "Tell me what's going on with your book? Have you heard anything else from your agent?"

"No, I need to hear about this, Aileen. This is important to me too. We're in it together now, right?" He gave her another one of his intense looks. He gripped her hand hard for a moment, and then released it.

The conversation pretty much dried up after that. Todd paid the bill, and they walked back to his car in silence.

"Listen," he said as soon as they got in, "I need to go ahead and take you home. I've got some things to do, and I'm sure you have stuff to do." He leaned over and gave her a quick kiss. "You don't mind, do you?"

"Of course not."

He headed back the way they came, then looked down and cursed. "I need to get some gas. I'll have to stop on the way."

He pulled into the next convenience store. He slid his credit card out of his wallet and climbed out, tossing the wallet down on the seat. He jerked the door back open after only a minute. "It won't let me pay at the pump. I'll have to go in."

He slammed the door shut and started across the parking lot. She could see a long line in front of the counter through the window. Todd entered the store and got at the back of the line.

Suddenly, musical notes filled the car. She looked around and found Todd's cell lying on the floorboard where it must have fallen out of his pocket. She picked it up and set it on the console without answering it.

She looked back up and checked Todd's progress. He was about halfway up the line now.

Something was nagging at her.

Now that she thought about it, she didn't think she had actually heard his phone ring before. He usually kept it turned down. But she had heard that ringtone before. She was still pondering if he had received a call in front of her when it came to her.

She knew where she had heard it before.

It had been the morning she had called Colleen back and Bobby had been there, not too long after they had started dating. She had heard it in the background. She had noticed it because it hadn't been Colleen's and it had sounded like the theme from the Twilight Zone.

But that would mean that Todd and Bobby had the same exact ringtone.

Or that Todd had been at Colleen's apartment.

Her cell went off, causing her to jump. She pulled it out of her purse and checked the Caller ID: *Colleton County Hospital*. Her heart in her throat, she answered.

"Aileen?"

"Yes?"

"Aileen, it's Steven. Listen, I have your test results. Where are you?"

My God, was it that bad, that he wanted her to sit down?

"I'm sitting down. *What is it?*"

"NO, I mean, where are you? Are you alone?"

She looked up. Todd was next in line.

"Yes. No, I only have a minute."

"The test results were positive. It came back negative for arsenic but they found a small amount of something unusual. It appears that someone gave you a dose of oleander, sometimes known as dogbane. In most cases it's fatal, but in small enough amounts it can just make you very sick."

Oh my God. She'd heard about that. Hadn't a young couple that had gotten lost while hiking died from eating the leaves? Her heart slammed in shock and disbelief.

"*Jesus.* How big was the dose?"

"It was a small amount, but it doesn't take much. You were lucky."

Todd was at the register now.

"I have to go."

"Wait!" she just had time to hear Steven say, and she closed the phone. She reached over and grabbed Todd's wallet. She flipped it open and jerked his license out.

He was coming out the door.

The name on the license was Robert Todd Jennings.

Robert. Todd. Jennings.

Someone poisoned her.

Robert Todd.

Bobby and Todd had the same ringtone.

Bobby was short for Robert.

Bobby Todd.

Everything clicked into place.

Todd and Bobby were one and the same. She and Colleen were seeing the same guy.

Aileen reeled in shock. She crammed the license back in and tossed it down just in time.

"Whom were you talking to?" Todd asked, climbing back in after he pumped the gas.

She thought furiously. "My mother," she said, working hard to keep the horror she was feeling from showing on her face. Her face felt hot from the effort and she was terrified he would see something was wrong.

Todd noticed his phone on the console. Out of the corner of her eye, she saw him spot the blinking light and quickly pocket it.

She was shaking all over, and she grabbed hold of the armrest and shifted in her seat, as if to better look out the window, to hide it. She held her purse tight against her side with the other hand.

"Are you okay?"

She looked over at him and tried to smile. "Just feeling a little sick again is all. Probably a good thing you're taking me home."

He seemed to concur and sped off towards her apartment.

It was all fitting together now. He always wanted to come to her place. He had probably made up the roommate that slept during the day to keep from having to take her to his place—where he lived with Colleen! He had been overly jealous of Carter. He must have thought, like most cheats, that if he was doing it, then she must be too. He didn't have any pictures from Redhill—because he never went there. And she had never met Bobby. He always seemed to disappear right before she came around. That night at the bar when she first met Todd, he had really been *Bobby* there to meet Colleen's best friend. The friend with her recent paranormal experiences that she had undoubtedly told him all about.

And Todd was desperate to publish again.

For once he didn't argue when she hopped out and told him he didn't have to come up with her. "Really, I think I'll just lie down for a while. Just pop the trunk and let me grab my bag."

She had grabbed her laptop just in case she wanted to pull up the picture she had gotten from Sadie. She had begged Sadie for the picture of them by the mouth of the cave, and since she had another one that was similar, Sadie had agreed to let her borrow it so she could scan it. She had planned on showing it to Todd, but had ended up leaving her laptop in the car.

She lifted the trunk lid. Working rapidly, she opened up first her bag then his, yanked his laptop out, shoved it down beside hers, and grabbed the little blue drive he had been using earlier from the front pocket where she had seen him drop it. She slung her bag over her shoulder and slammed the lid shut.

Throwing up her other hand at Todd, she hurried to her apartment stairs. Her heart was pounding more in fear than exertion by the time she made it to the top. Her hand was shaking so bad she could hardly get her key in.

She slammed the apartment door and locked it.

She had, at best, twenty minutes or so. Ten minutes there, and ten minutes back when he discovered his laptop gone.

She threw her bag down on the kitchen table and jerked his laptop out. She hit the power button and waited impatiently. Just as she had feared, it was password protected.

Foregoing the password for the moment, she took his flash drive over to her desktop and plugged it in.

There was nothing on it about cemetery art, only things to do with Rose Wood.

She found scans of every newspaper article she had copied, all the pictures she had taken, and every picture she had scanned, including the one she had gotten from Sadie just the day before. Her mind flashed back to her apartment right before they left. Todd had been on her computer when she came back into the living room.

There were also two Word documents: the article she had started for Ed, and a document called Shadows.doc. And she noticed something else. When she clicked on Properties, the scanned newspaper stories and all of the other pictures had earlier access dates. *Colleen*, the night she had stayed over, when she had asked for her password. And Colleen had brought her a cup of hot tea right before she got sick.

She clicked on the Shadows document, and the first page appeared. It was blank except for the words "In The Shadows". A title page. She scrolled down. Just as she suspected. He had written a first-person account of his time spent with Aileen during Emma's haunting of her. It seemed to be part memoir and part factual information, chronicling Aileen's encounters with Emma's ghost and the history behind it.

She checked the time. It had been twelve minutes.

Closing out Todd's document, she scanned the list of files again and found one other folder and an audio file. She opened the folder. It contained scanned copies of her discharge papers from the ER after she had been struck by lightning. Unbelievable. Colleen had even found the papers where she had thrown them in a drawer and copied them too. And if she had found those, she had surely found the password to her online journal that she had written on a Post-it note and stuck by her computer.

She clicked on the audio file. The media player box popped up, and after a slight pause, she heard some incomprehensible sounds, the sound of a phone ringing, and then her own voice. It was low quality but she recognized it immediately. Her tinny voice came over the speakers. *"I know why Emma won't rest now. She can't rest knowing Charlie blames himself."*

He had recorded her.

She advanced the file and heard herself ask, *"Do you smell that?"* *"Smell what?"* Todd's voice asked. *"Roses,"* her voice murmured, and Aileen closed it out.

She pulled the drive out and dropped it in her purse.

She walked back over to his laptop. The cursor blinked for the password. She sat down and tried to remember the placement of his hands on the keyboard. It hadn't been a long password and he had started typing it with his left hand. In her mind saw him hit the last key with a flourish. She was pretty sure he had ended it with a 1. She gave herself two minutes and then she was going to give up. She needed to leave before he came back. Her heart palpitated in agitation. She started typing anything she could think of that might be it. She tried the obvious ones like his name and zodiac sign and the car he drove then started on terms relating to his supposed new book. She tried all variations of things to do with cemetery and headstone art, and had just started typing ridiculous ones like *losernum1* and *devious1* when she typed in *scribe1* for the hell of it and got it right. She went to get up and realized she had actually cracked it.

She sat back down and quickly deleted anything of hers that had been saved on the laptop. Then she emptied the trash in the corner of the screen to be sure. She couldn't stop him from writing the book if that's what he was determined to do, but she wasn't going to make it easy for him.

Next she went over to her computer, and after making sure her own USB drive with her backup files was safe and secure in her pocketbook, she deleted everything off of it even remotely related to Rose Wood, and emptied that recycle bin, too.

Opening back up the Word document of his new book so he would see it first thing, she turned his laptop around facing the door, left the door cracked so he could get in, and got the hell out of there.

Chapter 31

She felt numb, except for the ache of betrayal in her chest. She closed her eyes. Someone blasted a horn at her, and she jerked the car back over the centerline. She tried to concentrate on her driving but gave up after a minute and pulled over.

Her hands were trembling where she gripped the wheel. A line from a Madonna song played insanely through her mind. *Nothing is what it seeeeeeeemmmsss.*

Nothing made sense. Her life felt out of control and fraught with peril. Death lie in wait, from earthquakes and storms and ghosts to even the people nearest and dearest to her. Everything seemed out of her hands, like chaos trying to drag her screaming from her orderly life.

She looked around slowly. Traffic passed on the road beside her, normal people living normal lives, going to or from their homes.

She couldn't go back to her apartment, and she wouldn't go to her mother's. Her bank account couldn't take the hit of a hotel room, so that left Carter's.

It was after hours and Rose Wood was deserted. She passed through the open gates and had just started around the side when the car started to skip. She gave it more gas and it rolled a few more feet, then faltered. The car jerked once more, coughed, and then died. She looked down at the fuel gage. She still had a quarter tank of gas, so why ...? The sharp floral scent of roses suddenly filled her nose and she nearly gagged. Pushing the door open, she got out and walked away, leaving the car where it was.

Carter wasn't home. The Harley sat parked to the side of the house, but the truck was gone. She knocked anyway and then sat down on his steps.

She looked at the top of the mansion poking up above the trees. She couldn't imagine how she had ever thought the place was idyllic. It was monstrous; the soil stained with blood, year upon year. People had been enslaved and then died there; children had died there; other people had gone crazy and then died since. Sometimes events were so resounding that they held a place in this world and tainted the very air. And sometimes they just kept reverberating, causing more death and grief to anyone they touched. It wasn't Emma's fault she had gotten trapped by her love for her brother. It was something in the very air, the very fabric of the place, like grooves worn into a record played over and over.

She leaned her head against the side of the porch railing. Had the place gotten a hold of Todd and drawn him in too? Because she was pretty sure she knew whom Carter had thrown off the property for using a flash on the oil paintings. She closed her eyes.

Someone grabbed her shoulder and she jumped and cried out.

"*Easy*, you fell asleep," Carter said, hovering over her.

She struggled to a standing position but she did it too quickly and immediately felt the blood rush to her head. Her vision dimmed and she swayed.

Carter caught her arm. "Are you okay? What's wrong? Did something happen?" He shot a look at the house in the distance.

Aileen shook her head. Her thinking still felt muddled and she could barely comprehend what had happened. It was just so unbelievable.

Even if he had wanted my pictures and all, he didn't have to poison me to get them.

"Who? Who poisoned you?" he said, and she realized she had spoken out loud.

She tried to think where to begin. When had it begun? When she had met Todd and told him about everything? No, before that. When he had met Colleen and she told him about her? No, *wrong again!* She gave a little titter that even to her own ears sounded a little unhinged. It had been before that, when he visited Rose Wood and had been thrown out by Carter for taking shots of the oil paintings. That night she had ran into him at the bar, Emma hadn't been warning her about the drunken redneck, she had been warning her away from Todd!

"Come inside," Carter said and began to propel her through the door. She had been lost in thought again, and now he was looking at her as if he truly did fear for her sanity.

She let him push her down on the couch. "I'm okay." She tried to make an effort. She ran a hand through her hair and sighed. "I've just had a shock is all."

"Don't move. I'll be right back."

He was back after a moment with two glasses and a bottle of Brandy. He set them down on the coffee table and poured each of them a measure. "Here," he said, handing her one of the glasses.

She took a small sip.

"All of it."

She rolled her eyes and killed off the rest of it, not even flinching. She wiped her mouth with the back of her hand.

"Better." He gave her a half-smile and poured her a little more. "Now tell me what the hell's going on."

She took another drink. It had the effect of calming her and clarifying things at the same time.

"Was it Emma again? Did something happen at the house?"

"No," she said, shaking her head. "I've had a few recent developments, but this is about Todd. Or Bobby. Or R.T., or whatever the hell else he calls himself."

"Who is Todd slash Bobby?"

"My boyfriend," she said in disgust.

"Does it have anything to do with me? With you coming down here?"

"No, but he did get mad about that."

He gave her a look and took a swallow of his own drink.

"He poisoned me."

His eyes went wide. "WHAT!"

"Or rather, he got my best friend, Colleen, to poison me. Turns out, her boyfriend, Bobby, and my boyfriend, Todd, are one and the same. A friend of my Mom's is a doctor and he met me at the ER and took a blood sample. I just got the results back today. It was positive for oleander. Not much, not enough to kill me."

Carter abruptly set his drink down and left the room. He came back a minute later with a belt and his very large, very black gun. She watched wordlessly as he strapped it on.

He dropped the gun into the holster and she felt some of the horrible apprehension she had been feeling lift a little.

"Big guns and brandy, oh yeah," she said, and giggled.

He frowned at her. "I think you've had enough."

"No sir, I don't think so. If you'd had the two horrible, SICK days I had and then found out the man you thought you were falling in love with was just using you, and your best friend in the whole world was helping him do it . . ." She felt her face crumple and she almost broke down. She turned her head into the couch cushion until she could control herself.

He poured another inch into her glass.

"Why would he have Colleen poison you?"

Aileen struggled up from the sofa. "Wait," she said when he made a move towards her. She pulled out her cell. She scrolled through all the pictures on her phone and stopped at the one of Todd she had taken at the zoo. "Ever seen him before?"

He took the phone from her. "It looks like the guy I had trouble with a while back. I caught him using a flash on the oil paintings."

"That's Todd. He told me he was working on a coffee-table book of gravestone art."

"Hmm. And he was really working on . . ."

"Me. And the book he was using me for."

"Yeah, but why did he have you poisoned? I'm not sure this makes sense, Aileen."

"I guess so Colleen could incapacitate me long enough for her to gather everything he wanted. Although it does seem like he could have found another way. Colleen stayed over while I was sick and I heard her that night on my computer. She copied all the pictures from my camera and the ones from Charlie and Sadie. She scanned all the newspaper articles I copied at the archives. She even found my discharge papers from the ER and scanned a copy of them too."

"Doesn't he have to have your permission to write about you? Isn't that an invasion of your privacy?"

Aileen shook her head, rolling her eyes. "It's basically Gonzo journalism."

Carter's brow wrinkled in confusion.

"It's a style of journalism where the reporter immerses himself in a situation and becomes part of the story. Todd's writing it as a first-person account of his time with me, which makes it essentially a memoir. And people write unauthorized memoirs all the time. I can't even do anything about him recording me."

"He recorded you?"

"Yes. He recorded me one night when I thought I detected Emma's presence. And in the state of Georgia you can record someone without them knowing it if you are a party to the conversation."

"But surely he can't use the pictures?"

"No. He probably just wanted copies of those for himself, or maybe he thought he would be able to talk Sadie or Charlie into letting him use theirs. If nothing else, he can probably get permission to use the photos of Emma accompanying the old newspaper stories."

"But neither one of you knows what happened to Emma."

"No, but I did find out something from Sadie. Did you know there was a secret tunnel under the house?"

He lifted a shoulder. "Sure. John, the constable before me, the one I told you killed himself?" She nodded. "He showed me the trapdoor when I came to work here."

"So you've gone down it?"

"No. John said you don't get far before you hit a wall of dirt and rocks."

"So unless we can get an archaeologist or whoever out here to excavate, then I'm at a dead end. I don't have anyone else to question and the only answers I might find are buried in the collapsed tunnel."

He shook his head, just as much at a loss as she was.

Later after she had finished filling him in on everything she had found out from Charlie and Sadie, he got up and checked the locks on the doors and windows. "You're staying here tonight and in the morning we're going to the police. Even if he has the right to do a book on you and Emma, he still had Colleen slip you the oleander. You could have died."

She agreed, and after she forced herself to eat some of the soup he heated up, he tucked her into the couch—she absolutely refused to take his bed—and left her to get some sleep. He kept the door to his room open to keep watch, and she was comforted.

Even with the brandy, if felt like forever before she felt the pull of sleep.

She was dreaming again.

Sadie tugged on her hand. "Ms. 'Lizbeth, the tunnel! They could be in the tunnel!"

Elizabeth turned from the window where she was looking out. "Well we better check it then," she said, her voice devoid of inflection.

In the distance she could hear the shouts of the men as they gathered to search for Emma and Leona.

"I'll take Sadie with me," she said to the few servants that had stayed in the house.

She handed a lantern to Sadie and opened the closet door under the stairs. She and Sadie crowded in. Elizabeth removed the linens from the bottom shelf, then knelt down and pushed against the back panel, and it swung inward. "Give me the light."

Sadie handed her the light, and she crawled through the opening and disappeared into the hidden space beyond.

After Sadie had crawled in behind her, Elizabeth lifted the trapdoor and led the way down into the darkness.

The Earthquake had done serious damage to the tunnel, but the entrance was clear. They went downhill for a ways before it leveled out. A small tremor sent a small cloud of dirt and rocks tumbling.

"Hurry, Ms. 'Lizbeth! It's not safe."

They hurried along the boulder-strewn passageway and discovered that a section of the roof had partially caved in.

"Hold the light up and wait on me here."

Sadie did what she was told, climbing the bank of debris and shining the lantern through the opening at the top.

Elizabeth worked her way over and disappeared through the hole. The tunnel shook again. "Please Ms. 'Lizbeth, hurry!"

Sadie waited, propping the arm holding the lantern with her other arm to ease the strain. Small tremors were hitting the tunnel every few seconds *now, raining more dirt and rocks down.* "Hurry Ms. 'Lizbeth!"

Sadie screamed as another stronger tremor shook them. "Ms. 'Lizbeth the whole tunnel's coming down around us!"

Elizabeth reappeared at the top of the debris. She shook her head. "They're not here."

She climbed down, and they hurried back the way they had come. A harder shock suddenly jolted them and the tunnel began caving in behind them. They raced for the steps leading up. Elizabeth grabbed the light for one last look down the passageway.

The tunnel was now completely blocked.

Chapter 32

Aileen woke up in utter blackness. When she had fallen asleep there had been the faint illumination from the bathroom down the hall and the TV Carter had switched on in his bedroom. Now there was nothing but complete darkness. She shifted, still caught in the remnants of her dream, and immediately knew she was no longer on the couch. Instead of the softness of the sofa cushions, she felt something hard beneath her. Coming fully awake, she realized she was nearly sitting up in a chair.

She knew what must have happened. Incredible as it seemed, she had been sleepwalking. She had gone through a strange period when she was little when she had roamed around the house while she slept. She'd never forgotten the paralyzing feeling of terror, waking up in total darkness, not knowing where she was or how she had gotten there. The worst time had been when she was about four, and she had woken up in a chair in the den and had to sit there frozen in fright, too scared to move, until daylight came.

She felt the same paralyzing fear now. She had no idea where she was. She kept still and listened to the sounds around her. It was raining. She could hear the thrum of it on the roof above her. The house ticked and creaked around her. *What was that?* She jerked her head around but couldn't see a thing. She thought she had heard the sound of someone walking. Was it Carter? Had they had a power outage? Yes, that was it. The power had gone out. "Carter, is that you?" she asked, sitting all the way up. Her feet found the floor and stopped her cold. The floor her feet were touching was hardwood. And Carter didn't have hardwood; he had carpet and linoleum.

Thunder boomed in the distance. She jerked her feet back up and held her knees tightly. *Oh please no*, she whimpered to herself.

Something creaked across the room. Creeping terror stole over her and she felt goose bumps break out across her body. Her mind was playing tricks on her. She couldn't see, so she was hearing things she normally wouldn't notice, that was all. The sound, it really did sound like someone walking towards her, advanced across the floor. She shook in fright, reduced to the long lost but not forgotten childhood dread of something *under the bed* or *IN THE CLOSET*!

Lightning cracked so loud and explosively that Aileen screamed, the sound lost in the deafening thunder that followed. But it was what she saw in the brief flash of light that had her up and out of the chair.

She was in Rose Wood and the thing coming towards her in the darkness was not of this earth.

Lightning flashed again and she saw two twin orbs of red reflected back at her where Leona's eyes should have been. She screamed again, and threw herself instinctively to the side away from her. She banged against furniture and managed to lose her sense of direction.

She felt herself brush up against cloth material and reached up and jerked the curtain to the side. Bolts were popping all around the house and she could see just enough around her to realize that she was in one of the bedrooms. She saw with the next flash that Leona was still in the room with her. She had continued on her original path and was now moving around the bed.

Aileen didn't remember a bed being there when she had come on the tour.

She was having a dream. That's what it was. Of course. She was dreaming.

Why else would there now be softly lit candles and lamps burning around the room, which was filled with things and furniture that hadn't been there before? She could hear Leona humming to herself. She finished smoothing the bed and turned back around. Aileen shrank back but she gave no notice of seeing her, merely gliding out the door. Eyes wide, Aileen followed. The house had been made over. It was no longer nearly empty rooms. Everything was as it had been in Emma's time, beautifully decorated and lived in, filled with all their possessions. She tiptoed down the stairs, following the ghostly figure of Leona. Halfway down, Leona looked back over her shoulder and

Aileen saw with surprise that she was now Emma. Of course, this was just a dream. She was really on Carter's couch asleep.

Where was she taking her? Was she finally going to show her what happened? Aileen reached the bottom step, and two things happened simultaneously: she jammed a splinter from the wooden step into her foot, and she was plunged into darkness.

This was no dream. Gone were the lamps and the furnishings and the beautiful paintings and drapes from the past, and she was left in the darkness of the here and now.

The front door blew open and slammed into the wall, and there stood Todd silhouetted against the storm behind him.

Aileen shrieked and fell back against the stairs. She wanted to wake up now. She wanted to WAKE UP NOW! Todd stepped through the doorway. Rain lashed in and hit her in the face, assuring her this was real and not a dream. He reached into his pocket, and she held her breath.

He switched on a small LED flashlight. "I thought you might come here."

Her breath wooshed out of her lungs.

He shined the light in her face. "Will you let me explain?"

He started to walk towards her and she shrank back. "That's far enough."

"What, you're afraid of me now? I can explain, Aileen."

"What's there to explain? You used me."

"I'm sorry. I never meant for things to go this way."

"Oh sure you did," she choked out.

"Aileen, this isn't just some little article for me. We're talking about a book deal here!" He stepped closer to her, wiping rain off his face.

She backed up a step. "Nor was it for me and you damn well know it!" She was starting to get angry and she liked the feel of it. Anything was better than the stark terror. "And get that light out of my face!"

He instantly complied, propping it on a side table.

"You *poisoned* me."

He looked at her in amazement. "What?"

"I was sick for two days. I could have died!"

"Now you're just being ridiculous. Look, I know you're upset, but no one's *poisoning* you."

"You had Colleen lace my drink with oleander."

"Olewhater? What the hell is that? Is that a flower? And why would I do that?"

"I don't know! To get what you needed for your precious book."

Todd looked dumbfounded. "Would you listen to yourself? You're not even making sense. Why would I try to hurt you when I need you? We haven't even got to examine the remains of the tunnel yet."

"*We?* Don't you mean me? *We* haven't done anything. I've been the one going through this."

"Now be fair," he chided. "We've been working together, haven't we?"

"Oh don't even try that with me, Todd." She came down off the stairs. "Or is it Bobby?" she asked, injecting as much contempt in her voice as she could.

"Listen, Aileen." He brought his hand up to cup her face, and she batted it angrily away. "I care about you! I did this for us. I knew I could get published." The way he emphasized "I" infuriated her even more.

"You did what for us? Nearly killed me?"

"Oh come on. Please."

"I have proof."

He tilted his head sideways as if trying to comprehend the absolute ridiculousness of what she was saying.

"I went to the ER. Steven met me there. You remember me telling you about him?" He nodded his head slowly. "I had him do a blood test. It came back positive for oleander, sometimes known as dogbane. It's almost always fatal. Apparently, mine was just under the lethal dose."

He stared at her in almost believable shock.

"What? Why ...? Who ...? He seemed to be talking to himself now. Either he was a great actor or he was genuinely puzzled.

"Colleen put it in my drink."

He raised his eyes and slowly shook his head. "You have to believe me, Aileen, I had nothing to do with that. I knew she copied your pictures and all, but I had no idea she had deliberately made you sick. I would never do anything crazy like that."

"I still don't know how you managed to get her to go along with any of thi—you asked her to marry you."

"Yes. It was the only way. She caught me coming out of your apartment the night I cooked dinner for you, and I had to play back the recording I made of you so she would believe me when I told her I needed you for the book, but that I loved *her*."

"How could you do this?"

"The night I met you, when I took you home from the bar, I didn't realize who you were. Imagine my surprise when you told me your name after we had just kissed. What was I supposed to say, '*Oh, I'm Bobby, your best friend's boyfriend*'? I had just kissed you!"

"And then you couldn't say anything."

He shook his head. "Nope."

"You were afraid I would tell Colleen and then you'd be cut out of the loop. She would have broken up with you, and more importantly, I would have never had anything to do with you knowing how Colleen felt about you."

"What other choice did I have? I had already been thrown off the property at Rose Wood. Sure I could have gathered some facts together, but I needed more than that. I needed firsthand experience. I needed you. I needed your account of the lightning strike and the encounters with Emma that followed. And I still need to know how it ends. Only you have a connection with Emma. You're the only one who can find out what really happened to her."

He looked at Aileen beseechingly. "We can still work this out. I do care about you."

She made a sound of disgust. "You just don't quit, do you? What about Colleen? You're supposed to marry her."

His mouth pulled down into a moue of disgust. "I would never marry someone like her."

Colleen stepped into the doorway behind him.

Aileen gasped and flinched back. Todd's head whipped around and she just had time to think, *How much had she heard?* when fire spit from the end of the gun in Colleen's hand.

Todd arched towards Aileen in the wake of the deafening blast, and he dropped to his knees. A red stain blossomed and spread across his shirt. He looked down and touched the blood pouring out of his chest. He raised his eyes to hers, a look of anguish on his face, and then toppled over. Aileen cried out and fell to her knees beside him.

In the circle of the flashlight she saw him blink once, and then no more.

She looked up in horror at Colleen. "*What have you done?*"

Colleen raised the gun again.

"WHAT ARE YOU DOING? I didn't know, Colleen. *I didn't know!*"

Colleen lowered the gun. "He said he loved me."

"I know. I'm sorry. I'm so sorry. He used me too." She kept her eyes on Colleen; she couldn't bear to look at Todd again.

Colleen was crying now, silent tears streaming down her face as she looked down at Bobby, the man she had loved and had just killed. "I didn't know either, until I caught him leaving your apartment. He told me he was only seeing you for the book. I didn't believe him until he played the recording he made of you."

"I know. The night you kept calling."

"Yeah, the night I kept calling and you couldn't be bothered to pick up." Colleen raised the gun again.

"And then he asked you to marry him," she said, trying to distract her and keep her talking.

"Yeah. He asked me to marry him. He said he needed you for the book but that he loved *me*."

"I'm sorry," Aileen said again, trying to keep her voice steady. "Was that when you decided to poison me?"

"I just gave you a tiny bit to make you sick. I just wanted the whole thing to end, for him to get what he needed so we could be married."

And you were pissed that I slept with your boyfriend too, weren't you, Colleen? she thought but didn't say.

Aileen took a step towards her. "It's okay, Colleen. We can fix this."

The gun wavered for a second, then started to drop.

She took another step. "Just put the gun down and let me help you."

"What are we going to do?" Colleen asked in a broken voice.

Thunder rumbled again, this time louder and closer. The whole house seemed to vibrate with it.

"There's extenuating circumstances, we can explain. I'll make sure you get the help you need, Colleen. And I'll help you any way I can."

Her face darkened into a scowl. "What do you mean you'll get *me* help? I'm not the crazy one around here. You're the one who's seeing ghosts!" She brought the gun up and pointed it at her. "I'm sorry but I have to do this. I won't let you turn me in. I can't go to prison."

The floor canted underneath Aileen and the door slammed shut behind Colleen. It felt as if the whole house dropped an inch or two and then settled. It did feel a little like being on an elevator. The house and ground beneath it was moving and shifting, just like it had before in 1919.

Fire shot from the muzzle of Colleen's gun just as Aileen felt another stomach-dropping lurch and she actually felt the bullet whiz by her ear. She dropped to the ground and rolled purposely towards the flashlight Todd had brought and snatched it off the table. Colleen shot again and grazed a burning path across the side of her neck. She clapped a hand to it and threw herself at Colleen. She slammed into her, knocking her off balance. Colleen fell over Aileen and Aileen bashed her in the head as hard as she could with the little flashlight. It barely stunned her, but it was enough to allow her to switch off the light and scramble away.

She didn't even try the stairs—too easy of a target. She weaved back and forth, low to the ground, through the dining room and over to the side door. She had just reached it and closed her hand around the knob when she felt it stick in her hand, and then the bolt above it slammed across.

What are you doing Emma!

She abandoned the door and ran towards the adjoining room just as Colleen reached for her. She felt her fingers brush the edge of her shirt, and she wrenched away. She flew through the room with her hand out in front of her to keep from hitting a wall. Lightning still arced in the windows in random flashes and she used it to see what she could. She made it out into the hall behind the stairs and lunged for the back door. It was frozen shut too! Almost crying in frustration, she turned away.

She met Colleen coming through the doorway. Adrenaline gave her strength, and she launched herself at Colleen, hitting her with her whole body. Colleen fell against the wall, cracking her head in the process.

Aileen got around her while she was still groggy. Switching on the little flashlight, she ran for the front door. The locks turned before she could get there, sealing that way out too. *Dammit Emma!* She backed up and heard Colleen groaning and trying to get to her feet. Spying the closet door under the stairs, she switched off the light and crept over.

As quietly as she could, she tried the knob expecting it to somehow be locked against her too, but it opened easily. She stepped inside, gave one quick flash of the light to orient herself, then shut it off and crouched down in the corner. She gave another quick flash of the light. The closet was nearly empty. There was a vacuum propped up against the wall and a few other cleaning products and odds and ends on the shelf of the open storage cabinet. Nothing she could use as a weapon.

She listened for Colleen.

She heard her scuffling around then heard the rasp of a lighter being lit. Aileen held her breath. If she found her, she was dead.

After endless minutes it seemed, she heard the stairs creak above her. She considered running for one of the windows and trying to break it, but she was afraid she wouldn't have time and Colleen would shoot her in the back before she could get all the way out. For all she knew, she was still standing on the stairs right above her listening and waiting on her to come out of her hiding spot.

Her dream came back to her. She switched on the flashlight, cupping her hand around it. Shielding it as much as she could, she examined the back of the storage cabinet. Maybe she could buy some time, crawl into what was left of the tunnel and hit Colleen with a rock when she came down after her. Her mind was working overtime even though she knew Colleen would probably just shoot her. Crouching down, she leaned in and pushed against the back of the cabinet. Nothing happened; the panel didn't budge. She shifted to a better position and pushed harder. This time the back panel moved about an inch and then stopped.

A creak and a scrape alerted her to Colleen's presence. Just like she had feared, Colleen hadn't gone all the way up the stairs.

With renewed effort she pushed with everything she had, and the hinged panel flew inward. Cold damp air drifted out, smelling faintly of dirt like a dank grave.

"I know you're in there, Aileen. Don't make this any more difficult," Colleen called out.

Aileen scrambled through the opening. She immediately saw the trapdoor in the floor—and the lock that was on it.

Aileen yanked on the padlock, and *merciful God in Heaven thank you Jesus*, the lock had been left open. Whoever had closed the trapdoor last had left it hanging from the hasp. *Or was Emma responsible again?*

She ripped the lock off, grabbed the ring, and heaved the trapdoor over.

On the other side of the wall, Colleen threw open the closet door.

Aileen dropped through the hole, nearly breaking her neck on the crude stone steps. She righted herself and scrambled down the stairs as quickly as she could.

Oh God, Todd was *dead*. What he had done was wrong, but he hadn't been trying to kill her. She knew she would never forget the anguish on his face when he knew he was dying. Her face had been the last thing he saw as his life passed away. And it was all because of that crazy bitch coming down the stairs behind her.

The passageway had mostly leveled out now and Aileen spotted the cave-in ahead.

She quickly shut off the flashlight and veered over to the side away from where she had been. Something clattered on a rock behind her and Colleen gave a muffled curse. She had just dropped the lighter. Aileen could hear her shuffling around feeling for it.

She threw herself on the edge of the mound that blocked the tunnel. She dug her feet in and began pulling and clawing her way up the side, expecting to feel a bullet in her back at any minute. One of her fingernails ripped as she neared the top, and she barely felt it. Trying not to fall, she started shoveling dirt and rocks off the top of the pile. She scraped and dug at the ceiling, tumbling rocks and dirt down behind her.

Colleen yelped and cursed again as a rock hit her where she was standing underneath her.

Colleen's lighter flicked again, and Aileen switched her light on too. The top of the mound no longer reached all the way to the ceiling. The tremor she had felt earlier had shifted the pile of dirt and debris causing it to settle differently, and now with her digging she had a hole nearly big enough to fit through.

Colleen's lighter went out, and Aileen switched off the flashlight. It was completely dark now, and for just a second it was completely quiet except for the light rasp of their breathing. And then in the silence, Aileen heard the unmistakable sound of Colleen cocking the gun.

She threw herself up and into the hole headfirst, praying the pile of dirt and rocks wouldn't collapse and smother her. Wiggling and burying like a mole, she wedged herself through the opening. There was one tight moment when she thought she wouldn't fit, and then she was out and tumbling down the other side. She held onto the flashlight and tried not to fall on her head. Probably the only reason Colleen hadn't already shot her was because she was afraid the bullet would ricochet if she missed.

Already she could hear her scrambling up through the hole she had widened at the top. Colleen was intent on killing her, and the coldness of it terrified her.

Aileen ran down the tunnel, praying her little light would hold out. The passageway curved around to the right and then started sloping up. Maybe she could get out. Maybe she could hide somewhere and when Colleen passed she could go back.

After she felt like she had gotten far enough ahead of Colleen, she stopped for a minute. She looked behind her to make sure Colleen hadn't caught up with her and tried to catch her breath. Her breath fogged the air. Despite all her exertion, the earth the tunnel was carved into was damp and cold and she could feel it seeping into her.

She pushed herself off the wall where she had been leaning and started forward.

A rock clattered behind her, and she picked up her pace. The tunnel narrowed, and then she was climbing over a lip into some kind of natural shaft. This part of the tunnel wasn't man-made and she had to alternate short periods of running with clamoring over rocks and uneven spots. She had no doubt that Colleen was following her light like a beacon.

She was concentrating so hard on widening the distance between them that she almost missed it. Her nose finally detected the familiar scent and she jerked up the flashlight, still moving fast. Emma stood almost directly in front of her. Aileen couldn't stop and she started to swerve to the left when Emma stepped in front of her and she was forced to go right. Suddenly the ground was gone and her feet were stepping onto nothing. She pinwheeled her arms and fell through the air.

She smashed down in a heap, banging the back of her head against a rock. Pain jarred through her, and she lay still, fuzzy from the blow.

After a second her head cleared a little, and she managed to pull herself into a sitting position. She had held onto the little flashlight somehow and it had landed right beside her. She picked up it and, moving her head carefully, used it to look around. She had fallen on a little ledge less than halfway down a crevasse. If Emma hadn't blocked the other way, she would have fallen to her death.

She looked up and pain shot through her head. Through her blurry vision she could see Emma still standing above her. And now she could hear Colleen, running then pausing, then running again.

Just like with her, Emma stepped into Colleen's path. But this time instead of causing her to fall onto the ledge, she caused Colleen to go the other way, and she fell shrieking into the darkness below.

Aileen listened for her to hit and heard a muffled thump a second later.

She made it to her knees, pain shooting across the back of her head, and looked over the edge. She felt herself losing consciousness and managed to move back a little, then darkness closed around her and she collapsed.

Emma had already cut out the heavy paper and written on it "Happy Birthday Charlie! Hope your birthday is just how you like it—with plenty of cake!" and signed it *"with fondest love, Emma".* Now she only needed to finish coloring it, add the ribbon, and put in the real Indian arrowhead she had gotten for him.

Charlie rapped on the door and opened it. Again. Emma grabbed her shawl and tossed it over everything before he could see it, and wished for the thousandth time that her door locked.

"Can I come in?"

"Not now Charlie. In a little while, okay?"

"Okay." He pulled the door closed.

She sat back down and started sorting through her different colors. Maybe yellow, or gold. She chose gold, and started shading the border.

Charlie came running in again a few minutes later, this time without knocking. Emma jumped up, covering everything again.

He grinned at her in delight. "Mammy says we're gonna have chocolate cake."

"That's good. I like chocolate cake too."

"Are you finished now?"

"Not quite."

"Well, okay," he said, his bottom lip out.

Emma suppressed a laugh. She waited until he had gone, then gathered up her things. She would finish up the card, then see if she could get a bit of cake batter for her and Charlie and show him the art of licking the bowl.

Everything was still wet from the recent storm, including her favorite little wrought-iron table and chair.

Lifting her skirt, she went down the steps around to the back of the house.

Mammy was just disappearing into the house with Charlie's cake when she came around the side. She ducked inside the kitchen. It wasn't too hot for once. Charlie's birthday cake lingered in the air. She jumped up on one of the stools by the long table and dropped her things. Pulling the empty cake batter bowl over, she ran her finger across the top and licked it off.

She had almost finished Charlie's card when she saw Leona go past. Mama had told everyone to stay in the house. Where was she going?

She tied a thin piece of gold ribbon to the card, stuck in the arrowhead, and then dropped it in her pocket to give to Charlie.

But first, she wanted to find Leona and tell her to get back to the house.

Aileen swam towards consciousness, but the dream held her there and continued.

Elizabeth rounded the side of the house and started down the path. Twigs and sticks pulled at her dress. David had left saying he was going down the river to check on some problem at the mill, but she didn't believe him. And not long after, she had seen Leona leave the house.

She soon caught up with the girl. She had a basket with her and she was pretending to pick berries. Leona hadn't seen her yet and Elizabeth looked around for David. She had been sure they were going to meet. Like they surely had many times before. Bitter hurt and jealousy coursed through her at the thought of her husband and the girl together.

She walked over to the edge of the riverbank where Leona was standing.

"Where is he?" she demanded harshly.

Leona jumped and spun around, spilling the berries she had gathered onto the ground. "Ms. 'Lizbeth!"

"I said where is he?" she demanded again.

Leona's eyes widened in fear and surprise. "He . . . he not here today."

"But you were going to meet him, weren't you? Just like you have plenty of other times, you little Jezebel!"

Leona's eyes widened even further. "It's not like that Ms. 'Lizbeth! He say he love me."

"He loves you?" She gave an incredulous laugh. Then her eyes dropped down to where Leona's hand was resting on her stomach. "No . . . you're not," she could barely say it, "you're not pregnant?"

"Yes ma'am. We's having a baby."

"NO." Fresh pain knifed into her heart. Giving an agonized wail, she flew at her and knocked her backwards. It wasn't until she had gone over the edge that she thought to wonder how far down the river was.

She heard a gasp and a little scream behind her. She spun around. Emma stood frozen in shock, a look of horror on her face. Elizabeth turned back to the girl below and realized she was dead. Her neck had broken and now lay at an unnatural angle. She lay splayed out on the rocks below, her head smashed onto the rock beneath her, a pool of crimson leaching into the river swirling around her.

She had killed her and the bastard love child.

There must have been some anger still left on her face when she turned back around because Emma suddenly turned and ran.

"Emma, wait! I'm sorry. I didn't mean it. Please, wait!" she called to her but Emma kept going. Agonized regret lanced through her at she had done, at what her daughter had seen her do, and the fear she had seen on her face.

She raced after her. "Wait Emma!" If she could just get her to listen. She hadn't meant to kill her. She hadn't meant to!

Thank goodness Emma was slowing, and she was starting to catch up. Emma suddenly veered away from the house. Where was she going? She realized abruptly where Emma was heading. "No. No, Emma. Don't go in there. It's not safe!" she screamed.

She just had time to see Emma enter the cave when she felt another aftershock. The ground was still wet from the recent storm and her shoes slipped in the mud. The earth trembled and she fell and hit the ground. After a second it quit, and she jumped up and ran in after Emma.

A large piece of rock had already cracked and fallen in the back of the cave, partially blocking the passage that led back to the tunnel.

"EMMA!"

She squeezed around the rock and started down the passage. She lurched from side to side, trying to keep her balance. She was feeling tremors every few seconds now and rocks and dirt were falling all around her. The ground sloped down and then leveled out, and there was Emma ahead of her. "Emma, please! It's not safe baby. Please!" she begged, afraid Emma would run.

The ground shifted again, more rocks raining down. "Mama?" Emma said, turning around to face her.

"It's okay, baby, we just need to get out of here!"

Emma started towards her, and almost weeping with relief, Elizabeth ran to meet her. She had almost reached her when she saw the crack in the floor. She put her hand out to stop her but it was too late. Mouth open in horror, she saw Emma's foot come down on the gap just as it widened. She threw herself the last few feet, desperately trying to reach her in time, and felt her necklace rip off her throat as Emma caught it and fell into the fissure.

Emma's scream echoed up then cut off abruptly.

Elizabeth threw herself half over the edge and looked down. Emma lay far below. Even with only the dim light coming from the cave entrance, she could see that her eyes were wide and blank. "NOOOOOOOOOOOO!"

Oh my God. Oh my God, nooooo.

"NOOOOOOOOOO!" she screamed in agony. "EMMMAAAA!" She felt like something burst in her head from the force of her agony. "EMMMAAAA!"

"NOOOOOOOOOOOO," she screamed over and over until her voice was nearly gone. The floor of the passageway and the walls around her shook and she

didn't care. She wanted to die. She wanted to die, broken and bloody for what she had done.

She sobbed and screamed and thrashed around in remorse and grief until she thought she would go mad. OH Jesus she had killed her baby. She ripped at her hair. Oh God, Charlie. Charlie would be so upset.

Charlie. She was all he would have now. A large piece of rock broke off and fell with a boom, nearly hitting her, and she got up—for his sake.

She gazed down one last time at her beautiful daughter, then walked back the way she had come, alone, her heart broken, her soul blackened.

She stepped out into the cave and heard another BOOM and felt the earth rattle as another huge piece of rock came down behind her, blocking off the passage leading to the tunnel.

Aileen regained consciousness slowly. Her head pulsed in the distance. She moved, felt a rock dig into her back, and came all the way to.

She sat up, head throbbing, and found the flashlight. Mercifully it was still working. She crawled to the edge and looked over. Colleen lay below her. From the angle she was laying and the distance she had fallen, she didn't think she could have survived.

Colleen was not alone. Lying not two feet away from her was a skeleton wrapped in a faded dress. She shined the light over the remains. Pieces of Emma's long dark hair were still attached. Moving down she could barely see the edge of something sticking out of her pocket.

She stood up and moved around gingerly. Other than the monstrous ache in her head, nothing else hurt too badly. She leaned over and examined the rock face beneath her. The way down was too steep and slick right where she was, but over to the side she could see small cracks and protuberances that might work for hand and foot holds. The distance wasn't extraordinary. She thought she could make it.

Holding the light in her teeth, she started down. She only had one close call about halfway to the bottom when her foot slipped. She dangled by one arm for a second until her foot found the ledge again. She clung to the rock wall, breathing heavily, and then started descending again.

Colleen's eyes were open and glazed. She had bled from the mouth and nose before dying. Was she with Todd now, wherever he was?

She moved over to Emma. In her skeletal hand she still grasped her mother's silver locket. Leaving the necklace where it was, she carefully reached into Emma's pocket and drew out what was in there.

Chapter 33

"... And some residents in Andersonville county were awakened by more than their alarm clocks this morning. An earthquake measuring a magnitude of 4.6 was detected in parts of Andersonville and surrounding counties. This was the first quake to have been felt in the area since 1919, and that one had followed on the heels of the famous Charleston quake of 1886..."

Aileen clicked the Power button on the remote control and the television mounted on the wall went blank.

"I still can't believe I slept through the whole thing," Carter said, standing at the foot of her bed.

He had awakened to find Aileen missing and had gone searching for her. After finding Todd's body and calling the authorities, he had eventually found her. He had helped her back up the crevasse, and then insisted she get checked out at the hospital. The police had questioned her extensively and then left for the time being, finally giving her and Carter a chance to talk.

"Well it was storming. The noise must have covered the shots."

Carter winced.

"I'm okay."

"I'm glad you're all right," he said in a husky voice. "And I'm sorry about your friend and Todd."

Aileen shook her head silently. Colleen *had* been her friend, at one time. And all she had ever wanted was to be loved.

And Todd ... she'd probably always wonder if any of his feelings for her had been real. Tears welled up and spilled from her eyes.

Carter moved over and sat down on the edge of the bed. He reached over and rested his hand on her leg.

"All these needless deaths," she said, wiping her eyes. "Leona and her unborn baby. Emma, Colleen, and *Todd*," her voice caught, and fresh tears coursed down her face. "And not to mention the lives destroyed—Elizabeth's, and Charlie's, and the poor boy who fathered Leona's baby. He was hurt in all of this too. All because of something that never even happened."

"You mean David and Leona."

She nodded. "He may have felt something for her, something more than a fatherly protectiveness, but nothing ever came of it. A boy that worked in the fields was the father. Leona had been meeting *him*. In a fit of jealous rage Elizabeth killed her thinking she was pregnant by David and caused the death of her only daughter."

"And there Emma lay, all these years."

"Yeah, Sadie never actually went all the way through the tunnel. She waited, while Elizabeth went on ahead and pretended to search for the girls. Remember this was before they had found Leona's body."

He nodded. "So Elizabeth says they're not there, and Sadie unwittingly backs her up."

"Right, and since the tunnel had collapsed and had already been searched, it was quickly forgotten. And after they found Leona they thought that Emma might have fallen into the river too and been swept away, although her body was never recovered."

She sat up and took a deep breath. "I need to get out of here." She flung back the covers.

"What are you doing?"

"I have something I need to take care of."

"Well can't it wait until you're discharged?"

"No, it can't wait. And the doctor said I only have a concussion."

"A bad concussion. And a bullet wound."

"It's just a scrape and I'm going, regardless. Are you going to help me or do I have to do this by myself?"

He groaned and then stood up. "*Fine*. But you're coming right back here as soon as you take care of this."

Kendra and Sadie were at Charlie's when they got there. Kendra took one look at Aileen's condition and ushered them inside.

"What's happened? You found out something, didn't you?" Sadie asked, coming slowly into the foyer.

"Yes," Aileen said, smiling softly and more than a little sorrowfully. "But I need to speak to Charlie first."

"He's in the library in front of the fire."

Charlie was sitting in his customary spot. He struggled to his feet when he saw her and watched her approach. His eyes moved from the bandages on her head and neck down to what she held in her hand.

"You never told me it was your birthday that day." She held out the card. "It's from Emma. Happy Birthday, Charlie."

He took the card from her, his hand trembling. He gazed down unblinking at the faded birthday card, his mouth slack with surprise. Carefully, reverently, he opened it. His eyes filled with tears as he read Emma's last words to him.

He looked up at her, his eyes wet.

Aileen blinked back tears of her own.

"We found Emma. She had this in her pocket. She left the house so she could finish making it for you. She just wanted it to be a surprise, that's all. She was going to give it to you later that day when they celebrated your birthday."

"They never did," he whispered, gazing down at the faded card, tears spilling onto his cheeks.

His finger traced the arrowhead. "I always wanted one of these," he murmured.

Epilogue

That night she stayed and talked with Charlie, Sadie, and Kendra for a long time before going back to the hospital. She answered their questions as best she could, and had a few of her own answered.

She heard no more from Emma. Charlie finally knew the truth and no longer blamed himself, and Emma was finally at peace.

There was a minor backlash from everything that had happened. The police had a lot of questions, the media got involved, and she became a minor celebrity, earning her fifteen minutes of fame, as unwanted as it was. Her mother had demanded lengthy and detailed explanations, and for once was encouraging Aileen to forgo dating in the near future and to "just focus on your work." Little did she know that one of the nicer things that had happened from all of it was her growing friendship with Carter. He had proven to be a strong, steady friend and if it never came to anything else, that was enough for her.

They buried Emma on a bright cold day in early April. There was a surprisingly large turn out for someone who had died ninety-one years ago. Jane,

Diana, and even Edith had attended, but only Aileen, Carter, and Ed, who had asked to be there, had followed Charlie, Sadie, and Kendra down to the little graveyard beside Rose Wood. The media, of course, had been kept out, but one or two camera crews down the road recorded the horse-drawn carriage as it made its stately way into the cemetery.

A few weeks later, she met Ed at his office. It was after 8:00 p.m. and everyone else had already gone home for the day.

She found Ed working under the small pool of light from his desk lamp.

He made as if to stand. "No, don't get up." She sat down across from him and opened her bag. She pulled out the story she had written for him. She had spent weeks thinking about everything, and writing it all down and putting it out there had helped her deal with everything that had happened.

He sat up. "What's this?"

"My story."

"Your story? Weren't you offered a book deal or something?"

"Yes I was, actually. And that's probably going to happen. But for now, you get an exclusive. And I've talked with Crystal Edwards, and she's agreed to visit Rose Wood with me to search and calm any *remaining entities*." She made quote marks with her hands. "You'll get coverage of that, same deal as before."

Ed smiled. "That's great, Aileen."

"I have a couple of conditions."

"Oh?"

"I want a raise."

"All right. Done."

"And I want a real office. With a window."

Ed sighed, but he was still smiling. "Fine."

"Okay," she said.

"Okay."

She left him and headed out.

Down in reception, she paused before going out the door. She turned around and went back to the potted plant she had just passed. She reached in, fished around, and retrieved the little Casper bobblehead, then walked down the hall to her dusty little cubicle area and the desk she hoped would be located in better surroundings soon, and placed it right square in the middle, front and center. She gave it a thump with her finger and set it to bobbing.

It was still wobbling when she walked out the door.

DON'T MISS SHARON MIKEWORTH'S
NEW NOVEL COMING SOON:

A Patch of Blue

Miraculously the rear deck was empty for the moment. And it was a good thing because my head was swimming and I was in real danger of actually throwing up. I got up and moved unsteadily over to the built-in bench seat on the back corner of the boat.

The boat rode up another hideous swell, and that was it; I felt it coming. Twisting around, I stepped up on the seat and leaned out over the side, and three things happened simultaneously: the boat dropped back down, my flip-flop slipped out from under me, and I lost my balance. And just like that, I flipped over the guardrail and plunged into the ocean.

Cold water closed over me, shocking in its suddenness. It happened so quickly that I sucked in a mouthful of water before I realized what was happening. My chest heaved and I clamped a hand over my mouth to keep from breathing in more water as my lungs tried to expel what I had inhaled. Shocked and horrified, I fought my way up and broke through to the surface, choking and retching, trying to stay afloat in the swells as I coughed and gagged up the water.

By the time I managed to stop coughing and got my breath back enough to call out, the boat had already moved a considerable distance away from me. Hadn't anyone noticed? *Was that possible?* I heard no shouts of "Man overboard!" and no one seemed to be looking in my direction. Incredibly, my falling overboard seemed to have gone completely unnoticed. I felt the tug of the ocean around me and realized I was caught in a current that was pulling me away from the boat

Taking a deep breath, I mustered all my strength and screamed as loud as I could, "HEEELLP! SOMEBODY HELP MEE!" I took another breath and screamed again, "HEEEYYY! OVER HEEERE! SOMEBODY HEEELP!"

Oh God, they weren't hearing me! I was screaming as loud as I could and they couldn't hear me! If they left me I would die. Panic hit. This time I rose up out of the water as far as I could and screamed so long and loud that I felt like I ruptured something.

I fell back down in the water, going under for a moment. A large swell, nearly a wave, caught me by surprise and washed over my face as I came back up, and once again my mouth filled with water. I spit it out, this time without inhaling, and fought to gain my equilibrium and keep my head above water.

The boat was even further away now. If they didn't hear me before, how would they hear me now? Maybe the music had been too loud; maybe they had stopped playing for a minute. I rose up again and renewed my efforts. "HEEELLLLPPPP! SOMEBODY HEELLLPPP! OVER HEERE! HEEEEYY!" I waved my arms and continued to scream off and on to no avail. The boat was receding at too fast a rate. I was definitely caught in some kind of current.

PREVIEW: *A PATCH OF BLUE*

How could this be happening? I rose and fell with the swells in the ocean around me. Up, then down. Up, and down. Weirdly, my nausea had disappeared. Not that it mattered. If the weather kept going the way it was, it was going to storm and then the waves would be huge and I would be hurled up and then flung back down until I was drug under and drowned. Panic swept over me again. I didn't even have a life jacket on. I couldn't believe this was happening. My mind fought against the reality of it, and I kept repeating in my head, *This can't be happening. This can't be happening.*

I fought to keep afloat in the increasingly choppy water, riding the swells as best I could, trying not to overtire myself. I twisted around in the water, but I could no longer spot the boat at all. It had gotten either too far away or the waves were blocking my view.

Had they realized that I was gone yet? How long would it take for James to come looking for me and realize that I wasn't in the bathroom or anywhere else? My mind seized on the possibility. Of course. James would come looking for me and realize I was gone. They would figure out what happened and turn the boat around. I twisted around again, scanning the ocean around me the best that I could, but it was impossible in the choppy water, and I gave up and hoped for calmer seas.

Sometime later the waves and swells began to die down. I could still see lightning way off in the distance, but the sky had brightened above me and the waves seemed to be smaller. The storm had passed on. There was no way to know how long it had been since I fell overboard. Two hours? Three?

I scanned the horizon constantly for any sign of the boat, but all I could see was endless water in all directions. Once I heard the distant sound of a helicopter and my heart leapt with joy, but either because of the remaining cloud cover, or because they were just too far away, I was never able to spot it, and the sound soon receded and was gone. The vulnerability of my position was even clearer to me now that I wasn't occupied fighting waves to keep my head above water. Open water stretched out as far as I could see. I was one lone person in a very big ocean, and I wasn't even wearing a life jacket. It would be nearly impossible for anyone to see me. Treading water, I told myself to stay calm, but I could feel the panic coming again, nipping at me from the dark depths. How long could a person stay afloat without a life vest? I could alternate treading water with floating if the water stayed calm, but wouldn't I get tired at some point? And what about water? I had to already be somewhat dehydrated from all the alcohol and the spitting up I had done earlier.

I lifted my legs and stretched out on my back, floating as motionless as possible to conserve my strength.

I prayed for rescue.

What followed was the longest night of my life. I floated quite a bit, but I had to keep my head tilted back to do it, which hurt my neck, and I could only manage it for so long. And worse, since the sun went down the temperature had dropped considerably, and now I was cold. Really cold. I couldn't even move around too much to warm up because I knew that sharks came out at night to feed.

Because of the partial cloud cover, only a few stars were out to give me light, and the sea around me was eerily dark. I tried not to think about what could be in the depths of the ocean beneath me. It was easy to imagine some giant sea monster rising slowly up out of the water to take me into its beaky mouth. Suddenly I had another horrible thought. What if they never even knew I was missing? The helicopter I had heard earlier might not have been looking for me. I was a last minute addition and my name wasn't even on the list. But surely the woman who had been checking off names would remember me. Wouldn't she? Or the hotel lady's cousin who had taken my money. Or James. Surely he would remember talking to me. But even if they had realized I was missing, it might not have been until they got back to the marina, which left a large area to search, from the boat's location when James last talked to me to the marina all the way back in Port Denarau. And even then, they would be looking in the wrong place because the current had surely swept me far away by now.

I had always been a strong swimmer, probably due to the summers I had spent immersed in the neighborhood pool when I was growing up, but even so, I was starting to get tired. The coldness and the constant motion I had to make as well as the constant strain to stay above water was wearing me out, mentally and physically. It wasn't too bad whenever I was floating, but then my neck would start to cramp, and I would have to drop my legs and tread water again. I was terrified it would attract a shark.

On and on the night seemed to drag. I had no perception of time. All I had was minute after minute of exhaustion, fear, and cold. And though I tried not to think about it, I knew lack of water was a real worry. After all the sun, alcohol, and the saltwater I had inadvertently swallowed, I had to be getting dehydrated. All it would take would be for me to pass out for a minute and then I would slip beneath the water and drown.

I flipped onto my back and tried to conserve my strength. Hypothermia was probably setting in, but it was all I could do. I was so tired. I relaxed as much as I could and let my mind wander. My thoughts drifted to the boys. I couldn't give up ... I had to think of them and all the things they would need ... me for ... graduations ... weddings ... and grandchildren ...

The first sharp sting jolted me awake. I hadn't been asleep exactly, but somehow I had managed to drift into a twilight state that I immediately wanted to go back to as I felt two more sharp stings on my leg and shoulder.

I let out a cry and jerked upright in the water. I reached down to my leg and my fingers closed around something gelatinous. Burning needles of pain immediately shot through my hand. I cried out and jerked my hand away. I felt another searing pain on my neck and realized that one was clinging to me. Reaching around I ripped it off and was stung again. With a shriek, I flung it off of me.

Translucent white jellyfish surrounded me in the water. More excruciating needles of pain began to strike me all over. I felt one on my foot and another on my lower back below my tank top, and then on my leg. Shrieking, I thrashed about in the water and tried to swim away from them. Relentlessly, I was stung over and over as I plowed through them and tried to get away. Crying out every few seconds in agony, I kept swimming even though there seemed to be no end to them because stopping wasn't an option. Just when I thought it would go on forever, I finally got clear of them. My heart was slamming in pain and exhaustion and drowning now seemed like a real possibility, but I forced myself to swim a little farther to be sure I was far enough away.

I rolled over in the water and managed to get onto my back. My limbs were trembling, and my breath whooped in and out of me. I had been stung too many times to count, and I had no idea what all that venom would do to me. I realized I was making a low keening sound and forced myself to stop.

For the first time, dying in this fathomless ocean seemed not so much a possibility, as a certainty. Jared had cast me aside and I had been left in the ocean to drown. I was going to die. Jared would be with Angie, and I would be left in this endless sea.

Made in the USA
Charleston, SC
07 April 2013